THE REFUGEE'S DAUGHTER

CAROLYN NEWTON

BLOODHOUND
BOOKS

First published in 2024 by Bloodhound Books.

www.bloodhoundbooks.com

Print ISBN: 978-1-917214-65-0

To Newt, who loved this story best.

O kur manęs laukia namai?
Toli pakrašty lygumuos Apauga žolę pelenai.
And where is home waiting for me?
On the far edge of the plains
Grass growing over ashes.

Evening on Foreign Fields by Kazys Bradūnas, 1945

Lithuania

Baltic Sea

Klaipėda

Šilutė

Tauragė

Stubriai

Jurbarkas

Kaunas

Tilsit

Memel River

Vilnius

Königsberg

East Prussia

PART 1

CHAPTER ONE

BRIGIT, 2010

Secrets. The room was choked with them. White lies, well-meaning ruses, and vile deceptions slithered between every hug, every pat on the back, every knowing tilt of the head. They screamed at Brigit through every somber attempt at condolence.

"I'm so sorry for your loss," offered a man who looked vaguely familiar. "Who'd've thought Joe would..." the man searched for the appropriate euphemism.

"Die?" Brigit filled in the awkward gap abruptly, struggling to control her need to scream. *Don't shoot the messenger*, she chided herself. "It's really shocking that someone like Joe could have a heart attack," she added for what seemed like the hundredth time. The offers of condolence were looping back on themselves, and Brigit was suffocating under the pretense.

"Yes, well right," the man stammered, surprised by Brigit's directness. "The man seemed to be in tip-top shape, and during a marathon no less. It's just a tragedy."

"It is. Thank you for being here," Brigit said while fighting the desire to throttle this friend or colleague or confidante, whoever he was. *Did you know? Did Joe tell you? What else do you think Joe seemed to be?* She searched the bearded face for any glimmer of knowledge, but if the man knew, he was holding his cards close to the vest.

He wrapped both his hands around Brigit's own clammy fingers and squeezed. "Oh, Barbie, we'll miss him so much. He was always the life of the party, you know?"

"He was and thank you." She pulled her hand out of his meaty grip. "It's Brigit."

He persisted. "Listen, Barbie, if you need anything, you promise to call me, right? Joe would want to make sure we're taking care of his sweetheart."

"I promise,' Brigit lied.

Her living room, stiflingly hot despite the January day that was bone-chilling even by Boston standards, reeked of wet wool and stale coffee, and the mourners had tracked in black slush from the sidewalk and planted it in wet puddles all over the tidy carpet. They occupied every square inch of her modest cottage, but there were few she knew. Joe's family was there, of course. A chatty Boston clan, all randomly connected through marriages and remarriages, led by Joe's mother, Wanda, and her third husband, Roy. Margie, Brigit's mother, was there too. She sat primly on the edge of the sofa, the only member of Brigit's own family in attendance.

As much as Wanda seemed to marshal the energy in the room around her, Margie repelled it. Her mouth, set in a stern line, lent her face an unreadable yet off-putting quality as she smoothed out the delicate lace ruffles on her sleeve and occasionally cleared her throat. She gave the appearance of a woman wrestling with her emotions, but Brigit knew it to be her mother's sign of impatience.

Dr. Hiyashi, Brigit's supervising professor, and a few of her fellow grad students had dropped by right after the funeral, but it was awkward, and Brigit could tell that they were searching for an opportunity to escape. It was a relief for all of them when

Joe's family barreled in and they could ease out the door unnoticed.

The rest of the crowd belonged to Joe, his colleagues mostly because he'd had few true friends. His success had been meteoric—a young, handsome doctor brimming with charisma and a specialty for mending Boston's elite athletes—and he preferred his shallow, transactional world of publicity and fame. Their marriage had been puzzling to most, that of the local celebrity doctor and his introverted wife, but Brigit understood the arrangement. It's not that she dwelled to any extent on her capacity for beauty, although with her thick chestnut hair and arresting eyes, she often drew admiring glances. Rather she knew that Joe depended on her unwavering support, endless well of patience, and scant demands for attention. She gave him the foundation he needed to soar with the assurance that she would only complement and never eclipse. And never question, apparently. For ten years, she devoted herself to him and never once saw it coming. She grieved his loss, but it was tangled in hurt, embarrassment, and anger.

His secret lurked in the crowd like a fault line, unseen, cataclysmic. She scanned the faces, watching for tells and seeing none. Brigit silently challenged the mole to reveal himself... or *her*self. Were any of these women part of the plan? Brigit couldn't conjure an accomplice from this group. There were no signs that he had told anyone of his intentions.

Brigit thought back to her own last moment with Joe, the man she had supported through medical school and for whom she had delayed her own graduate work in deference to his demanding career. As he zipped his bag shut and headed out the door to catch his flight to Honolulu, he'd kissed her on the head and said, "You'll come to see it's for the best, Brig. Don't hate me for long." Sleepy and befuddled, she had watched him walk out the door into the predawn darkness and climb into the taxi. She was questioning whether she had heard him correctly, but her mind was cluttered from staying up too late, rearranging her dissertation notes and organizing her lecture. She had stumbled back into bed and fallen asleep.

Wanda took a fork and began beating it against a coffee cup now, demanding the group's attention and forcing Brigit back to the present. "Let's take this back to our house, shall we? Don't be a stranger now, you're all welcome to come. It'll give Brigit and her mother some time together in private," she announced, managing to ignore Brigit and disinvite her at the same time. "We can gather around the fireplace and share special memories together!" And with that, they all raced to exit.

Brigit had to assume that those special memories were unlikely to include stories of the wedding. As Brigit recalled, Wanda cried longer and louder on that day than at his funeral, so she was eager to close the door on the last departing Lewin relative and relieved not to have to make an excuse to decline an invitation to join them.

Margie remained anchored to her spot in the sitting room, fiddling with a napkin and sipping a cup of lukewarm coffee. She was too well-bred to make disparaging remarks about Joe's family, but she had mastered the art of communicating exactly how much she disapproved without a single word. She was equally averse to filling in the quiet spaces with mindless chatter, so the two women sat in silence.

"Mama, shall I freshen up your coffee?" Brigit inquired, searching for a way to find a connection.

"No, dear, I really must get going." Margie consulted her thin gold watch. "I should be getting on to the airport. Your father will be waiting for me."

Margie sighed, and Brigit wondered if her father's interest in Margie's return was a comfort or an annoyance to her mother. She could never tell. The concept of family for Margie was complicated. She had been estranged from her own parents for years, and Brigit had never met any grandparents, aunts, uncles or cousins. Brigit's father, Otto, who remained in Charleston too ill to travel, was an orphan and an immigrant; for Brigit, family meant traversing a minefield of suppressed heartache, simmering resentments, and thinly veiled slights. She had thought her life with Joe was different, until now. Naively, she had comforted herself with the notion that she had created a different path, but it seemed that distrust was lodged in her genes.

"C'mon, Mama, at least let me take you to the airport," Brigit pleaded. "We can talk on the way."

"No, Brigit," Margie reached out to squeeze her daughter's hand, but didn't allow the gesture to linger. "I can take a taxi. You have things you need to do here, I'm sure."

Brigit started to protest and then decided she was too fatigued to argue. Margie had spoken and was unlikely to change her mind. Brigit picked up the phone and ordered the ride.

After a blessedly short wait, the taxi pulled up to the curb with the driver honking impatiently. Margie stood up, smoothed out her immaculate wool skirt, dabbed her mouth delicately with her napkin, and cleared her throat. "Brigit, you have a lot of decisions to make right now. You've always been stubborn, and I don't see that changing anytime soon. Joe was the best thing that ever happened to you, and you have to decide for yourself how to go on. This doctorate in Psychology, working with *refugees...*" Margie paused as if the very word was an intrusion on polite discourse, "for heaven's sake, try to do something uplifting with your life. Your father survived being orphaned in the war, then escaped the communists to make a better life. He managed to shake all that messy business, and I don't see any benefit to your dwelling in unpleasantness. Especially now."

Brigit stood quietly, absorbing the blows of her mother's assessment. She thought about revealing Joe's secret, just to demonstrate to Margie how wrong she really was, but the driver honked again, and Brigit chose instead to accept the criticism. She collected Margie's wrap, holding it just right so that her mother could grasp the sleeves of her cardigan and don the coat without mussing up her clothes. Margie had a system. She turned back to Brigit, reaching out to straighten a flyaway curl that had escaped from her thick braid. Brigit froze, not wanting to break the spell of this tender moment.

"Brigit dear, you know I love you, and I'm just trying to help." She hesitated, watching Brigit for a reaction. When there was none, Margie pressed ahead. "You should really consider cutting your hair. Thirty-five is too old to have your hair as long as this. Something short and chic is much more appropriate. You know I just want the best for you." She dropped her hand and walked out the door without a hug or a kiss.

Brigit stood at the window long after the taxi had disappeared down the street. Only the secret remained, lingering in the house as a dastardly intruder. She picked up a handful of coffee cups and plates and carried them to the kitchen sink.

When she noticed the junk drawer was ajar, she panicked. Who had been rifling through her things? Did anyone see what was inside? She yanked the drawer open, but nothing seemed amiss. Rubber bands and matchboxes commingled with crumbs, paper clips, and expired coupons. The note lay as she had left it, crumpled and shoved to the back. She had found it the day Joe left, after she woke up the second time feeling unsettled and off-balance. She had searched her memory for clues to her unease, doubting her recall as she poured herself a cup of coffee, and then she had spied the envelope propped against the microwave. 'Brig' was written in Joe's bold handwriting.

Dear Brig,

I don't have the heart to tell you this in person. Please forgive me for taking the coward's way out and writing you a note. It's better this way, I am sure of that. You'll hate me and I'll hate myself, and I'd rather have the image of your smiling face in my mind.

I think it's time that we admit that our marriage has run its course. We have both created the lives we need and want, but they are no longer compatible, and we need to recognize that it's time to go our separate ways. We have no children to consider, and perhaps this was God's plan all along. Please know that there is no one else, no girlfriend or mistress or flirtation, only the knowledge that I'm holding you back, and you're holding me back, and it's just not fun anymore. Do you remember when we were at college together? You, the gorgeous bookworm, happy to bury yourself in the library carrels and spend all day researching dusty facts and stories from long ago. I was the reckless one, drawn to your intelligence and your strength. You got me through medical school and helped me set up my practice, and for that I will be forever grateful.

Now, I am living my dream. I love the fast pace, the cameras, the travel. You love the library, your graduate work, your classes. Two different worlds, and I know that somewhere out there, there is someone better suited to you than me.

When I get back from Hawaii, we'll go to the lawyers, and I won't fight you for anything. We'll get you set up so that you can finish your dissertation and finally be Dr. Brigit Lewin, and I will be really happy for you. Be happy for me and know that deep down, I will always love you.

Joe

Brigit balled it up again. She wanted to set it alight, watch it burn, but it was just a piece of stationery, and Brigit would never be able to purge the hurt and surprise that way. That would linger after the paper and ink turned to ashes. She thrust it back in the recesses of the drawer, vowing to let it rot there.

The tears finally came, and she collapsed on the floor and sobbed. She was an expert at plumbing the depths of others' emotions, but her own so often remained elusive, a toxic blend of grief, hurt, betrayal, and shame. "No!" she screamed, and she embraced the release. She screamed at Joe, at Margie, at herself for being such a dupe. She screamed at all the high-fliers and bigwigs who had traipsed through her home today offering platitudes. They had aided and abetted Joe's need for attention in a way she never could. She screamed at the world, and then she was too hoarse to scream and too tired to fight. She leaned against the cabinet, sucking great gulps of air into her lungs, and vowed to herself that she would not be anyone's patsy again. She thought of Otto, and for a moment, she berated herself. Her father had endured much worse than she, and he was fighting a losing battle with his failing body. If *he* could manage, then so could she. She would find a way out of this dark tunnel, and she would start now.

Normally, Brigit sought out peace and solitude. She reveled in moments of introspection, but in the wake of Joe's treachery, the funeral, her mother's departure, and the disapproval that still hung in the air, the silences in her home were oppressive. The clock ticked intrusively as if to emphasize all the many ways that Brigit's life was a cluster of regrettable compromises and misunderstandings. The weak winter sunlight was casting the kitchen in somber blue shadows, and Brigit decided that it was too early to crawl into bed. She would banish the demons in her midst.

In a burst of resolve, she attacked the downstairs,

channeling her rage into action. She swept up the rest of the cups and napkins and jammed the last of the snacks in the fridge, where she discovered a plastic dish labeled 'chicken a la Wanda.' She chucked that in the bin and allowed herself a smile. She dismantled the industrial-sized coffee maker, a seldom-used wedding present, flinging the loose bits in the sink and plunging them into a billowing pile of suds before she tossed the cleaned and dried parts haphazardly in a box, a move that would have earned Margie's ire.

Brigit teetered on a chair in front of the hall closet and heard Joe's voice warning her to be careful. "I'll be reckless if I want to be!" she hollered aloud as she hoisted the whole kit up to the top shelf and tried without success to push it all the way in. After two or three attempts, she swore in frustration and set the box back on the floor, then she reached up to feel for whatever was in the way. Dust flew off the shelf as her fingers swept across the upper reaches of the closet. Finally, her fingertips brushed against the seams of a large, padded envelope. She managed to grasp it enough to nudge it forward, and she pulled it down off the shelf along with a cascade of spiders' webs.

"Oh my God!" Brigit exclaimed when she noticed the return address. Deutsches Rotes Kreuz, Carstennstraße, Berlin. It was the response from the German Red Cross that she had been waiting for. When had it arrived? Brigit examined the postmark. Three months ago. "Damn you, Joe!" she blurted out. He must have gotten it from the mail and set it aside. Surely, he didn't hide it on purpose? Brigit climbed down from the chair and took the envelope, a big fat bundle swathed in tape and bulging with odd-sized documents, to the dining room table. She swept the centerpiece aside and dumped out the contents of her package.

Brigit assessed the clutter of letters, newspaper articles and grainy pictures, and cautioned herself that the jumble of brittle yellow papers and smudged photocopies were most certainly another dead end to her search. She put her head in her hands and fought back a wave of discouragement. Her father's plea had been so loaded with despair that she couldn't refuse him, but now she was reeling with self-doubt and grief. Would she be able to find the information he needed so desperately? They had tried so many avenues: contacting embassies and aid agencies, scouring through dusty microfilm reels of death records and compensation claims. Nothing. Joe had been annoyed with her doggedness and accused her of chasing ghosts.

The letter to the Red Cross had been at best a Hail Mary, a crazy idea with no real expectation of progress. Now here was their response, and it had been hiding in her closet for months. Brigit took a deep breath and reminded herself that she had resolved this very day to be a woman of action. This mission—a fool's errand, perhaps—was a way for her to start again on a positive path, and it had literally fallen right in her lap.

Brigit went into the kitchen and splashed cold water on her face, then she checked the clock: 4:08pm. "Close enough," she said as she poured herself a generous glass of wine. Then she forced herself back into the dining room to survey the spoils of her fledgling search.

A brief note was on top:

Sehr geerhte Frau Lewin,

Thank you for your inquiry. As you can imagine, in the final days of the war, the situation in East Prussia was rather chaotic. Many families were separated, deaths went unrecorded, and people dispersed across Europe. Your father sounds like one of the lucky ones to have survived.

We checked our files for your aunt's name, and we could not find any records relating to Brigit 'Giti' Binz. I am also unable to find a record of anyone searching for her with us before. As you can imagine, the files from the post-war years are incomplete;

however, I have sent you photocopies of some documents we have related to East Prussia. While we normally share digital files, we are pleased to be able to send you paper copies as you indicated that your father might have difficulty with email attachments. In addition to the East Prussian files, I have also included a few documents and photographs we have from the post-war period in southern Lithuania, as many ethnic Germans made their way there. Perhaps you or your father may see a face, a place, or a name that you recognize? If you wish to send me your father's name, we will be honored to continue our search on his behalf.

Mit freundlichen Grüßen
Ilsa Schneider

Brigit set the letter aside and began organizing the contents. She ignored the telephone and doorbell as she sorted through the piles of documents and deciphered cryptic letters in old-fashioned German. There were people in these pages who had faced the unimaginable and survived. Finding stories of hope and resilience became Brigit's refuge.

At first, it was mindlessly satisfying to abandon the tasks around Joe's death and focus entirely on separating the contents of the envelope into piles of photographs, newspaper clippings, copies of family trees, letters written in splotchy ink and shaky hands, sorting them into groups, then stacking each category in chronological order. This was what she did best: glean truths from old documents and bring history to life. Eventually, she began to pick up on threads of people's stories: cruelty, loss, betrayal, amid the tiny voices of hope. She read obituaries of long-lost fathers and letters imploring the Red Cross for information on absent mothers, daughters, and sons. She stared at the weathered faces in the pictures. Occasionally, she broke down and cried in solidarity with the wan figures trapped on the pages, but mostly she felt empty and adrift in her own pain.

Just as the last few rays of timid winter light washed over the table and reflected off Brigit's first dram of merlot, she found it: a double-sided photocopy with a photograph of a woman on one side and images of the photographer's markings on the other. The original, faded with age, was clearly the work of a professional. Brigit was drawn to the woman in the image, her scarf pulled low on her head and her hand raised in a futile attempt to block the low winter sun. If Brigit concentrated too hard, the individual elements of the woman's face blended together in a cluster of muted grays, but if she let her eyes glance delicately over the image, she could discern the features of her face: pale almond-shaped eyes with a strong gaze, a short-bridged nose with a perky tip, and a rosy full-lipped mouth, open just a bit as if she was about to say something. Curly blond hair peeked out of the back of the scarf, and a thick braid coiled over one shoulder. A group of men to her left wrestled with the broken wheel of a wooden cart, which was mired in mud and snow, but the woman was staring past them, to something compelling right outside the photographer's frame.

Brigit went to her bedroom to the polished mahogany box that held her treasures and drew out the old, tattered photograph that her father had given her, reluctantly, but necessary for her search. This one was an original, frayed around the edges and stained with moisture from long ago calamities and adventures. It was of a girl, her soft curls spilling out of the disheveled blond plaits framing her face as she clutched a bleating goat and laughed at an unseen accomplice. Her eyes squinted into the sun, and deep dimples tickled her face. Behind her was a plain timber and stone farmhouse with an unremarkable façade. It gave the impression of a solid structure built over time with second-hand supplies. Small, mismatched windows and a solemn front door seemed to indicate a dark and utilitarian interior.

Brigit took it back to the dining room table and set it by the photocopy. She drew out a magnifying glass. Dismissing the severity of the house and surroundings, she focused on the girl—her aunt Giti—whose heavy woolen dress, thick gloves, and serviceable boots marked a sharp contrast to her joyful demeanor and mischievous grin. Brigit memorized her features, then quickly darted her gaze to the woman, eager to find definitive evidence that the young girl teasing the goat had somehow survived and was indeed the grown woman in the second picture, part of a group of earnest farm workers assembled for winter chores. Brigit's attempts to reconcile the physical features were inconclusive except for one detail: the woman's hands. The left one rested on the woman's hip and featured long, thin fingers, elegant despite the callouses. The right one she held aloft, pressed against the sweat-stained scarf, and fully visible were the brittle, misshapen fingers, curled rigidly inward. The child holding the goat had suffered no such injury, but that was consistent with the memories her father had shared. *Could* it be Giti?

Brigit puzzled over the image, putting it in the pile and then pulling it back out again. Although it was the hand that intrigued her, Brigit searched for other clues. In the photograph, the woman was standing in front of a barn. There were at least six other men and women in the image with evidence of several more inside the structure. The men were focused on the repair of the damaged cart. Snow was piled in dirty heaps around the barn, and the women were clustered around large pots suspended over fires. Apparently, it was laundry day, and except for the woman who was peering off in the distance, all other women appeared to be deeply committed to the process of sorting and bundling the linens. A dog sat at the woman's feet, an old hunting hound who lay in a lethargic heap, perhaps dreaming of chasing foxes and rabbits down holes in the forest.

Brigit flipped the image over. *'Litauen, Winter 1952'* was scribbled on the back in pencil and farther down, stamped in black ink, *'Fotografijos stilius Lukas Galinis, Kaunus 73.'* Based on Otto's telling, Giti was born in 1930. In 1952, she would have been twenty-one or twenty-two; the woman appeared much older than that, yet in spite of some contradictory evidence, it was the woman's hand that continued to haunt Brigit. She grabbed her phone and booked a flight to Charleston for the next day. Otto would know and she needed him to see it.

CHAPTER TWO
GITI, 1945

Before the soldiers came, Giti had never been farther from her home than the cemetery that lay just beyond her grandmother's strawberry fields behind a cluster of oak and birch trees. From her earliest memories, her life centered around the solemn stone and timber farmhouse with the mismatched windows, which gazed out onto the rutted lane winding alongside the Pregel River. The house, like other East Prussian farmsteads, was an austere yet functional structure full of the laughter, quarrels, and robust activity of an extended family. Other than Giti, her mother and grandmother, the Binz family had always been a bustling brood of men and boys, and together, they wrestled a living from the rich soil of the fields and the yield from the livestock.

The cemetery was Giti's outermost universe, a silent witness to those who existed in the margins of memory. It sat on the rise of a small hill with a broad view of the river and small farms that dotted the flat East Prussian plain. On hot summer days, Giti liked to sit among the mossy stones and conjure stories from names on the tombstones, fanciful tales of love, treachery, and adventure that wildly embellished the simple seasonal rhythms of the farm.

Now, deep in the winter and deeper still in the constant deprivations of war, Giti felt like the cemetery had reached out its deathly tentacles to claim the exuberance of the house. Her father, Walter, her uncle Karl, and her two older brothers, Paul and Stefan, had left five years ago, marching down the dusty lane wearing their crisp uniforms and disappearing into the clutches of the German army. There had been no word since Stalingrad, and no one spoke of them with hope. Giti's grandfather, consumed with despair, became a prisoner of dementia. Opa had wandered out toward the family plots during a blizzard, where Oma found him hours later, frozen and entombed in a snow drift. The women had pried him loose and buried him in the crude and shallow grave that they had hacked out of the unyielding ground. Otto and Giti helped round up heavy stones to cover him and thwart the wild animals' desperate scavenging. Giti and Otto shed the only tears, the deep well of grief too recently plumbed to rouse the women.

The reduced family was now dominated by the women: Giti's mother, Ruth, and her grandmother, Oma Elise, both strong personalities who had not up until now been natural allies. Their relationship had been forged tenuously through the men, and in the wake of their disappearance, the women figured out how to lay aside their natural competitiveness to focus on survival. Giti, at fourteen, had enough experience to recognize the power shift and had come to fear the detente in the women's relationship. The days of them arguing openly and challenging each other's authority had been replaced with simmering resentments, tight-lipped resignation, and fear.

Eleven-year-old Otto was now the only man in the house, unless one counted Wally the dog or Rufus the cat. He was a light-hearted boy full of chuckles and tricks, impervious to the dark undercurrents that Giti associated with their last few years on the farm. It was in Otto's direction that all the meager family goodwill flowed, and he delighted in the attention. Otto alone was convinced that his father, uncle and brothers would return, and he felt that it was his job to keep the family spirits up in preparation.

"You never smile, Giti. Papa wants us to be strong," he would urge.

Otto moved to sit next to Giti on the low stone wall, and he nudged her with his shoulder. She smiled back and offered him a corner of the thick wool blanket she had draped across her knees. He accepted the warmth gladly and started to sing a German nursery rhyme.

Giti laughed at the song of the hapless rider, the tune that Opa always sang when they were little, lifting them up and swinging them around. "You are right as usual, Otto. We will be happy and strong."

In the absence of school, Otto and Giti took their precious books and school supplies to the cemetery as often as they could escape their chores and Mutti's shadow. While Otto delved into mythical tales of medieval knights and chivalry, Giti addressed more practical matters. She wrestled the crinkled sheet of paper out of her pocket and spread it out on the blanket. With her supplies arranged, she faced the wooden cross that Otto had fashioned for Opa's headstone and imagined her grandfather's deep tenor voice. Talking to him helped her organize her thoughts. "Opa, we have three bushels of potatoes and a dozen jars of Oma's tomatoes left in the root cellar," she read off her list. "Helga is still producing milk, and we've managed to keep the mice out of the grain. We still have a few cabbages. If we manage it well, we may have enough to last until we plant the first crops, as long as the soldiers stay away and don't try to take any more of our supplies."

Giti remembered the last time the soldiers had banged on the door. Two came to the porch, and two others ransacked the barn. They were young and reminded her vaguely of Paul and Stefan, but these boys were gaunt and each held a cruel gaze as they surveyed the limited options available for them to steal. Before they had left for duty, Pappi and Uncle Karl had constructed an ingenious false wall in the cellar so that Mutti and Oma could hide most of the food. So far, it had worked.

With the farm animals, they weren't so lucky. The cows, chickens, pigs, goats, and horses had all been taken early in the war, along with Pappi's truck and Uncle Karl's rusting motorbike. Other than Wally and Rufus, only Elsa the aged mule, and Helga the goat were left. Elsa was too decrepit to entice, and Helga had proven to possess an astonishing ability to wander off into the woods just ahead of ravenous invaders.

Giti had worked out the sums to devise a plan for the food to last. She felt confident that she, Mutti, and Oma could cut back and reduce their portions, but Otto worried her. She remembered when Paul and Stefan were home, and they could eat three times what the women ate. Otto was already so thin. His cheekbones formed sharp ridges on his face, and he had sores on his mouth, which Mutti said was from not having fresh vegetables.

Giti continued with her report to Opa. "Oma wants to know if she should try to sell your watch to buy another chicken and some feed, but I was thinking that maybe that would bring attention to us, that it will be a sign that we have food to spare. If we get a chicken, the soldiers will just come and take it."

She was worried. She needed a sharper strategy than the simple scribblings on paper, because she had heard Mutti and Oma arguing at the table late last night. Mutti was telling Oma that they needed to leave. The Germans were losing their hold on East Prussia, and the Russians were poised to invade. Oma said no. They should stay put.

Even as recently as Christmas, the Nazi leaders of East Prussia had forbidden anyone from escaping. Civilians trying to leave had been accused of deliberately undermining military morale, and they were being very publicly shot. Yet despite the draconian orders, Mutti was undeterred. Frau Klettner's sister from Königsberg brought news that the Russian army had broken through the German defenses and made it all the way to Vistula Lagoon. Horrid stories of Russian barbarism were spreading among the towns and villages.

Mutti pleaded with Oma to pack up Elsa and the wagon with provisions and secure their escape across the frozen lagoon toward the western territories, but Oma continued to resist. She reasoned that if they left, they might fall into the hands of the Russians anyway. Pappi, Karl, and the boys might still be alive. What if they came back and the family was gone? What if they packed up Elsa and left, but were not able to make it across the ice? Where would they go then?

Giti listened with alarm and began to formulate her plan. It appeared that Oma would win out. If she refused to go, Mutti would not leave her behind. That much was certain. They were all staying together, and Giti felt like a tiny mouse in charge of disarming a massive trap.

In late January, the Russians arrived. Giti was in the barn milking Helga when she heard the truck pull up in the lane and stop. She hadn't heard the sound of a truck on their road in months and knew right away this was a bad sign. She set the pail of milk behind Opa's workbench and shooed Helga out the back door. This time, however, Helga refused to go. She nosed her way back in and retreated to the corner of the barn. Giti was already scrambling up the ladder to the rafters, tripping over the hem of Oma's large wool cape that she had grabbed by mistake in her haste to finish the milking. She crawled over to where she had hidden her project: a bag with a few essential provisions, just as she had promised her Opa. She retrieved the bag, cradled it to her chest, and crept to the side of the barn where she could see the house through the cracks in the ancient siding.

The truck was a Soviet army transport with a small cab up front and a large canvas tarp covering the back. It was pointed towards the barn, so Giti could see only the driver, standing off to the side watching his comrades walk to the front porch. Another truck pulled up and parked behind. Five more Russian soldiers climbed out. The second driver joined the first while the remaining four headed to the house.

The soldiers didn't knock. Giti's heart lurched when she heard wood splintering just before the solid door crashed in on its hinges. Mutti and Oma screamed, and minutes later, one of the soldiers rushed back out onto the porch, his face covered in scalding porridge. He leaned over the bushes and shook off the burning paste before he grabbed a gun and charged back in, his cheeks red and mottled with blisters. Mutti and Oma were pleading, and Giti could hear pots and pans hitting the floor amid a hail of bullets.

Giti crawled to the corner of the loft and wedged herself behind a pile of old traps. She heard another crash and curled up tight in the stale hay, balling her fists beside her ears to shut out the terrifying noises coming from inside her home. She struggled to breathe with her heart pounding erratically in her chest. Lying on the floor with her eyes squeezed shut and her hands over her ears, Giti saw Opa. He was reaching out his hands to her, and then he spoke. "Otto."

Otto. Giti raised her head and tried to think clearly. Otto

needed her. She wrapped her arms around her chest and rocked back and forth, fighting the paralyzing fear. Think, Giti, think! She had last seen Otto this morning taking his sketchpad into the cellar. Likely he was still there, trapped and terrified. Giti drew aside Oma's cape for long enough to secure the bag on her back, using the handles as loops over her arms, and then pulled the cape back over her shoulders. She returned to the ground floor and armed herself with a sharp pair of farm shears. She was thinking that she could make it to the back of the house and into the rear entrance to the cellar if only she could evade the two drivers standing watch out front.

Giti moved toward the entrance, but once again she tripped over Oma's cape and fell forward, her thick boots hitting the packed dirt floor. Helga sprung to her feet, bleated, and trotted forward as Giti pulled herself up and crept to the door. As she feared, both the drivers had heard Helga and were now walking toward the barn. She grabbed Helga by the neck and positioned her by the door, edging it open just enough for Helga to fit through. The goat resisted and bleated again, so Giti thrust the shears into her backside, forcing her into the yard squealing with pain. Helga bolted for the woods, and the two drivers gave chase.

Giti slipped out of the barn through the small side door, keeping herself hidden from the drivers until she saw them wrestle Helga to the ground. She ran to the back of the house where the cellar door lay under the high kitchen window, and she paused as she considered how to operate the squeaky hinges without drawing attention to herself. She heard her mother sobbing and imploring the men for mercy. One of the soldiers offered a crude response, and a foul chorus of guttural laughter erupted.

Propelled by fear, Giti grabbed the latch. She eased the door up just enough to squeeze herself through, but the weight of the bag pushed her forward causing her to tumble headfirst and land with a thud against the stone floor. The cellar door clattered back down, and Giti hovered in the darkness, her breaths coming in ragged gulps. Mutti's muffled cries were directly overhead through the sturdy floorboards. Giti retreated into a corner struggling to adjust her eyes through her tears and the enveloping darkness. The only illumination came from a gap under the door above, the one that led from the cellar into the kitchen. Another loud thud above sent dust swirling in the stingy light. She choked back her sobs and wiped her face. She briefly considered charging up the stairs with the kitchen shears, but a fresh round of gunfire erupted. It was then that she heard Otto.

He was to her left, and as her eyes acclimated to the dimness, she lay the shears aside and crawled toward Mutti's low herb table where she could see him flattened against the ground. Behind this table was Pappi's false wall and the secret door that led into the rest of the cellar. Giti whispered, "Otto Liebling. I am here." He made no response. Giti reached out to touch him, and he batted her away. "Otto, it's me. We're going behind the wall," she pleaded. "Look at me." But when she reached out again, he cried out and kicked her with his legs.

Giti backed away, and Otto cowered, his muscles taut with terror, ready to lash out at any provocation. He was breathing heavily, and as a new round of thumps and crashes began, he diverted his attention from Giti to stare up at the floorboards.

Giti reached out her hand. "Otto, you must let me get behind you to open the door. We're going to help Mutti and Oma, but we have to hide first. Please help me, Otto. Please."

Otto whimpered and rolled into a ball. It was just enough to move his body away from the door, and Giti inched her way to his side while running her hands along the rough wooden partition to feel for the hidden latch. As her hands grasped and pulled on the ring, the door sprung outward, crashing into the table and knocking off Mutti's glass jars and metal lids. Giti scooped up Otto. He tried to fight back but her adrenaline was surging, and she managed to wrestle him into the tight space. Once again, jars and lids crashed to the floor, splintering into glass shards against the stone. Giti lowered her head and ducked in behind him.

She pushed Otto farther into the tight space and arranged herself so that she was facing the door. She reached out to pull it shut, but it wouldn't budge. She thrust out her arm and patted around to feel for whatever was blocking the door, and her fingers closed around the toe of a worn leather boot. A big hand reached down and dragged her out into the open. Two soldiers stood in the middle of the cellar. One had a deep gash running down the side of his face. The other had a bite mark on his hand. The door into the kitchen stood ajar, and Giti could see broken dishes on the floor and bullet holes in the walls.

The soldier with the gash reached down, grabbed the collar of the cape, and yanked Giti to her feet, but the other soldier put out his arm and pushed his comrade back. He shoved the table to the side, toppling it and scattering the remaining baskets and bottles across the floor. He then knelt, thrust his hand inside the hidden door, and laughed crudely as Otto tried to wiggle out of his grasp. He grasped the boy's foot, dumping him in a heap at Giti's feet. She drew Otto into a strong embrace, as much to steady her own nerves as to comfort her brother, and she watched as the soldier pulled out the remaining supplies of food from the secret cellar. She glanced helplessly at the shears, lying on the other side of the cellar.

The two soldiers argued briefly before they were summoned upstairs. They forced Giti and Otto to their feet and pushed them up the stairs into the kitchen. The floor was covered in bullets, glass, and splinters. Oma lay face down, unmoving. Otto screamed and lunged out at the soldier who held him, but the man simply picked him up and tossed him through the gaping hole that had once been their front door. Otto landed with a thud on the frozen ground dirt at the base of the stairs.

Giti ran to follow Otto and caught sight of Mutti, crumpled in the deep ruts beside one of the trucks. Her eyes were swollen shut, and she had an angry wound on the side of her mouth. Her dress sagged where it had been ripped open, and blood snaked down her legs, pooling into the folds of the stockings that were bunched around her ankles. Her precious silver locket, the one with Pappi's and her pictures inside, still hung around her neck. She moaned softly and then yelped in pain when the soldier with the bite on his hand picked her up and threw her in the back of the truck. Otto was hurled in next and landed in a pile beside her. Mutti reached out her hand and clasped his cheek before collapsing on the floor.

A brawny officer reached for Giti. She evaded his grasp and ran back into the house toward Oma, but she stopped in the hall when she saw the last soldier light a match and toss it onto a puddle of oil on the kitchen floor. Giti grabbed a blanket off of the bench, prepared to charge into the flames, but the soldier picked her up and dragged her screaming to the truck.

Remnants from their food stores were loaded carefully as the engine roared, and the truck began to move. Giti strained to get one last glimpse of her home, willing against hope for Oma to appear on the porch. As the timber and stone farmhouse receded into the distance, she heard an explosion and saw flames shooting out of the front door and dancing in the windows. The light flickered across the yard where Giti spied Helga, her lifeless body crumpled in the snow.

CHAPTER THREE

OTTO, 2010

The nurse adjusted Otto's IV drip and rolled him over to the window so that he could see the harbor and monitor the progress of the sailboats and yachts racing across the choppy, steel gray water for the safety of their slips. Giant thunderheads massed in the sky, and the wind was picking up speed.

"Ach, a storm is brewing, Inez," Otto observed in his thick accent. "You better get yourself home before the streets start to flood." He winked at his nurse, and she reached out, her warm brown fingers enveloping his skeletal hand, crisscrossed with ropey, bruised veins and scarred from the need for constant IV drips.

"Now, Mr. Binz, spoken like a seasoned sailor, but you know I'm here for the full shift—rain, shine, floods, and earthquakes. You can't get rid of me quite that easily." She adjusted the settings on his chair, and then stepped back to make sure he was as comfortable as possible.

Otto Binz was her favorite patient, and she doted on him like he was family. This was his third trip to the hospital in as many months. The surgery had seemed routine, but the resulting infections and reactions to different medications had wreaked havoc on his fragile constitution. Years of smoking had damaged his lungs, and when the cancer appeared, it had spread with gusto. Now the treatment seemed like the biggest threat to Otto's frail body. The oncologist was running out of options and, with Otto's blessing, had begun reaching out to her colleagues about experimental treatments to try. Regardless of the outlook, Otto was relentlessly cheerful, and his sunny disposition endeared him to the hospital staff and the legion of caregivers who assisted Margie during his infrequent trips home. It was always Otto asking after *them,* inquiring about their families, worrying that his care was costing them sleep. He seldom complained.

"*Jeder Tag ist ein Geschenk Gottes.* Every day is a gift from God," he would explain to anyone who asked how he managed his endless well of good cheer. "Just think," he would add, "if I hadn't gotten sick, I wouldn't be having this conversation with you!"

His illness, however, had prevented him from attending Joe's funeral, and it was on that one day that Otto seemed defeated because he longed to be in Boston to hug Brigit, support her, and dry away her tears. They talked every day on the phone, and she had called to say that she would be traveling to Charleston to see him tomorrow. She even hinted at a surprise, and Otto was intrigued at this revelation so soon after Joe's death.

Three weather delays stalled Brigit's trip, but she made it to the hospital in time to see her father before the last round of medications for the day left him groggy and confused. In the taxi on the way to the hospital, she had checked in with Dr. Hiyashi to go over plans to cover her classes for the next two days. Her mentor, a pedantic and methodical academic, was progressing from mildly to fully annoyed at the constant disruptions to her schedule. Joe's death he understood, but this new trip out of the blue was costing Brigit good will with her colleagues. "We were expecting you back, Brigit. I don't know how long I can hold your position open," he complained. "Your work is suffering, and there are others eager to take your place."

Brigit had assured him that she would be back in two days. She needed to see her father in person and ask him a question. She'd be back on the red-eye to Boston no later than Wednesday and in class to teach Thursday morning's freshman seminar. Dr. Hiyashi relented, but Brigit was well aware that she was running out of good credit in the Psychology department. He was right. Jobs in academia were hard to find, and there were scores of eager young doctoral candidates that would love to have her spot.

She tiptoed into the hospital room where Otto was dozing in a chair by the window. The monitoring equipment emitted a constant but irregular regimen of beeps and chirps, and the compression socks around his legs occasionally whooshed with air. Margie stood up and smoothed out her skirt and matching cardigan before giving Brigit a half-hearted hug.

"You are good to come, dear," Margie whispered as she reclaimed her seat. They both peered over at the thin figure in the big chair, strung up with tubes and bandages. Margie leaned toward Brigit. "He tries so hard to keep his spirits up, but he's failing, and he knows it. He's become obsessed with Giti. It's not helpful or healthy, all this talk about long ago hurts. I wish he would give it up."

Brigit shook her head. "Mama, I don't agree. Maybe it's better to find answers. I might have something. I don't know. Is he strong enough to handle it?"

Margie sighed. "I guess any hope is better than none, and

he's lived all these years with the memories. He never shared with me what happened, and these old ghosts have lived with us and between us for years." She crossed her arms tightly over her chest. "I don't believe he can be hurt more. Let's see if you can give him something to live for."

Brigit had spent her childhood basking in her father's devotion, much to Margie's ire, and she treasured time with him as much as he was eager to be with her. Brigit knelt by Otto's chair and gave his shoulder a gentle squeeze. He opened his eyes and put his hand on her cheek. "Liebling, you're here," he said. He searched her face for any signs of sadness or distress, but her piercing green eyes sparkled, and her curls were elegantly tucked into a messy but stylish bun. "*Du bist sehr schön*. You are so beautiful," he said, "unlike me. Your papa is rather frightful at the moment."

"Papa, you are never frightful. Just tired, I think. Mama said you had a difficult night."

"Ach, it's just bad dreams, Liebling, but you're here now, and I only have happy thoughts." He clasped her hands and kissed them gently. He noticed that she was not wearing her wedding ring and regarded her quizzically.

"I'm moving on, Papa, taking a page out of your book."

Otto wasn't that easily distracted. "This isn't about me. I need to know you're all right, Liebling. It's still so soon. Mama and I worry about you and Joe."

"Dr. Joe would want you to concentrate on getting well." Brigit flashed her parents a reassuring smile. "Besides, I have something for you. I need your help." Brigit reached into her computer bag and pulled out a plastic sleeve containing the pictures. She fished out the photo of Giti with the goat and laid it on Otto's lap. "What year was this, Papa?"

Otto cradled the small, yellowed photograph tenderly in one hand while using his other to trace the outline of the girl.

"*Oh, Giti—meine liebe liebe Schwester.*" His eyes filled with tears as he implored Brigit. "You are like my sister, *ja*? So pretty and strong and smart. And don't forget you have her name. And have I ever told you that you look so much like her—the same eyes, the dimples, and the lovely smile?"

"Of course! How could I forget that? Now, what year was this photograph taken?" Brigit repeated.

"I'm not sure," he admitted. "It was in this little bag of treasures that she packed in case we had to leave suddenly, which we did, of course." His brow furrowed, and the corners of his mouth quivered.

"Are you okay, Papa? We can talk another time."

"*Nein.* Not much time left, Liebling." He smiled. "We need to talk of such things. My dream..." He faltered and then regained his strength. "I want to know what happened to Giti. I want to know before I die. This is in the days before the war, *ja*? Maybe 1937 or 1938? She would have been a young girl, and I was just a little fellow. The goat was Helga." He stared at the photograph, lost in his thoughts.

Brigit glanced at her father, so thin and frail. All her childhood, he had been full of life, a natural charmer who never met a stranger. Now the disease had diminished him, and he seemed to retreat deeper into a well of sadness that Brigit had not known existed within him. She searched for a way to lighten the mood.

"Tell me again, Papa. Tell me how you came to America. How you came to be in Charleston."

Otto closed his eyes. He became so still that Brigit put her hand on his heart to feel its timid beat. Without opening his eyes, Otto started talking. In a voice so soft that it was almost a whisper, he repeated the tale he had told for so many years.

"*I came to America on board a big ship, so big it was like a country all to itself. The first time was in 1966 or maybe '67. At* that time, I was living in Hamburg, and before that, I had been in East Germany. I ended up there after the war because I had been separated from my family, and I found my brother Stefan living in East Berlin. I thought he had died, and I was overjoyed to find him, even though I barely remembered him. Stefan survived the battles at Stalingrad, but he had lost the tip of his nose and both his ears to frostbite. We never found our other brother, Paul. There were many of us in those days, searching, trying to piece our families back together. The war had scattered us, and we didn't know how to find our way back.

Stefan had a job working in a factory, and I was soon working there with him. All day, we stood in the dust and fumes with only the tiniest windows way up near the roof. Sometimes birds would fly in, but mostly it was dust and noise and rodents. We built these awful little cars; they looked dreadful and drove just as badly. During the long days on the factory floor, I used to look up at those birds when they flew in and wonder what they saw when they were flying over the countryside. It was bleak in those days, and we all thought that we would never feel the warmth of the sunshine again.

The factory was in an area just outside of town that looked out over the Teltow Canal. One long summer day, I spied a bird trapped up in the rafters, and at the end of my shift, I climbed the ladder up to the catwalk that surrounded the factory floor in hopes of helping the bird get out. I managed to shoo the bird back out of the window, and that's when I noticed a second ladder, a concealed one that led all the way to the roof. I climbed up and was amazed to see the most incredible view of the canal, and beyond that, West Berlin. The thought struck me then that I wanted to follow the birds over the wall and into the free part of Germany. It was not so easy in those days. We had all heard stories of people who'd tried to hide on trains or in the trucks that were allowed to pass into West Berlin. Those people were shot, and the police made sure we all knew when an escape attempt had been unsuccessful.

As soon as I could, I took Stefan up to the roof and showed him. It was his idea that we should try to swim across the canal. I thought he was crazy, but he convinced me that we had nothing to lose by trying. Stefan was so sad, you see. His injuries were bad on the outside, but worse inside, where you couldn't see. His face was so scarred that no woman would even glance at him. He was lonely, and when he had the idea to swim out of East Germany, the thought consumed him. The only problem was that neither of us knew how to swim. Stefan had his injuries, and I was so afraid of the water.

There was a swimming center near our apartment. It had been built by the Nazis during the war for the health and fitness of German youth. After the war, it was taken over by the state and used as a training center for East German athletes. I arranged to meet the caretaker of the pool, and I promised him that Stefan and I would help clean the complex if he taught us to swim and allowed us to use the pool at night. In those days, you didn't ask questions. You only said yes or no, and we were lucky that he said yes. So that's just what we did. We would leave the factory each night and eat a scrap of dinner while walking to the pool. First we swam, and then we cleaned. We would get home at midnight and fall into bed exhausted. We were awake again for the factory before the sun was up, but those were happier days for Stefan and me. We dreamed of what our life would be like in West Germany, and we talked about finding Paul and Giti again.

We trained until we could swim for two hours without stopping, which is much more time than we thought we would need to swim across. Of course, we could not expect to slip into the water right at the border—too many guards there—so we planned to enter the water deeper inside East Berlin and swim several miles to the point where we could climb out on the bank *of West Germany. The main concern was Stefan's nose and ears. He had a much more difficult time holding his breath and keeping the water out. Nevertheless, we planned around it. We would slip in the water at dusk so that when we passed the guards, we would be covered by the darkness.*

The day arrived, and we were so excited. Stefan talked of walking arm and arm down the Ku'damm and tipping our hats to the ladies of the West. We were so intent on our plans that we didn't stop to worry about the clouds gathering in the sky or the wind that was growing stronger. We finished our factory shift and hurried back to our apartment to grab the bundles we had arranged with a change of clothes, all the money we had, and our papers. We had wrapped it all in oil cloth and made straps to hold it together on our backs. We didn't stop to say boo to anyone, we were so scared of someone turning us in. We walked straight to the point we had chosen to enter the canal, and we slipped into the water just as the sun dipped below the horizon.

We had about three miles to swim to the point where we thought we could get out on the West German side, and the first hour or so went according to plan. I swam out first, and Stefan followed close behind. But soon the rain began falling, and the wind picked up. It was blowing us back the way we came. I noticed Stefan was starting to fall behind, and he labored to breathe. I swam back and stuck by his side to encourage him, and he picked up speed.

We got close to the place where we thought we could climb out to safety. At this point, we had been in the water for hours, and both of us were exhausted from fighting the wind. That's when our luck really changed for the worse. A guard on the East German side saw us when a spotlight flashed over our oilskin packs. He came running to the bank and shot wildly into the water. I dove under and held my breath, but Stefan struggled at the surface. I swam back up to help him, but soon other guards joined the first, and more bullets were fired. We could feel them zipping by, and one of them hit Stefan. He grabbed my face in his hands and kissed me hard. Then he pushed me toward the shore before he began sinking. I tried to pull him along, but with his last bit of strength, he pointed me to the opposite shore and then sank out of my grasp. A bullet split the water between us, and I lost him. That is the last thing I remember before I woke up on the shore, surrounded by people trying to help me. I was in West Germany, but I was alone all over again.

In the days that followed, I was in the hospital but all I wanted to do was dive back into the water and find Stefan. I didn't have the strength to get out of bed, and I had developed a severe lung infection. Several newspaper reporters visited me, and I met with someone from the Red Cross. I asked her about Paul and Giti. She brought me confirmation that Paul had died after Stalingrad. Giti's whereabouts were unknown. There was no record of her at all.

When I was finally able to get out of bed, I opened my bundle with the soggy clothes, ruined papers, and worthless money. Only two things had survived. There was a note from Stefan. You see, he knew all along that he would not make it. He wrote that I was to be the lucky one, out of all of us: Paul, Stefan, Giti, and me. He told me to be strong and to live well for them. And there was this picture of Giti and Helga. Until I gave it to you, it was with me every day and gave me hope that I would find her.

One of the reporters wrote a story about me, and when it was time for me to leave the hospital, there was a letter waiting. A man who ran a shipping company in Hamburg had read about me, and he offered me a job. He wrote that he needed strong and dependable men to work aboard the ships taking goods from Germany to America, and he hoped I would accept his offer of employment. And that is what I did. I sailed with that company *for many years until one day on shore leave in Charleston, I decided to go to the moving pictures."*

Otto's eyes remained closed, but he smiled. He had gone quiet. Margie reached over and patted his hand, and he slowly opened his eyes.

Brigit gently stroked his cheek. "Papa, I have another picture to show you. I wrote to the German Red Cross. I read they had compiled pictures and stories about the lost children during the war, and they have collected more, much more than when you first asked for their help. They sent me a box of clippings with letters and photographs. Most are useless, but then I found this." She drew out the mottled copy of the picture showing the woman at the barn. "Look at her hand, Papa. Could it be?"

Otto took the picture and brought it up close to his face. His eyes darted across the image, trying to tease out every detail. His gaze came to a halt over the woman's hand. His face clouded with worry. *"Ach, Gott im Himmel."* Tears welled in his eyes and spilled over the papery skin of his shrunken cheeks. Brigit moved quickly to prop him up, but he waved her off. He laid the photocopy on the tray table pushed up next to his chair, and ran his fingers across the woman's features. His tears flowed freely, and he began to cough.

Inez rushed into the room, casting stern glances at Margie and Brigit. "Mr. Binz, you need to calm yourself down," she said, as she swept up the picture and handed it to Brigit. "I think you're done for the night."

But Otto batted Inez's hand away and motioned for Brigit to give the picture back. Reluctantly, she returned it to him.

"Don't worry, Papa. Maybe it is Giti and maybe it's not, but I'll keep searching. Let's go with what we know and see if we can figure out a plan." Otto peered at her plaintively as she fished a magnifying glass out of her satchel. Margie brought the lamp closer and positioned it behind Otto's head.

"First of all, Papa, do you see anything that tells you that this isn't her? A birthmark that is missing, or something like that?"

Otto scanned the photo, seeking clues. Then he turned his red and watery eyes back up to Brigit. "Oh, Liebling, it's just been so long."

"Papa, I don't want to give you false hope, but this woman looks like the girl in the other photo. She also has an injured hand, and you've always said that Giti might have done horrible damage to hers on a train. That's all I know. Can you try to tell me that story?"

Otto began to cry again. She reached down and held his face with both her hands. "Papa, it's okay. Don't tell me until you are ready. You've done a lot of reminiscing tonight. Here—look at the back. More clues! It says, '*Lithuania in 1952*,' and it has the name '*Lukas Galinis*,' a professional photographer in Kaunas. Maybe he's still alive. If there's no reason to think that this is Giti, then I'll keep hunting."

He struggled for a deep breath and shuddered with the effort. "What did you say the photographer's name was?" Otto asked.

"Lukas Galinis, Papa. See, it's written here."

Otto put his face in his hands, and his shoulders shook. It frightened Brigit to see her father so upset.

She persisted. "Papa, I'm going to try to contact Lukas Galinis or his family, and we'll keep trying. You have to hang on."

He seemed like a small child as he nodded at her, then he reached for Margie's hand. A round of hacking coughs shook his fragile body, and Brigit tenderly rubbed his back as he settled back in his chair. He kept one hand over his face as he sobbed and gulped for air.

"Papa, you calm yourself and rest. I'm going to make inquiries about Lukas Galinis, starting tomorrow," Brigit promised.

Otto heard Brigit, and he nodded, but his crying continued. Inez plunged a syringe into the IV, sending him into a drug-induced sleep.

CHAPTER FOUR

GITI, 1945

Mutti lay on the rough wooden floor of the truck and moaned. The bitterly cold wind whipped through the holes in the rotten canvas roof as the truck rumbled over the rutted lane. Giti took the blanket and draped it across her mother's prone body. It covered her legs and her skirt, but Giti noticed a burn on Mutti's cheek, seeping into her soiled white collar. It was the shape of a knife blade and smelled of seared flesh. Giti reached under the blanket into Mutti's apron to retrieve the handkerchief that always nested in the broad front pocket, and she used the soft cloth to dab at the wound. Giti felt the faint pulse on Mutti's warm neck and knew she was still alive. Barely.

Otto was curled tightly in the corner with his face buried in the thick wool sweater he had worn to play in the cellar. He too was silent. His fingertips were turning blue, and his legs were shaking. Two soldiers rode in the back of the truck with them, the thin one with angry blisters on his face and a bigger bear-like man who had a scruffy black beard with bits of dirt and food dangling from his whiskers. He had stains on his hands and neck, but no apparent wounds. Giti averted her eyes.

The two soldiers yelled at the driver in the front and

laughed wickedly when he volleyed back. Giti didn't need to know their language to understand the cruelty of their banter. She watched through the open back as the farmhouse faded from view and saw that the rest of the soldiers followed closely behind in the second truck. Long after they had left the limits of the Binz farm and Giti had seen the path to the cemetery pass by, she could still see billowing black smoke from the fire consuming all she had ever known as home.

Keeping her eyes on the floor, Giti eased over, intending to comfort Otto, but a thick, foul-smelling boot landed in her path. The soldiers snickered, and one pulled at the collar of Oma's cape. With his other hand, he grabbed a fistful of Giti's thick braids and dragged her back across the splintered floor. She yelped in pain as an exposed nail bit through the skin on her knee. The blistered soldier stood over her, a wicked grin exposing the black nubs of his remaining teeth. He was knocked off balance as the truck came to an abrupt halt. He fell on top of her, pushing her onto the bag strapped to her back and sending jolts of pain into her muscles and spine. The soldier cursed and wrapped his hand around Giti's neck, but the driver hopped down from the cab in front and the other soldiers scrambled out to join them. The soldier pushed himself up using Giti's throat, and as she gagged and gasped for breath, he rushed to join the party heading for yet another house. A red-faced guard from the other truck peered into the back ignoring Giti's distress and positioned himself so that he had lines of sight into the backs of both trucks.

Through a gash in the canvas, Giti could see bits of a farmhouse. She did not know the family that lived here, but it had the same timber and stone as her home. She put her hands over her ears as she heard shots ring out followed by the cries of women and babies. Neither Otto nor Mutti seemed to rouse at this newest assault taking place just beyond the thin veil of filthy canvas that separated them from the violence. Giti heard every sound: pots and pans flying, a woman sobbing, a gunshot followed by a thud as a victim fell to the ground. At one point, the soldier with the blisters reappeared at the back entrance to the truck. He was in his shirt sleeves now and carried a small girl, perhaps no older than six or seven, under one arm. The child was screaming and wailing, but neither the blistered man nor the red-faced guard seemed perturbed. He squared up to the back of the truck and tossed her in, right at Giti's feet. Two other children were thrown into the back of the other truck, and for the first time, Giti wondered if there were people in that truck who had listened to the carnage at her own house.

By the time the two trucks barreled into Königsberg, they had stopped three more times and had been joined by other convoys. All stops followed the same pattern: attack, collect the survivors, and torch the house. Each time, a different man or two kept watch over the trucks while the rest plundered and terrorized. The soldiers seemed to feed on the grief, and the trucks rumbled on.

There were ten people in the back of the truck, all women or children, plus the same two soldiers. The women and older girls were traumatized. Many wore little but aprons covering their ripped wool dresses. Thick stockings designed for warmth were shredded or pooled around their ankles, the same as Mutti's. Giti realized that she too might have been attacked, but Oma's oversized cape had made her appear younger than she was. She needed to keep the cape on, both to preserve the illusion of her youth and to protect the supplies she hoped would keep her family alive until they got to wherever they were going. She remembered Opa's watch and despaired. It remained on Oma's dressing table. It had purchased neither chickens nor safety.

As they rumbled through city streets, Giti held Mutti's and

Otto's heads in her lap and tried to keep them warm. She had surrendered the blanket to a woman who was thrown into the truck with her dress ripped so thoroughly that her bare breasts were exposed. The cape was stretched over Giti, Otto, and Mutti. Giti had tried to position several of the smallest children under it as well. When the soldiers began to snore, Giti allowed herself to glance up, and she stared into the face of a boy about her age. He was in the shadows at the far end next to the back flap, his eyes darting from person to person, seemingly in disbelief that so much suffering could be contained in such a small space. She noticed that he was missing a chunk of his left ear. Blood streamed down his neck, but he was not in shock like the others. Some of the passengers were stirring, others resembled scarecrows—frightened, defeated, and frozen in place with vacant stares.

The trucks converged on the train station where the soldiers scrambled out and then barked at all the passengers to follow them. The truck had made no stops for water or for the prisoners to relieve themselves. The floorboards reeked, and their tattered clothes were soiled. A few people managed to climb out, dazed and blinking in the fading daylight. Most stayed rooted to the floor. Similar scenes played out all over the staging area. Soldiers were dragging women and children from trucks and corralling them into groups. Giti watched a woman exit a truck, then turn around to coax someone else to follow her. She pleaded and cajoled, but whoever she was talking to was too ill or too scared to come out. A soldier, no more than fifteen or sixteen years old himself, walked up behind the woman and pointed his pistol into the back of the truck. A shot rang out, and she screamed and collapsed. He then turned and walked away, leaving her sobbing in the dirt.

People began spilling out, shocked into submission. With fat tears streaming down her face, Giti nudged Otto harshly, and he slowly turned his head. "You must come with me. We cannot stay here. Get up, Otto!" She hissed. He obeyed numbly, and together, they roused Mutti and dragged her to the edge of the truck.

Catching her breath, Mutti implored Giti. "I cannot stand, *Schatzi*. What can I do? We must stay together."

They continued to hear sporadic gunfire. Giti tamped down her panic and tried to keep her thoughts from racing. She noticed the boy from the truck standing close by, staring at her. She motioned to him. "Please, we need help."

Without speaking, he approached and wrapped his arms around the left side of Mutti's waist. Giti mirrored his movements from the right and together, they lifted her down. Otto climbed down behind them, wordlessly trailing them toward the cluster of women and children assembled in the yard close to the platform. The truck pulled away, and Giti realized too late that the woman and their blanket were still inside. As night fell and the temperatures plunged, they had only Oma's cape, the contents of her bag, and each other to ward off the bitter cold.

Women with sloshing buckets of water and baskets of bread circulated among the gathering. Giti assumed they were from Königsberg and wondered if they too had been victimized when the Russian troops rolled in. They walked silently among the gathered, their eyes cast down, giving no clues and no reassurance. Giti and the boy set Mutti down, and Otto curled up beside her. A woman approached and gave each a sip of water from a rusted ladle and handed out small pieces of hard, tasteless bread. The boy devoured his slice, crumbs falling from his mouth as he wrestled with the tough chunk of rye mixed with what appeared to be wood chips. Otto whimpered and nibbled around the edges while the boy eyed his and Giti's slices. Giti tore off little bits and put them in Mutti's mouth, but she gagged. Giti wiped the spittle from the edges of Mutti's mouth with the hem of her coat and divided the remaining piece of Mutti's bread between Otto and the boy.

Giti studied their companion and helper. He still hadn't uttered a word. "Let me see your ear," she said. He slowly turned his neck, and Giti gasped at the crusted nub of flesh left on the side of his head.

"Does it hurt?"

He nodded.

Giti reached under her skirt and tore off a long strip from the bottom of her petticoat. The back section was soiled where she had been sitting in the truck, but she wrapped the cleanest part close to his ear and wound the soiled section to the other side of his head.

"That will keep it from getting dirtier at least. What is your name?"

He cast his eyes down and ate the remaining piece of Mutti's bread, slower this time, either refusing or unable to answer. Giti ate her meager portion while keeping her eyes on Otto and Mutti, who dozed fitfully.

The train approached in a thick fog of coal dust and steam, prompting the soldiers to herd everyone up on the platform.

"Make a line!" Someone ordered in heavily accented German, "You will be taken away from the frontlines to safety. Stay together, and board quickly!" Giti began to rouse Otto and Mutti, and the boy fell in beside her without being asked. They got Otto to his feet, lifted Mutti between them, and shuffled into line. When the train rounded the bend and entered the yard, Giti noticed that it was pulling cattle cars. She had never been on a train before, but she had seen them crossing the plain from her perch in the cemetery, and she knew that the cars for people were very different from the cars for animals. These were definitely not cars for people. The boy tilted his head, concerned, and locked eyes with Giti. She was grateful that he was not talking. It wouldn't help to alarm Otto or Mutti, but it was clear. These cars were not meant for safety.

The boy helped Giti and Otto push Mutti up to the platform and into the train car. She staggered with every step, and when they hauled her aboard, Giti noticed that there was fresh blood streaking her legs. They settled her in a spot next to a crack in the siding and near the giant door. The cold air was racing in, but it was fresher air than what they breathed in the car. An impossible number of people were shoved in before the door was pulled shut, casting the panicked crowd in darkness. Giti watched through the crack as a soldier reached up to close the lock and seal them in. Out of her line of sight, a scuffle broke out. Shots were fired, and the soldier scurried away. The lock was never engaged.

Giti's eyes began to adjust, and she tried without success to see past the legs and backs of the people pressed against her. The crowd of passengers were eerily silent, shocked into a numb stupor. A few babies whimpered as motherless children were passed among the adults. Some of those who were next to the slatted walls, like them, were able to sit. Most in the middle of the train were forced to stand. No one noticed Mutti as she slumped toward the floor, propped up only by the crushing weight of people pressing against her.

There were no comforts in the car. A single bucket sat in the middle, presumably the toilet, but no one could get to it. Bits of grimy hay were strewn across the floor, but not enough to soften the hard planks of wood. There was nothing to heat the space except for the collection of bodies. The boy stayed close to Giti and Otto as the train chugged out of the station heading east, back along the Pregel River. Mutti moaned as the train gained speed. She was burning with fever. Giti implored the boy to help, but neither of them knew what to do. Giti drew Otto near, and together, they nuzzled close to her as much for warmth as for solace.

The train settled into a taunting rhythm. Clackety, clackety, clackety. The passengers could feel and hear the vibrations of the rails, but there was no sight to guide them other than the nefarious shadows shifting across the inside of the car. The smell of so many humans combined with coal dust was nauseating, and several of their fellow passengers retched as the train navigated the bends of the tracks. Mutti moaned and reached out her hands. Giti grabbed hold of Mutti's fingers and brought them up to her face. "Mutti?" she asked. "Mutti, we're here. It'll be okay, Mutti." Giti begged her mother to rally.

Mutti opened her eyes. "Otto?" she asked, and Otto pressed his face into the soft flesh of her chest.

"I'm here, Mutti," he mumbled.

"You two listen to me." Mutti's voice was raspy and weak, but her words were clear. "You were raised to be strong. You were raised to be smart. Don't ever forget that I loved you with all my heart, and I will be with you." She coughed. Blood trickled from her nose, and Giti wiped it away with the sleeve of her own dress.

"You stay together and take care of each other," she pleaded.

Giti pulled her mother's hand to her own cheek and nodded. "We will, Mutti. I promise."

She heard a gurgle and a rattle as Mutti gasped for her last breath. Her head pitched over and her body slumped. Giti screamed. She pulled her mother back up and thumped her hands against her lifeless chest. All the reserves of strength that had propelled her through this horrific day were gone, and she was a scared girl once more.

She felt hands on her shoulders and around her waist as she wailed and threw herself on her mother's body, the warmth of the fever disappearing in death's icy grip. She writhed, sobbed, and lashed out at anyone trying to comfort her, but Otto's plaintive cry finally brought her back. She heaved ragged breaths and thrust her arms out for him through all the strange faces crowded in. Giti and Otto were on their own now, and Giti knew that she had to get them off this train.

CHAPTER FIVE

BRIGIT, 2010

Brigit fumbled with her bags as she pushed the key into the lock of the cottage. She was not accustomed to being here alone. Every time she walked in the door, she expected to hear Joe's voice, or see a note from him on the counter, or find his running clothes tossed to the floor on the path to the laundry room. Now whatever she saw was whatever she herself had left. The silences of his absence were jarring.

Before Brigit had departed Charleston, she went back to the hospital to tease as much information as she could from Otto to aid her in her search. She had scoured the internet looking for references to Lukas Galinis and had found only one clue. A small gallery in Vilnius had featured a show of his Soviet-era photographs, but the exhibit was long past. She called the gallery's phone, but got a voice recording in Lithuanian, a message she did not understand. She needed to get back to Boston and broaden her search.

Considering the limited time and her father's fragile emotions, Brigit knew she needed a strategy. Whenever she tried to quiz Otto about his last memories of Giti, he became distraught, either reluctant or unable to speak of those events.

To get to the details of his childhood, she needed to start with facts and steer clear of emotions. She led with questions that he could easily answer:

"What year were you born?"

"1933."

"Where were you born?"

"A farmhouse outside of Königsberg in what used to be East Prussia."

"Who were your parents?"

"My mother was Ruth. I do not know her maiden name. Schneider, maybe? She never talked about her family or where she was born. My father was Walter Binz. He was born in the same farmhouse."

"When was your father born?"

"Ach, Liebling, I do not know."

"Who were your siblings?" Here, she was getting into dangerous territory.

Otto sniffled a bit and wiped his eyes. "Giti, Paul, and Stefan," he said, then slumped in his chair. Brigit gave him a light kiss on his cheek as he nodded off. It was a start, but offered her no new information.

Brigit glanced over at her mother who sat in the shadows, her arms tightly crossed over her chest. Margie embraced disappointment as an entitlement.

"What's upset you, Mama?"

Margie batted the question away with a flick of her wrist and shook her head. The machines monitoring Otto's vitals beeped and chirped in the thick swirl of unspoken resentment that sat heavily between the two women. Margie cleared her throat and without looking up, she said, "He never talks to me like that." She straightened her back and smoothed out her skirt. Her voice cracked ever so slightly when she added, "I asked. Lots of times, I asked. I should know those things."

"Oh, Mama!" Brigit picked up her chair and moved closer to Margie. She offered a hug but met stiff resistance. Brigit backed away as Margie sought to reclaim her composure.

"It's nothing, Brigit. I shouldn't have said anything." Margie paused, and then she blurted out, "You and your father, just always thick as thieves. How did that happen? He didn't even want to be a father. And then you and Joe..." She fiddled with the delicate bracelet on her thin wrist as her voice trailed away.

"Wait! Stop right there! What are you saying?" Brigit's mind was reeling, trying to make sense of what her mother had just divulged. "Mama, are you jealous of me?"

They locked eyes. Margie, long practiced at keeping a stiff upper lip, found herself in the uncertain terrain of being on the verge of tears.

Brigit reached out and clasped her mother's hand. After a long minute, Margie squeezed back and rubbed her thumb over Brigit's ringless finger.

"Mama, there's something you need to know." Brigit told her everything. The fissures in her relationship to Joe, the note that ended their marriage, and the shame of carrying it all by herself.

Margie absorbed the news, mentally adding Joe's betrayal to the list of things she didn't deserve. "Well," she said when Brigit had finished, "it appears we both know what it means to marry a man with secrets." She patted Brigit's knee briskly with as much warmth as she could muster. "Best not to dwell, dear."

"Maybe, Mama, but perhaps there's another path. I'm not ready to forgive Joe, not yet, but I'm determined to try." Brigit cajoled Margie into a tender embrace.

Back in Boston once more, Brigit pulled out the box of clippings. She rummaged through them one more time, seeking any information that might have slipped by her before. Nothing from Lukas Galinis, and nothing with the name Giti or Binz. The gallery was her only lead, and she needed someone who could listen to their phone message and help Brigit contact them. Who did she know that could speak Lithuanian?

A quick internet search confirmed that there was no Lithuanian consulate in Boston, but Brigit found a link to a Lithuanian Society. She jotted down the address, and as soon as class was over the following day, she was on her way. The building was an impressive brownstone on a leafy street on the outskirts of the business district. Clearly this used to be an upscale residential area at one point, and despite creeping commercialism, the neighborhood had retained its air of exclusivity. The grand facades now held discreet signs indicating that they were offices for high-priced lawyers or hedge funds, hardly the type of businesses that needed to hawk their wares through gaudy advertisements.

The door to the Lithuanian Society was locked but there was a button for an intercom, and a woman answered on the first ring. She politely explained that the director, Dr. Balkus, had stepped out to a meeting and would not be back until late-morning. When Brigit described the message that she needed to decipher, the woman said that Dr. Balkus would be the only one who might be able to help. She offered to buzz Brigit in, but only when the director returned, so Brigit walked across the street to an overpriced coffee shop and secured a table at the window.

After Brigit's third latte, she noticed a distinctive woman, small in stature but brimming with confidence, making her way purposefully down the sidewalk. She wore a fuchsia coat that to Brigit's eyes appeared quite expensive, and she carried a chic leather satchel draped over her shoulder. She stopped at the Lithuanian Society, fished a set of keys out of her pocket, strode up the stairs, and disappeared behind the heavy door. Brigit tossed her cup in the trash and dashed across the street in pursuit.

This time, she was buzzed in as soon as she pressed the intercom, and she entered a serenely elegant foyer presided over by a prim woman who emerged from behind a massive oak desk. On the front of the desk was a brass sign that read 'Mrs. Penworthy, Executive Assistant.' Despite her formal appearance and diction, Mrs. Penworthy's eyes projected warmth.

"Dr. Balkus just returned from her meeting, and I informed her that you were waiting," Mrs. Penworthy offered. "She asked for a few minutes and will be down to assist you directly. Feel free to wait in the parlor." She gestured to the formal room opposite.

Brigit took a seat on the expansive Duncan Phyfe sofa and tucked her feet back, hoping her scuffed shoes were out of sight. She recognized the refined features of the room even though she had grown up in much simpler surroundings. Margie was always ready to educate Brigit on the finer things in life, even if, or perhaps because, Otto's salary could never allow them to indulge beyond their most basic needs.

Framed antique maps were on display along with a single photograph on the mantel of the ornate fireplace. Brigit walked over and examined the image. It was a family portrait from the 1950s with a handsome man in the middle, his blond hair swept off his tall forehead. He was surrounded by his wife, son, and daughter. Brigit heard soft footsteps on the rug and turned quickly, embarrassed to have been caught snooping. She was immediately struck by the fact that the wife in the photograph was a carbon copy of the woman standing before her now.

"I'm Dr. Rachel Balkus, and that is a picture of my family shortly after we came to America in 1955."

Brigit replaced the photo on the mantel and reached for Dr. Balkus's outstretched hand. "I am so glad to meet you, Dr. Balkus. My name is Brigit Binz Lewin."

"Please, call me Rachel!" Rachel explained to Brigit about the Lithuanian Society and how it came into being. Her family was from Vilnius originally, where her father worked as a chemist at the university before the war. In 1937, he had been offered a prestigious position at Berlin's Humboldt University. In retrospect, it was clear that Hitler was laying the basis for his program of *Lebensraum*, which was his strategy of grabbing land in the east.

"My father did not know that at the time. He and my mother planned to return to Lithuania at some point and then the war intervened. My father resisted the Nazi machine and spent the remainder of the war in prison. He was released in 1945, and my parents found themselves in the American sector of Germany. When his professional skills became known, he was offered a position at Harvard, and they came to the United States in 1952. My parents never returned to Vilnius.

"My father's heart was always in Lithuania. His work here in America was very lucrative, though. He made a small fortune advising agricultural companies in the sixties, and my parents gathered a growing group of Lithuanian expats in the States around them. They started this society for the preservation of pre-Soviet Lithuanian art, literature, and music. He applied for permission to visit Lithuania several times when it was in Soviet control, and he was always denied. Sadly, he died in 1977 and did not live to see the end of the Cold War. At that time, I was a college professor of Baltic studies." She glanced around the room with reverence. "My mother has since died, and this is my labor of love in honor of my parents. I can work here and still teach classes to inspire love of my homeland, which I didn't visit until I was an adult. We have an extensive library upstairs, and we get a steady stream of requests for our reference materials. It's a privilege, really, and I would love to help you."

Brigit explained to Rachel all she knew of her father's story, her discovery of the photograph, and her call to the gallery in Vilnius. Rachel asked to see the photographs, and she took her time seeking out Giti's distinctive features from the earlier photograph, then checking for similarities in the picture of the older woman. She turned the copy over and examined the scribbles on the back.

"Does the name Lukas Galinis ring a bell?" Brigit inquired.

Rachel shook her head. "No, but that doesn't mean anything. The fact that a gallery featured his work means that he had a significant body of work, and there must be someone in Lithuania who knows of him and can shed some light on this particular photograph. I can certainly ask Mrs. Penworthy to check through our library to see if anything turns up."

She paused, clearly considering an idea. "There's something else that may be relevant here," Rachel continued. "Have you ever heard the term *Wolfskinder*?" Brigit appeared confused so Rachel pressed on. "At the end of the war, the treatment of Germans at the hands of the Russians was pretty horrific. Women and young girls were systematically and brutally raped; many men, women, and children were killed. The ones who survived were taken to gulags in Siberia and endured awful conditions. Some children were orphaned or separated from their families and lived like feral animals in the forests. The luckier ones were taken in by farmers and became field hands, and many made their way to Lithuania. Those children grew up without family or schooling. Many changed their names, forgot how to speak German, and have never been reunited with their families. Your father and aunt seem to fit that description. If this picture is your aunt, then she made her way into Lithuania. I wonder how they became separated and what Lukas Galinis might add to the mystery?"

Brigit pulled out her phone. Together, she and Rachel listened to the message from the gallery in Vilnius.

Rachel nodded as Brigit ended the call after the beep. "The gallery is closing, and the building is scheduled to be torn down. They are holding a final sale of all their remaining works tomorrow night. After that, they cannot guarantee any response to calls or letters. There is no forwarding number or name." Rachel pressed the photos of Giti and the woman back into Brigit's hand. "I think you have to attend that closing tomorrow night, my dear. Perhaps someone will be able to tell you about Lukas Galinis."

Brigit quickly agreed and suggested leaving a message, so she dialed the number again, and this time, at the beep, Rachel explained in Lithuanian that Brigit would be attending the closing with the hopes of gaining information about Lukas Galinis. She left her number in case anyone tried to contact her.

Buoyed by the new lead, Brigit hugged Rachel and effusively thanked Mrs. Penworthy. For the first time, she felt hopeful. Rachel and Mrs. Penworthy consulted briefly and then Rachel pushed a piece of paper into Brigit's hand.

"We had a researcher here from Vilnius several years ago, Peter Mazieka. He attended MIT as a graduate student and was invited to some of our events. I think he was quite bored with our programs, but he was homesick, and he was searching for a lost family member just like you. He would spend hours here reading the old books and translating some of our documents for us. He even taught Mrs. Penworthy some Lithuanian phrases, and she had him over for dinner at her house a couple of times." Rachel winked at her assistant. "I think we both had a little crush on the lad."

Mrs. Penworthy blushed. "There was nothing untoward, mind you! Mr. Penworthy passed many years ago, and I took a motherly interest in the young man, not having any children of my own. He was always so kind and mannerly. He was raised well."

Rachel chuckled. "Well, we truly enjoyed his company, but we haven't heard from him in a while. I'm sure he has much to keep him busy beyond corresponding with a couple of old friends in Boston, but it occurs to me that you might need a translator or an interpreter, and perhaps Peter can help, or at least point you in the right direction."

Brigit felt her spirits soar with this unexpected show of interest and generosity. "Thank you both. I promise to let you know what I find."

She left the Society feeling both elated and something else she couldn't quite pin down. Encouraged? It was validation. Neither Rachel nor Mrs. Penworthy had dismissed her search as folly. In fact, wasn't Rachel the very vision of a woman who had dedicated her life to achieving her family's dream?

Brigit felt more emboldened to tamp down the nagging voice in her head that was badgering her to back down, be reasonable, go back to work, and think all this through. She dreaded facing Dr. Hiyashi to request a longer leave. He would think less of her, be disappointed in her work ethic. Doubts began to creep back in, determined to derail her momentum. Then she thought of what Joe might say. He would pat her on the back and then tell her how much he needed her help updating his website or choosing clothes for his publicity shots. Brigit would swallow her plans, do what made him happy, and convince herself that it was fulfilling. "Well, not anymore!" Brigit blurted out, and her confidence began to rise. She had a purpose and a mission, and maybe it was worth chucking in her work, her grief, and her responsibilities to pursue Lukas Galinis.

Despite her surge of courage, it wasn't until Brigit settled into her flight to Reykjavik that she called Dr. Hiyashi. She was relieved to get his voicemail even though she knew she should talk to him in person. The flight attendant was motioning for her to turn off her phone, so she left a quick message over the roar of the engines. She turned off her phone under the glare of the flight attendant and put her head back on the seat for the first leg of her journey. It would be a long trip. At the last minute, the best the internet could piece together was a two-hop flight arriving in Vilnius late afternoon. If all went well, she would have time to check into her hotel, change clothes, and get to the gallery before it closed for good.

CHAPTER SIX

GITI, 1945

As the train rattled and swayed through the night, Giti assessed their bleak options. She didn't know where they were headed, nor what would happen when they arrived. She had the bag with a few supplies: a candle, matches, three sweaters, two books, three apples, two potatoes, and photographs. She gave sweaters to Otto and the boy, and both hastened to pull them on over their clothes. Then she slid out the photographs. It occurred to her that they might be useful if they got separated. She held them up to the last bits of light peeking through the cracks in the siding and selected the one of her and Helga. She was much younger in the picture, but it was the only one of herself that she could find. It would have to do. She reached over to Otto and tucked it into the pocket of his middle layer sweater. "In case you need to find me, Otto." He nodded automatically and didn't check to see what she had given him.

She put a photograph of Otto in the pocket of her coat along with a picture of their entire family taken just before the men had left for war. There wasn't enough light to see it now, but she had the images committed to memory: the men in their new uniforms, proudly holding their kit bags, the women in their aprons, called out of the kitchen when the traveling photographer arrived. Oma and Opa with their dour expressions. Giti knew that they were awed at having their pictures taken and had never learned to smile for the camera. Opa was a jovial man, but you would never know it from the few photographs of him. She rearranged the rest of the supplies back in the bag, and the meager possessions rolled around in the bottom of the canvas sack.

Giti worked her way to Mutti's side, and she arranged herself next to her mother's body so that she could cradle her lifeless head in her lap. Even though the family never had much in the way of fancy possessions, Mutti had always taken great care with her appearance. Her hair was always meticulously pulled back in a bun, and her clothes were thoroughly patched, cleaned, and pressed. It grieved Giti to see her bloodied and unkempt.

Giti tried to smooth back her hair and reorder her frock, but the train was just too cramped and bumpy for Giti to make much of a difference. Giti thought about what her mother would tell her right now—*stay warm, take care of Otto, be practical.* She took a deep breath and slid the woolen stockings, dirty but thick, off her mother's legs and rolled them up over her own, doubling the warmth on her limbs. As she wrestled with Mutti's body, a shaft of light pierced through a crack in the siding and glinted off of Mutti's throat. Her locket. Giti reached inside her mother's blouse and grasped the cold silver case. It was too dark to see, but Giti didn't need to view it. Mutti loved that necklace. It was her wedding present from Pappi, and inside, Giti remembered, were pictures of Mutti and Pappi when they were young and their life together was mostly in their dreams. Giti reached around Mutti's neck and unclasped the necklace. She fastened it around her own neck and tucked it in under her coat.

"Danke, Mutti," she mouthed quietly.

Then Giti remembered the lock on the train door. The soldier had never finished sealing them into the train, and there was a possibility that it could be opened from the inside. She stood up and felt around the edges; there was a gap along the side. Giti poked the boy and motioned for him to stand next to the door and cup his hands. Intrigued, he pushed his way across Mutti's body and positioned himself next to Giti. He allowed her to put her foot in his hands and use his shoulders to hoist herself up. She felt along the top and determined that it was a giant slab of wood mounted to a metal rail that ran along the top, just like a barn door. The rail stopped about where she was standing, which meant that the door opened by pushing it away from them. She climbed back down, applied her shoulder, and pushed on the edge. It moved an inch or two. If Giti could push it a couple of feet, they should be able to jump out. Giti had now aroused the curiosity of the people resting up against the door, and they slowly stirred and watched to see what was happening.

Giti ignored the others and pulled the boy closer. "We can jump out," she said urgently. "There is snow along the banks, and if we can jump far enough out and away from the train, we can get away." He nodded quickly, helped her pull Otto up, and stood by patiently as she explained her plan. She would go to the door first and push it open. She would jump out, then Otto would be next. The boy would probably have to pick up Otto and push him out to help him leap beyond the tracks. Then the boy could jump out after him. As soon as the train got far enough away, Giti would light the candle so they could find each other.

With her plan in place, Giti realized that they had to act fast. Others on the train were stirring, and while she wasn't trying to prevent anyone else from getting out, she wanted to make sure that she, Otto, and the boy were first. She touched the boy's cheek and forced him to look at her eyes. He was feverish and unsteady, but Giti had to trust that he would do what he must to help. She leaned down and kissed Otto, telling him to stand up and stay close to the boy. Finally, she secured the bag on her back under Oma's cape.

She hesitated for only a moment before she and the boy gave the door a strong push. It moved a few inches before getting caught on something above. Giti leaned in with her shoulder and shoved. The door lurched forward a bit more, enough to knock her off balance and topple an old woman leaning against the other side. The freezing air was rushing in, causing a confused scramble among the other passengers.

She steadied herself and reached for the side of the doorway with her left hand. The opening was narrow but it was enough for her to wedge herself and the bag out. Now on the outside of the car, and facing back in, she held on to the side of the door with her left hand, and with her right hand, she grasped a metal handle on the inside of the car's doorframe. She glanced down at the snowbanks falling away from the tracks, took a deep breath, and prepared to leap.

Just as she pushed off with her feet, the tracks took a sharp turn, and the train lurched to follow. The door slammed back into place, trapping her hand. She screamed as she ricocheted back against the side of the car, the weight of her whole body supported by her crushed fingers. There was a metal bar on the outside of the door that she was able to grasp with her left hand, but her feet dangled free, dangerously close to the tracks. She was now clinging to the outside of the cattle car, the wind whipping at her cape and pulling at the bag drooping from her back. She could hear people inside scrambling to open the door and free her fingers, and she could hear Otto wailing uncontrollably. She tried to yell to him but her voice was drowned out by the biting wind. Up ahead, Giti could see that the train was approaching a bridge over a river. She felt fingers prying at her hand, and the effort was helping to push her out of the door. The pain was worse than anything Giti had ever experienced, but adrenaline was taking over and keeping her focused. She took another deep breath and pulled her right hand as hard as she could at the same time as she pushed off of the side of the train with her feet. She sailed backwards and tumbled down the snowbank just as the train with Otto still aboard hurtled over the bridge and beyond the broad river.

CHAPTER SEVEN

BRIGIT, 2010

Brigit glanced at her watch and discovered that she had a few minutes to spare, so she logged on to her computer and checked her messages. Dr. Hiyashi had responded quickly to her message, and his email was short and to the point. She needed to be back by the start of class on Friday or the committee would reluctantly consider her withdrawn from the program. She resisted the urge to email him back. She would get the information she needed tonight and be back on the plane tomorrow. Friday would find her back on campus exhausted but working to get back in his good graces.

Galerija Emilia was a compact storefront on a broad retail thoroughfare between Vilnius's fabled Old Town and the city's sleek new business district, Šnipiškės. It was clear that the neighborhood had once been an area of some wealth before the Soviet occupation had brought more bleak and utilitarian structures. Like a mismatched set of dentures, formal brick townhomes dotted the block interspersed with dismal concrete structures. Clearly a new phase was underway, with several of the less distinguished buildings in various stages of demolition and gleaming metal and glass structures springing up to take their place. Light spilled onto the sidewalk near a smattering of cafes where tables were filled with chatting patrons and smart young professionals relaxing after work with a smoke and some wine.

Brigit hesitated in front of the gallery and shifted her black leather bag from one shoulder to the other. She peered in through the small windows and took a deep breath. Right now, the evening was full of possibilities, and she was hopeful that she would get a valuable clue. There was also the chance that she would leave here with nothing to show for her visit while risking her work on a fool's errand. There were already several patrons inside, but it was a thin crowd. A sign on the window advertising the closing was plastered right next to the demolition permit. Brigit didn't need to read Lithuanian to understand its intent. She pushed on the door and let herself in.

Brigit observed straight away that most of the people in the small crowd looked young, about her age in their late twenties or early thirties, and they all seemed to know each other. There was an atmosphere of easy camaraderie in the room, not celebratory, but supportive. Bare walls riddled with cracked plaster and the marks of previous exhibits dominated the space. The smattering of art that remained on the walls and easels was sparse but eye-catching—bold splashes of color on canvas, a tall sculpture assembled out of spare bicycle parts, and a series of stark black and white photographs. Brigit decided this was the last clearance event for the pieces that hadn't been sold, or one last excuse for a party, but nothing seemed to match up with anything Lukas Galinis might have produced.

Tables of snacks with random assortments of beer and wine were placed around the room with no special attention to aesthetics. Most of the men and women wore jeans, T-shirts, and scruffy jackets. Brigit stifled the urge to run back to her room and grab her favorite jeans. She was embarrassed to be at a trendy gallery wearing clothes that only her mother would appreciate, carrying a photograph that was almost sixty years old. That no one seemed to take any special notice of her calmed her insecurities; she bit back the urge to take herself too seriously and walked around to find a person who might be in charge.

Glancing about, she mustered the courage to approach a pair of young women and ask for help. They were minimally dressed in snug black jeans and tank tops that showed off their colorful tattoos and ample piercings. Brigit was grateful when the women were friendly, fluent in English, and keen to help. The dark-haired woman steered Brigit to a table and poured her a cup of white wine while her pink-haired companion set off in search of the owner. She interrupted a man who was deep in conversation with a dour couple contemplating the virtues of a massive canvas covered in black paint. The man, eager for a distraction, tilted his head as he listened and followed her hand as she pointed out Brigit.

He certainly defied Brigit's image of an art dealer. Tall and fit, he wore faded jeans with a rumpled blue jacket, and his mottled tortoiseshell spectacles, slightly askew, mirrored the color of his thick, coppery hair. He gave the appearance of a charmingly befuddled professor. He mumbled apologies to the couple and followed the pink-haired messenger over to where Brigit stood.

"I am Milo, the owner of Galerija Emilia. Are you possibly Brigit?" He shared a curious smile. "I listened to my messages this morning and am intrigued that you would fly from Boston for our little gathering."

Brigit was too intent on her mission to engage in small talk. She thrust her hand into her bag and fished out the photograph by Lukas Galinis. She gave it to Milo and explained her search for the photographer. Milo studied the picture, flipped it over to read the back, and chuckled softly.

"Ah! This is interesting," he said. "My uncle was Lukas Galinis. My father is Andrydas Galinis, and Lukas was his much older brother. For a brief time in the 1950s, Lukas was a professional photographer. This clearly is one of his photographs."

Milo explained that Lukas had been a photographer during the Soviet occupation of Lithuania. In 1950, when he was quite a young man, he set out to document post-war life in the country. "He produced quite a body of work. In the process, though, he became a vocal critic of the Soviets and got involved in a branch of the partisan movement known as the Forest Brothers. He was arrested and killed, I assume shortly after this photograph was taken, and it was illegal to possess or share any of his work after that. Some of the photographs disappeared, such as this one that is apparently in the possession of the German Red Cross. The rest were hidden by my family."

Brigit was crestfallen, not only because Lukas Galinis wasn't alive, but also because of the tragic nature of his story. "What about your father?" she asked. "Does he know anything about Lukas's travels?"

Milo shook his head and said that his father was just a boy in the early '50s. The family feared repercussions and rarely talked about Lukas's work. "That is, until I opened Galerija Emilia a few years ago. I decided to observe Partisans' Day by hosting a showing of Lukas's photographs. I assume that is what you found on the internet. Lukas is not well-known, and the work of the partisans is controversial to this day. To my knowledge, it is the one and only showing of his work."

In Brigit's mind, she was already sorting through Milo's stash of Lukas's work. "The photographs... do you still have them here?"

Milo sidestepped her question. "Unfortunately, tomorrow morning, I lock the door to Galerija Emilia for good. I planned to take a little vacation to lick my wounds and mourn the passing of my big dream." His eyes scanned the gallery and its small but enthusiastic cohort of supporters.

Brigit was determined to see those pictures, then she realized that she had reached out and clasped Milo's arm. She blushed at her immediate reaction and uttered a second bashful apology.

Milo brushed aside her concern. "I think Lukas would be honored to know that his work brought someone hope. Sometime, I plan to start on my next project, which will be a book of the resistance featuring Lukas's photographs, but," he sighed and surveyed the room again. "I have other more pressing concerns. I'm sorry you came all this way. It was nice to meet you." Suddenly distracted, he sauntered off, leaving Brigit clutching a thin plastic cup of wine and nursing a deep well of disappointment.

CHAPTER EIGHT

GITI, 1945

Giti lay in the snow and wailed, great wracking sobs that careened off the frozen river and assaulted the stately birch forest. She had lost Otto, she was alone in the woods, and her hand was crushed and bleeding. She sobbed for her mother and her grandmother and Otto. She sobbed for Helga and the timber and stone farmhouse. She sobbed for her father and brothers and Opa and even the boy who was now Otto's only companion. With her wounded hand thrust into the snow, she curled the rest of her body up into a ball and sunk into her despair, her sobs diminishing into low guttural moans. She was unable to move, consumed by the searing pain.

The shrill whistle of an approaching train roused Giti, and she felt the whoosh of the passing cars followed by the vibrations of wheels clattering across the bridge. She was surrounded by inky darkness punctuated by flashes of moonglow and receding train lights glinting off the river ice. The snow had settled into her crushed fingers and dulled the pain a bit, but when she stirred and moved to shake the bag off her back, the pain shot through her body once again. She doubled over and concentrated on calming her ragged breaths.

When she was able, she reached into her bag and fished out a potato, by now frozen solid. She wedged it into her right hand, then she gritted her teeth and folded the twisted fingers around the papery potato skin. She managed to stand up and pull off another section of her soiled and tattered petticoat, which she wrapped around her hand in a clumsy package. It would keep her fingers curled around the potato and hopefully prevent further damage. She closed her eyes for a few minutes then she began to stagger forward, heading away from the tracks and into the woods.

Voices of the owls and wolves swirled in the wind that whipped through the trees and propelled her forward as she trudged in circles. She shuffled unsteadily through the sparse, frozen undergrowth and bare winter trunks, dodging the menacing shadows that loomed over her path. She fought nausea and dizziness as the forest floor pitched under her feet. The train returned as a phantom, rocking her back and forth. She clutched onto prickly branches to keep herself upright, and when she eventually collapsed into the snow, she made no sound.

Giti woke and felt the comforting cushion of a pillow behind her head, the coarse homespun fabric achingly familiar. For a mere moment, she imagined she was home, but the smells and the erratic swishing of a broom were oddly foreign. Despite being covered with a thick blanket, she shivered in convulsive waves that caused her teeth to clatter and her joints to ache. She tried to lift her head and the pain shot down her neck. She cried out.

A man shuffled over and gently pushed Giti's head back down. "Shhhh," he warned. He placed a cool cloth on Giti's forehead and patted her arm. "Ye best lie still. Ye pretty near died out there last night." Giti held her head steady and searched around using just her eyes. Even that was painful.

The man pushed himself up off the bed and resumed sweeping. Giti noticed that he had only one arm. The sleeve of his thick wool sweater was pulled up and pinned over the nub that hung from his shoulder. As he swept, he lurched back and forth. Something was wrong with his leg too, but Giti couldn't see beyond the edges of the rough woolen blanket pulled up to her chin. His lank, gray hair draped around his face, and his threadbare clothes hung on his thin frame. Every so often, he would steal a peek at Giti. He didn't attempt any further conversation, and Giti closed her eyes. His sweeping lulled her back to sleep.

When Giti finally woke on the third day, she labored to lift her swaddled right hand and fretted over the condition of her fingers beneath the thick bandages. Seeking solace, she felt for Mutti's precious locket, fearful that this man or someone else would have stolen it. Her fingers caressed the smooth oval of silver, warm from lying against her fevered skin. She used her nail to pry it open and was relieved to see Mutti's and Pappi's young faces staring back at her, their expressions joyful as if they looked forward to a life of contentment.

The man hobbled over and felt her forehead. "Your parents?" he inquired tenderly, and Giti said nothing. He patted her shoulder. "Well I think ye've passed the worst of it," he said, and he moved over to the fireplace and returned with a cup of weak broth. He helped her sit up and take little measured sips. "Still worried about that hand of yours. My name is Tomas. Can ye tell me what happened?"

Giti stared back at Tomas. Everything about him was worn and tired and gray, but his voice was kind and soft. She was not scared of him but she had no words. She couldn't process the thoughts that would allow her to recall the jump from the train and the flight into the woods. She couldn't summon emotions. She lay propped on the pillow and sipped the broth.

Tomas seemed to understand that she was in shock, and he didn't push for more information. He told her simply that he had found her in a snowdrift when he was out checking his traps. What he didn't tell her was that she was crumpled in a heap and burning with fever. With difficulty he got her to his tiny cottage. He didn't have to ask why she was out in the woods by herself. He knew all too well what was happening in the countryside, and he had heard of children wandering aimlessly in the forest. It wasn't uncommon to find bodies by the railroad trestles, tossed from the cars headed east when death took the weakest and most infirm. He tried to stay away from the tracks. He was a simple farmer and carried his own demons from the war—the shame of being a survivor, of finding his family murdered. When he found Giti, she was the first person he had seen alive in three months.

Now that she was awake, he endeavored to allay her fears. He had taken the cloak she was wearing and the bag that lay on the ground beside her and spread them out by the fire to dry. He took the two photographs that were in her cape pocket and set them on the table next to her. She glanced over and picked up the picture of Otto. Wordlessly, she touched the image of his face with her good fingers and then set the picture down. She showed no emotion, but Tomas could see the grief in her eyes.

Tomas motioned toward her bandaged hand and asked for permission to check her wounds. Giti recoiled, and the two silently faced each other over a chasm of communication before she offered it up. He slowly unwrapped the bandages and exposed the full measure of her broken hand. He had done his best when he first found her to treat the crushed bones. In place of the potato, he had fashioned a wooden splint and wrapped her hand around it with clean bandages. He had seen many injuries like this in the hospital, his own arm for one, and amputation was the first order of business. He had neither the tools nor the stomach for the process, so he kept it clean and bandaged, and hoped for the best. Her fever was subsiding, but the hand remained dangerously swollen. The only sign of hope was that the tissue looked alive still. There were none of the grisly black fingers he had seen in his own recuperation.

Giti crawled out of bed on the fifth day while Tomas was outside collecting dried herbs and checking traps. She gathered her things by the fire and put them all in her bag, which she stowed by the bed in case she had to make another swift escape. Then she explored the single-roomed cabin. No photographs, no books. A simple fireplace for cooking and a well-worn table. She spied a chamber pot in the corner behind a screen and blushed to think that Tomas probably had to care for her with this most basic and intimate need. Random bits of crockery were piled on a shelf above a cabinet, and inanition to the bed, there were two crudely stuffed but solidly built chairs. At the foot of the bed, a ladder led up to a small loft. Giti slowly climbed the stairs using her good hand to steady herself. At the top were two mattresses on the floor covered with colorful quilts. A chest against the wall held dolls, a toy soldier, and a slate with a small piece of chalk. Giti took the slate and gently tossed it on the bed below and scrambled back down the ladder. On the slate she wrote "Thank you. My name is Giti Binz." She set it on the table, climbed back into bed, and curled up into a ball.

Outside, winter gradually lost its hold. Small green shoots pushed through the snow on the ground, and the trees began to sprout tiny leaves and buds. Giti defied the earth's gentle call to renewal and remained in a deep well of despair. She was mute. With the bleak resources at her disposal, her silence became her armor. She found an odd comfort in solitude. Tomas didn't prod, and in truth, after years of battlefield terrors and the shrieks of the dying, he was at peace with her need to draw inward.

They cobbled together a pattern of easy camaraderie. As the swelling in her hand subsided, and her fingers curled into rigid claws, she began helping him with the chores as she was able. He taught her how to accomplish complicated tasks with one functioning hand, and soon, she was chopping and cooking the meager supplies he was able to scrounge for them to eat.

They walked often through the forest, and Tomas pointed out the berries that were edible, the plants that were not, and clues to what the forest would yield if one knew the signs. It was all confusing at first. Some plants were edible when they were young sprouts, but poisonous when mature, or edible in spring and poisonous in the fall. *Avoid plants with a milky sap,* he cautioned, *and always stay away from the three-leaved ones.* He showed her wild asparagus and reedmace. They sampled a few bugs, and Tomas laughed at Giti's grimaces. She found the mushrooms most intriguing. Tomas mused, "They are intricate, are they not? A reminder that nothing exists in isolation. These beautiful stalks are all connected underground to nutrients, other living creatures, and decay. The decay marks both loss and new beginnings."

Giti nodded. She understood.

A tenacious drought ravaged the summer. Tomas and Giti were able to keep a simple garden going with buckets of water they hauled several miles from the river, but the garden yield was scant for their summer needs, and they resorted to foraging for wild vegetation to fill their gnawing bellies. Both worried about what they might be able to put away for winter. One day they wandered much farther from the cabin than was their custom, in search of berries or wild animals, and they stumbled on the remains of a makeshift village. The fires were still smoldering, and there were bodies strewn among the wreckage.

"Russians," seethed Tomas under his breath. "These poor folks weren't hurting a soul. Fleeing is all they were, and now look. Evil, pure Russian evil."

They scoured the tents and wagons and managed to find a few potatoes and jars of summer preserves. They bundled the provisions into their cart along with the bits and pieces they had gathered along the way, and set off toward home. On the trek back, Tomas talked to Giti with a seriousness and a forcefulness that he had previously avoided. He explained to her that Soviet troops were now in control of East Prussia, and that none of them were safe. He told her of his wife and children, all killed, and Giti's lack of reaction confirmed for him that she had experienced the same. He also oriented her to where they were. His cabin was west of Tilsit in the northernmost territory of East Prussia. The river that flowed near his cabin was the Memel River, and beyond it lay Lithuania.

"I have heard tales of children who managed to get to Lithuania and found safety there." He forced her to hold his gaze. "If the Russians come, ye must promise me that ye will go there. Ye are older now, and they will see ye as a woman. Ye are not safe with them, understand?"

Giti stared down at the lumpy clothes she was wearing, odds and ends from the trunk in Tomas's cottage. A woman? She pondered her situation and couldn't settle on *what* she was. Childhood was an illusion.

They walked in silence for the rest of the journey back to

the cabin, both contemplating the repercussions of what they had witnessed, and when they arrived, Tomas went straight away to his cabinet and pulled out a small map. He showed Giti the approximate location of the cabin, where Tilsit lay, and again he pointed out the river. "Stay away from Tilsit. The Russians are there. Here is the best spot to cross the river—farmers and fishermen are often there with boats." Then he folded up the map and tucked it into Giti's bag.

Winter again, and Christmas was approaching. Tomas told Giti that he had family: a brother, nieces, and nephews, but that they lived far away. It was two days' journey but before the war, they had often spent Christmases together. He proposed that they set out in a week's time to see if the family was still there. He needed to tell them about his wife and children and felt strong enough to make the trip. "They have a daughter not much older than ye, Giti. That would be nice, eh?"

Giti eagerly set about making gifts. She labored over the fire rendering wax from honeycomb to make candles and balm. She tried to unravel an old sweater she found in the loft chest and knit a new scarf for Tomas, but she couldn't make her broken hand work with the needles, so she gathered vines from the woods, soaked them, and began weaving them into serviceable baskets. It was difficult at first, but she eventually developed a rhythm and produced two good-sized containers. She added it all to her bag for the journey.

Four days before Christmas, the snow that had been steadily falling abated, and timid sunshine leaked through the clouds. Giti decided to venture out to check their traps and scavenge seeds and nuts that might still be clinging to the trees. Both she and Tomas had lost more weight as they rationed out their dwindling supplies, and they needed food for their journey. With the drought and the war, they couldn't just show up at his family's door and expect to be fed. She passed the first three snares and found nothing, but the fourth produced a thin rabbit that Giti collected. She reset the trap and wandered a bit farther collecting rose hips, acorns, and burdock before she turned toward home.

She was lost in her imaginings about celebrating Christmas with a houseful of people and didn't hear the soldier until he stepped into her path, his gun leveled directly at her head. She gasped and dropped her basket, the rabbit falling in the snow with a dull thud, and the acorns spilling out in all directions. She stayed rooted in place as the man inched his way to her, a malevolent grin forming in his scraggly beard.

He uttered something in Russian and crept close enough for Giti to gag at his wretched smell. When he reached out and yanked a fistful of Giti's hair, she gritted her teeth, pulled back her right hand and aimed for his head. Her wooden splint hit him in the temple, not enough to do any damage but enough to stun him momentarily. Giti bolted to her left and ran toward the cabin. The soldier rubbed his head, grabbed his gun, and darted after her. He tripped once on a tree stump, but otherwise kept pace with Giti, narrowing the gap as she approached Tomas's cabin. Her shriek brought Tomas to the door with his gun. With his one hand, he lifted it to his shoulder and fired at the intruder, grazing his shoulder. The soldier paused long enough to glance at his wound and watch Giti run to the shed, then he hoisted up his gun and aimed at Tomas. Giti heard the shot pierce the forest, and as she turned back, she saw Tomas pitch headfirst into the snow. A trickle of blood soaked into the dirt-filled ice under his head.

The soldier then turned and glowered at Giti, his venomous eyes boring into hers. She backed into the shed up against

Tomas's workbench and watched the soldier advance on her through the door. Giti had no means of escape. The door was her only way out. The soldier dropped his rifle to the side while he licked his lips and kept his gaze on Giti. She stood still, breathing heavily, watching every move. When he was close enough, he grabbed her by the neck with one hand and slammed her head backwards while he ripped open the front of her dress, then he fumbled under her skirt for the underclothes. Giti tried squirming but he wedged his legs between hers and pinned her to the table.

He struggled to maintain his balance and briefly loosened his grip on Giti's throat. She swiveled to her left, scooped up Tomas's awl and slammed it into the soldier's back. She wasn't strong enough to thrust it very far, but she managed to wound his shoulder. Startled, he spun around, grasping at his back. She hooked her leg around his, brought her hands together, and pushed him backwards. He hit the dirt floor with a thud, briefly stunned.

Giti tried to step over him to reach his rifle, but he grabbed her ankle and pulled hard. She fell over and landed with her chest on top of the wooden splint around her hand. The pain shot through her arm, and the blow knocked the breath out of her. The soldier was pulling on her leg, and for a few seconds, he reeled her back toward him. She summoned her remaining strength and kicked with all her might. Fueled by fear, her flailing legs loosened his grip, allowing her to push away and lunge toward the rifle. Her fingers closed around the cold steel, and she pulled the weapon toward her. Jamming the butt against her shoulder, she spun around and pushed the rifle into his torso before she squeezed the trigger.

The shed was quiet but reeked of the violence of their struggle. Giti scrambled up from the floor, refusing to look back. She didn't want to see the man, didn't want to know if he was dead or alive. She was consumed only with the need to flee. Once out of the door, her stomach lurched, and she lost the remains of her scant breakfast into the slush by the side of the shed. She stood sucking in the cold air as her stomach cramped. She managed to scoop up a handful of ice and run it across her face and her mouth. Then she darted into the house, covering her eyes as she passed Tomas's prone body, then ripped off the remains of her dress.

Giti pulled on Tomas's extra shirt, thick sweater, and trousers, cinching the waist with a piece of rope. She wrestled her arms into his heavy coat, pulled on a pair of his clunky boots, grabbed her bag and the blanket off her bed. Her fingers reached through all the layers of scratchy fabric to feel for the shape of the locket. Then she tucked her photos in her bag.

She stood in front of the mirror and stared at herself with disgust. Her cushion of safety living under Tomas's roof had been destroyed and once again, she felt raw, exposed, and vulnerable. Tomas's words echoed in her memory. *They will see ye as a woman now.*

She dropped her bag and pulled out the sewing basket. Sifting through the thread, needles, and measuring tapes, she found the scissors. She stood back in front of the mirror and grasped her thick, blond braid as well as she could with her right hand. Holding the scissors steady, she sawed through her beautiful hair as close to her neck as she was able. Then she tossed her braid, the last vestige of her youth, into the fire. It sputtered as it melted in the flames, filling the cabin with a caustic odor. She pulled Tomas's winter cap low over her forehead, and studying her image in the cracked mirror, she searched for signs of her lost girlhood. She was at odds with her body. It seemed disconnected to her mind, and Giti no longer recognized the person who stared back at her.

She retrieved her bag and peered through the window at the

shed. Seeing no one, she crept out the door and crouched by Tomas's body, already as cold as the ground where he lay. She put her hand on his chest and kissed his shoulder. Then she ran into the shed, covering her eyes as she caught sight of the lifeless soldier on the dirt floor. She took Tomas's hunting knife and flint from the shelf on the wall and stowed it in her bag. She doubled back and knelt by Tomas one last time. She held his hand and thought of the many ways he had shown such kindness to her.

She retraced her steps from earlier in the day when she had been idly planning their Christmas celebration together. Now, she was focused only on survival. She retrieved the skinny rabbit as well as a smattering of acorns and nuts, stowing everything carefully. Then she faced the wall of trees and began walking to the river.

CHAPTER NINE

OTTO, 1945

The train pulled into the station deep in the starless void of night. Otto and the boy had lost track of how many days they had been sealed into the cattle car. It reeked of death, vomit, and excrement, and the floor was littered with the bodies of the people who didn't survive the journey. It had been more than a day since they last stopped for food and for the soldiers to pull out the dead. Otto had hidden Mutti's body from them, terrified of what they would do to her. She remained in the car, slumped and undignified as the rigor mortis passed.

The door to the car lurched open, exposing a gaggle of soldiers on the platform surrounded by dazed and depleted prisoners. The soldiers were yelling at people to get into line. Those that hesitated or refused received a sharp blow to the head from the butt of a rifle. "Schnell!" screamed a young private in a crude Russian accent, pointing his weapon into the car and just over Otto's head. When no one moved toward the door, the soldier grabbed the nearest person, an older woman with a festering gash on her forehead. He yanked her from the car and threw her to the platform. The rest of the passengers, barely alive, began picking their way to the door, stepping around bodies, some dead and others near-dead, drawn equally by fear and the prospect of fresh air out of the open door. Disoriented and weak, they formed lines and shivered in the cold.

Otto caught sight of the boy being pulled upright by meaty, well-fed hands. He disappeared into the line of people streaming out of the car and onto the platform. Otto remained rooted to the filthy floor as he clutched Mutti's cold arm. He wouldn't leave her. He squeezed his eyes shut and remembered his mother's rough hands and how they used to hold his fingers tight. He remembered that her fingers were thick and calloused, with short nails and ropey veins that twisted across the backs of her hands like a tangle of blue yarn. But always her hands were warm and strong, and when Otto watched his Pappi and brothers march away down the road leaving him behind, it was Mutti's capable hands that enveloped his own and made him brave. He needed her back.

The blood was roaring in his ears, so he felt rather than heard the rough thump of boots on the train floor. "Get out!" yelled the soldier as he grasped the collar of Otto's sweater and flung him through the open door. Otto hit the platform with the side of his body, and several panicked people stepped on him as he tried to sit up. He glanced back into the train to see Mutti's body tossed to the middle of the car. One, two, three bodies followed until he couldn't see her any longer.

Otto searched the platform for the boy, but he was lost in the crowd. Otto was jerked up to his feet and thrust into a line. When he tried to break free to search for his friend, a soldier grabbed his arm and pushed him back. Otto called out, and the woman behind him shushed him quickly.

"You'll get us all killed," she seethed.

Otto didn't care about dying at this point. He screamed, but the soldier in front ordered the line to march off the platform toward the woods. The woman behind pushed on Otto's shoulders, propelling him forward with hands that were cold and sharp. Otto was forced to walk away from the only friend he knew.

They trudged through the snow for two days, stopping only for brief breaks to pass out water and stale bread. Otto tried to bite into the brittle slices, but his gums bled and his teeth were loose. In the middle of the night, he fell over in the snow. The woman picked him up. The acid was gone from her voice, and she hooked her arm through his, nudging him along.

On the second afternoon, they walked out of the forest and into a prison. It was set in a desolate valley at the edge of the woods, surrounded by fields and quarries. As he was led through the massive iron gate and thick stone walls, he spied the men in the guard tower pointing their weapons down at the bedraggled group. The old men and boys were separated from the women and girls as they were forced into long halls. They stood on cold cement floors where the guards shaved their heads and forced them to strip off all their clothes before herding them through ice cold showers. The smell of human filth and visions of emaciated skeletons wearing only their own pale, slack skin surrounded Otto. He pulled the photo of Giti out of his trousers as he removed his clothes and held it tightly in his fist under the frigid water. After the showers, Otto was handed scratchy trousers, a shirt, and a pair of wooden shoes. The right and left shoes were different sizes, and both were too big for his small feet. Shuffling forward to the next station, he was handed a thin blanket before being herded once again into another long hall with rows of crudely built bunkbeds.

This room was filled with boys about the same age as Otto. Several were crying but most just stood still, lost and numb. The boys were positioned in two lines in front of the rows of beds, their uniforms either puddled around their feet or clung to their wasted bodies with too short sleeves and too short legs. The boys stood for several minutes until a sturdy woman strode into the room with a sneer on her face and a horse crop in her hand. She spoke impeccable German.

"My name is Frau Petrov, and I am your new mother." She paused to glare at the boys assembled in the hall and sucked on her tobacco-stained teeth. Spittle glistened along the edge of her mouth. She tapped her palm with the end of the short whip for emphasis. "You have been saved by the mercy of the Soviet state, and you are now home. If you behave and do as you're told, you will be fine. Those who disobey will be punished. Do I make myself clear?"

Otto's life fell into a grim, predictable rhythm of long days in the fields punctuated by fitful periods of sleep during the interminable nights. Many of the boys cried out in their sleep, some continued to suffer from diarrhea, the brown stains running down the legs of their trousers and the revolting smell permeating the sleeping hall.

Otto's job was to help the men in the fields. During the winter, they cleared new ground to build more barracks for the guards and barely habitable quarters for the prisoners. From dawn to dusk, Otto hauled rocks and stumps from one spot to another. As the weather improved, and winter turned to spring and then to summer, they labored in the fields, growing vegetables and potatoes. Otto didn't know who the vegetables were for since the diet in the camp never varied; always it was thin turnip soup and stale bread. His hands grew calluses that matched the scab that was growing over his heart. Once, five or six months after his arrival, he thought he caught sight of the boy from the train, but when he called out, he received a sharp rebuke in the form of a rifle butt to the temple. His head buzzed for days.

Otto befriended the boy who slept in the bunk just below his, and they shared stories of their families. Werner suffered from hacking coughs, and each night, Otto took his blanket and crawled into Werner's bunk so the two blankets and two bodies could generate more heat. One morning he woke up to find Werner dead in his arms, his lips blue and his eyes wide open. Otto kept to himself after that.

One night, Otto returned from the fields, two pieces of stale bread in his hands. He saw a new boy in Werner's bed. He was several years older than Otto and seemed to be too old to be placed with the children. He was tall and, unlike others in the camp, he carried a little meat on his bones. Otto walked past him to the troughs at the end of the hall and splashed water over his face. He rubbed his hands across the downy stubble that was accumulating on his chin, and he adjusted his trousers. He had lost track of how long he had been in the gulag. Months ago, he had outgrown the original trousers he had been issued. As bigger boys succumbed to illness and died, Otto was able to trade up for new trousers and shirts, all in the same prickly cloth. Now his shirt and trousers were close to fitting but one of his mismatched shoes was still too small. Otto returned to the bunk and climbed up, ignoring the newcomer. He was too tired from moving stones all day to react when the boy jumped up and grabbed Otto's leg, tossing him to the floor and stepping on his chest.

"I'm Boris," he said as he put his face right up to Otto's nose. "You'll do as I say." He grabbed the thin mattress and moth-eaten blanket off of Otto's bed and laid it on his own. Giti's picture fluttered down to the floor, and Boris picked it up. He whistled loud and long.

"Is this your little whore?" he hissed. He yanked the crusts

84

of bread out of Otto's hands, turned his back, and left Otto lying on the floor. Otto glanced around the room, but none of the other boys would look at him. They stared away, trying to avoid attracting the newcomer's attention.

Then Otto saw Frau Petrov. She had been in the shadows in the back of the room, watching. She sucked on her teeth, turned on her heels, and strode out of the hall. Otto crawled up on the bare boards of his bunk and curled into a ball. His face burned with shame. He remained that way through the night and came to a firm conclusion. He would not surrender like that again. He pledged to reclaim his photograph of Giti, and he would fight back. He would rather die than suffer humiliation like that again.

Otto returned from the fields the next day and walked down the corridor between the bunks. He saw Boris on the lower bunk, snoring like a sputtering engine, curled up on the two mattresses. Giti's picture was propped against the wall. Otto stood over him, breathing heavily as Boris shifted slightly and burrowed back into the blankets. Otto pulled up his right hand, clutching an apple-sized rock in his fist. He slammed the rock into Boris's head, the sound of bones crunching from within Boris's ear. Otto hit him again and again while the other boys circled behind him, silently watching the attack without any move to help Boris or stop Otto's anger. Boris clutched his head and whimpered.

Frau Petrov's whip landed sharply on Otto's shoulder. He cried out and dropped the rock as she grabbed his arm and pulled him out of the hall and into the yard. He was taller, but she was better fed. He had no strength to fight back. Two guards picked him up and carried him to a concrete building on the edge of the camp. Once inside, they tossed him in a tiny cell and slammed the door shut. There was no light, and the ceiling was too low for Otto to stand up. He curled up and whimpered himself to sleep.

For over a day, Otto stayed wedged in the black hole. Occasionally he heard voices, but mostly there was nothing: no light, no noise, no ticking clock, nothing to signal the passing of time or the movement of one hour to the next. When the door finally flew open, Otto was assaulted by light and the smells of food. Real food. The guards pulled him out and forced him upright, and he found himself staring directly at Frau Petrov. She put her hand on his arm and led him to a table.

"Sit," she commanded. And Otto complied.

In front of Otto was a bowl of stew with vegetables and meat. The aroma was overpowering, and Otto's stomach lurched. It had been years since he had eaten such a meal. Right behind the bowl was a loaf of fresh bread with a downy center and soft crust, and next to that was the photograph of Giti. Frau Petrov positioned herself across the table from Otto, and the guards backed away.

"Boris was one of my best boys," she said. "You took care of him in one day."

Otto sat still with his hands in his lap.

"Eat," she coaxed and tore off a hunk of bread, which she placed in front of him. He snatched it up and ate it whole. The soft dough stuck in his throat, and he gagged. Frau Petrov waited and stared. She picked up the picture.

"Your sister?"

Otto nodded.

"Do you want to see her again?"

Otto took a sip of the stew and tore off a smaller piece of bread. He nodded again.

"You know I can make that happen." She leaned in, and he could smell her toxic breath. "If you help me, I'll help you." She waited for him to respond, but he just stared at her, mashing the bread with his weak teeth. "You'll have to be better than Boris, though. He shouldn't have picked that fight with you."

The deal was struck, and Otto was allowed to finish the food before he was kicked back outside, clutching Giti's photograph. Only a few feet away from the door, Otto was dismayed when his frail body rejected the savory treats, and he hovered over the ground gasping for breath as his stomach cramped.

It was a simple arrangement, really. All he had to do was listen to the conversations in the hall and in the fields and report them back to Frau Petrov. It was for the safety of the boys, she insisted. She couldn't be everywhere, but she was responsible. Otto would be her eyes and ears, and in exchange, she would help him find Giti and put extra food rations in his kit.

Most days were uneventful. Otto resumed his work in the fields and reclaimed his bunk in the hall. Giti's picture returned to the spot at the side of his bed so he could see her when he rested his head for the night. Every few days, Otto was taken from the fields at the end of the shift to the concrete hut where Frau Petrov and a hot meal were waiting for him. While he ate, she quizzed him about the boys, the men's chatter in the fields, any talk he may have overheard from the guards. He related what little he heard; often it seemed inconsequential. Once, Otto told her that one of the boys in the hall had talked of disappearing into the woods during the labor shift. The boy bragged that he had hidden supplies behind a tree. Otto did not know the specific tree, but he explained where the boy usually worked. Frau Petrov nodded but said nothing. When Otto returned to the hall, the boy was missing. He never returned.

Otto began to put on a bit of weight. That and his frequent absences made him a pariah among the other boys, now turning into young men. They never confronted Otto, and he kept his counsel, but talk dwindled around him, and soon he had nothing of importance to report to Frau Petrov. She became frustrated with him, and she called him less and less for meals and conversations.

It was a surprise when the guard motioned him out of the line from the fields and led him back to the concrete hut. There was no food on the table, and Otto heard the faint stirrings of another person behind the door to the hole where he had been kept so many months ago. Frau Petrov stood in the corner, tapping her leg with the whip.

"Your sister is dead," she said. She stared at Otto, daring him to react.

He lifted his head and challenged her. "How?"

Frau Petrov picked at her raggedy fingernails. "Her body was found in the woods near Königsberg. The wolves got her." She glanced at Otto for a reaction and was disappointed that he seemed not to register the details. "Her body was ripped apart, so it was difficult at first to know who she was."

"So how do *you* know?" he challenged.

"She was clutching a picture of you."

"Which hand?"

"How would I know?" she spit out. She advanced on him and leaned into his face. "The little runt was food for the animals. There wasn't much left."

She brushed past him and stormed out the door.

"I don't believe you!" Otto hollered after her, just before the guard slammed the butt of his rifle into Otto's kidney. Otto doubled over and clutched at his side. "You're a liar," he insisted, but Frau Petrov was gone.

CHAPTER TEN

BRIGIT, 2010

Brigit's mind was a tangle of thoughts, mostly irritation at being dismissed by Milo and embarrassment that she had allowed herself to think that this trip would yield any clues. Her discomfort began to coalesce into anger, both at herself for risking precious time and resources to scamper across an ocean to grasp at straws, and at Milo for his disregard of her clear and compelling interest in his uncle's work. She tossed her clothes roughly on the floor and pulled on Joe's oversized shirt. It was late afternoon in Charleston. She thought about calling her parents, but couldn't face telling her father about the failed encounter with Milo.

Brigit knew she also had to confront the decision about her work. She conjured the image of Dr. Hiyashi's kindly face. He had been so attentive to her, a great mentor. She had never knowingly let anyone down in her life, and so she reconciled herself to plunging back into her studies. She clicked on her email hoping to find a nugget of encouragement. The fourth message down immediately caught her attention. It was from Dr. Hiyashi and the subject line read simply, 'Sorry.'

Dear Brigit,

I hope you made it safely to Vilnius and found the answers you are seeking. I can imagine that this is a difficult time for you to have your father's affairs unresolved so close to your loss of Joe. We care about you and hope that your endeavors on behalf of your family bring you peace.

This is difficult to write, and I would prefer to talk to you in person, but I know where you are and what you are doing. I do not want to interrupt your work. Dean Hollis has learned that you missed class again this week. In response, he called a meeting of your doctoral committee this morning. In light of your recent attendance issues and the delays in your work, the committee has decided to suspend your teaching grant for the remainder of the year. You will not lose the classwork and progress toward your degree. After the academic year is complete, you may reapply for your grant. I cannot promise, however, that you will be successful. Competition is strong, and the committee is disappointed that our efforts to work with you through your family difficulties were not better received. Please know that we all wish you well. Call me if I can help. I enjoyed working with you and want nothing but the best for your career.

Sincerely,
Nathan Hiyashi, Ph.D.

So that was that. The last support had fallen away. She had no marriage, no job, no prospects, and no luck with the one thing her father needed more than anything—a glimpse of his sister. Was Giti even out there to find still? Brigit retreated under the covers, too dejected to cry. She fell into a fractured slumber, assailed with visions of packing up her life in Boston and returning to Charleston. She saw herself moving back into her old bedroom, now refurbished as Margie's pristine and bland spare room reserved for the guests she would never have.

The next morning, Brigit emerged from the hotel exhausted from a bruising night and dismayed to be greeted by an ebullient taxi driver waiting at the curb. She considered requesting another less gregarious helper, but the desire to extricate herself quickly won out. She allowed the driver to stow her bag with much fanfare in the front passenger seat and rush back to open the door for her to climb into the back of the car. As soon as he maneuvered the taxi away from the curb, he began to chatter about the history of Vilnius and recent developments in the area. Brigit laid her head against the cool window and let the words wash over her. A couple of quick turns, however, and Brigit realized that the taxi was nearing Galerija Emilia. Her pulse quickened, and she sat up in the seat in time to see Milo place a rubbish bin on the sidewalk and disappear back inside.

"Stop!" she blurted out, interrupting the driver, and then she softened, "Please, stop. I'm so sorry but please stop!"

The driver abruptly ended his recitation and steered the taxi to the curb, mildly panicked at the interruption. Brigit fumbled with her wallet and handed the man a wad of bills, likely many times over the cost of the short journey around the block. She scrambled out of the car before the driver had a chance to open her door. He set her bag down on the sidewalk and drove away in search of a more compliant customer.

Brigit stood outside the gallery, and all the uncertainties from the night before flooded back. This was folly. Her flight left in three hours, and she had no plan of what she hoped to accomplish here. Brigit tried the door, but it was locked. She peered through the glass and saw only bare rooms, piles of trash, a few frames stacked on a folding table, and the sculpture of bicycle parts dismantled and splayed across the floor. Then Milo walked into view, a broom in one hand and a cellphone to his ear. Brigit knocked again, and Milo looked up, confusion written across his face. Clearly, he didn't recognize her. He slowly approached the door.

"Mr. Galinis? Milo? It's me, Brigit. We met last night. May I have a minute of your time?"

Milo nodded and signed off on his call. He straightened his glasses and opened the door.

"Brigit? Yes, of course, my new American friend." Milo smiled warmly but didn't move to invite Brigit in. "What can I do for you? If you left something, I'm afraid it isn't here. The place is pretty much cleaned out."

Brigit held her ground and leaned in through the door. "Actually, Milo, I'm not sure what I want beyond a few minutes of your time. May I come in?"

Milo waved Brigit in, reaching for her suitcase. "Of course, my apologies! I didn't mean to leave you standing there. I'm a bit..." he searched for the right word, "preoccupied at the moment." He set down her bag by the door and disappeared briefly, returning with two folding chairs. "Please have a seat and tell me what's on your mind."

Brigit glanced around the gallery. "You've been up all night," she observed.

Milo nodded. "A good bit, but not all."

"Look, I know I dropped in on you at a really bad time. I am so sorry about ..." Brigit paused, trying and failing to summon the right word, "all this. Can you hear me out for a minute, though?"

Milo listened patiently as Brigit explained her father's history and the urgency around her search for her aunt. She stuck to the facts and tried to compress her speech into as tight a narrative as she could.

"You see, I have to know if my aunt is alive. If there's any chance that I could help my father know what happened to her, it would mean the world to an old man to find his sister before he dies."

Milo ran his fingers through his hair and adjusted his glasses. He had deep circles under his eyes, and Brigit's story seemed to have resonated.

"I don't know, Brigit." He sighed. "Maybe if you'd come a month or so ago. But things are complicated right now."

"Milo, can I just see the pictures that you have from your uncle? Then I will leave you alone. I promise. I have a flight to catch this morning, so I won't be too much of a bother."

He looked up and smiled. "Sure, why not?"

Milo retreated to a back room and returned with a large faded black box. He pulled out two pairs of special gloves, handing one set to Brigit and tugging the other pair onto his large hands. She popped hers on easily while he continued to pull and adjust.

"Lint-free," he explained, "to preserve the pictures." He opened the box to reveal dozens of photographs that had been mounted on museum-quality boards. In addition to the mounted photographs, there were journal entries, maps, and additional loose photographs. Milo began by lifting out the framed photo on top. A young man with a head full of hair tucked under a military-style cap stared back at the camera, his mouth curled into the beginnings of a smile and his dimples lending his face an aura of joy and carefree confidence.

"Lukas, right before he was murdered," Milo said simply.

"What a tragedy," Brigit responded. She used her gloved hand to wipe dust off the glass. "So young! He was a handsome man, and I see the family resemblance. Looks as though he had reddish hair, just like you. A family trait?"

Milo chuckled. "Sort of. I think I resemble Lukas more than my own father."

He began laying out the mounted photos. Lukas's work was

far-ranging, which was astonishing considering his youth and inexperience. There were images of factory workers laboring over machines and assembly lines, street scenes of Soviet-made cars dodging pedestrians along urban thoroughfares, and shots of agricultural workers toiling in the fields or displaying their produce. Brigit and Milo took out all the photographs and sifted through them to isolate the ones featuring farms and the countryside. Once they had them all arranged, Brigit pulled the copy of the woman from her bag and laid it out with the others.

It was like a giant jigsaw puzzle, scanning the images for similar faces, features, or buildings. Milo saw the first connection—the barn in Brigit's photograph appeared in another shot of six men posed before a threshing machine. Milo turned it over and saw the same markings on the back. This one was stamped 75 whereas Brigit's photo was stamped 73.

Brigit began turning over the images to view any additional numbers, and Milo showed her how to expose the backs of the mounted ones. They organized them by number, and a pattern began to emerge. Brigit was disappointed to see that the woman with the wounded hand was not in the other pictures, but maybe there were leads in the piles of journal pages.

"Do you think that Lukas might have recorded where he took the pictures in his journals?" Brigit asked. "Maybe the numbers give us a location."

Milo knitted his eyebrows together and drew his mouth in tight as he concentrated. "I haven't really delved into the journals yet. I was so excited about the photographs and getting them on display. The journals are my next task. I've got copies to share, but they are all in Lithuanian and in Lukas's handwriting, which frankly is rather difficult to read. And they are water-damaged in places." He waved his hands across the scattered files. "All of this is my next project: learning more about Lukas's life and his death. But I have debts from the gallery, and I don't think I can afford to stop and work on this. I have to fund it somehow."

Brigit placed her gloved hand on Milo's arm. "Would you allow me to make photocopies of Lukas's journals and some of these maps? I could take them with me to Boston and let my friend at the Lithuanian Society make some calls."

"Brigit, no!" Milo exclaimed. "These photographs and documents are all I have. I can't allow you to take them and show them to anyone." Milo began packing up Lukas's work and arranging each piece back in the box with tender precision.

She needed to be on her way to the airport. Her mind began racing through the possibilities. She could fly back and tell Rachel about the journals, but what good would that do? No. She needed someone to decipher those journals and find anything Lukas may have written about the woman on the farm that winter day.

Milo was replacing the lid and peeling off his gloves. This can't be it; it just can't be the end, Brigit thought.

"Milo, listen. I need to know more about Lukas and his journals, and I think you might want to know more too. I know I just blew in here with a crazy emergency and a lot of demands, but maybe there's something here for both of us?" She paused to gauge his reaction, and when there was none, she plowed ahead. "If you'll take a chance with me, my friend may be able to help you with your project. Maybe she has connections, or even knows a potential donor. Are you willing to take a leap of faith?" She added, "What would Lukas say?"

Milo contemplated the request, and Brigit saw determination behind his crooked spectacles and weary eyes. He sighed. "I think Lukas would say... yes."

CHAPTER ELEVEN

GITI, 1945

Giti stood on the banks of the Memel and stared across at Lithuania on the other side. Same snowy plains, same pine and spruce trees, same cold, and same questions of fear and trust as on the Prussian side. But Tomas had promised her there was safety there. She had spent days trekking through the dense forest following his map as best as she could, dodging the bands of soldiers scouring the countryside for supplies and survivors, eager to exact their revenge on the most frail and infirm. Now, she stared across the frozen river and wondered what could be so liberating on the other side. Giti thought people were like the trees: some tall, some short, some beautiful, some straggly. What difference could a river possibly make? She observed her own footprints in the snow. To follow them led back to danger and heartache. She faced the frozen Memel and plodded forward.

Three days before, she had entered the thickly wooded plain from Tomas's cabin and followed the directions that he had drilled into her. She had fallen into a morass of loneliness and self-doubt, punctuated only by moments of confusion and waves of panic. Snow swirled around her, taunting her and obscuring the way forward. The cold plucked at her skin, burrowed into her bones, and seized her lungs. She couldn't trust her vision. The mottled trunks of the birch trees blended into the bleak landscape to erase reference points. The trees grew more densely packed, saving their branches for the uppermost canopy, so all Giti could see was a limitless supply of gray and white trunks, standing sentry like a stealthy and formidable legion. She felt both claustrophobic and terrifyingly exposed. Occasionally, she crossed a road or a creek, but the view remained largely unchanged. Miles and miles of tree trunks.

She had gathered a few more rabbits from Tomas's traps and tied them to her waist. When she stopped the first night, she ate the bread and jerky that she had taken from Tomas's table. By the second night, those supplies were exhausted, and Giti skinned a rabbit in the dying afternoon light. Too scared to start a fire for fear of attracting unwanted visitors, she tore at the raw meat with her teeth. Tough and slimy, the flesh gagged her, and she heaved up all the wretched bloody contents of her stomach. The diarrhea set in later, and the skin on her buttocks burned from exposure to the cold.

Each night, she labored to sleep, fighting demons while listening to the wolves howl. Opa stood over her. "Giti? What have you done?" he cried over and over. "What have you done?" She tried to answer him, but the words wouldn't come. He put his face in his hands and sobbed, and she reached out to him, but he faded away.

The next day, as she trudged forward through stands of birch and leggy pines, she emerged in a clearing to find a farmhouse. It was small and unadorned, and nearby there was a barn, a rusty well, and an abandoned chicken coop. Smoke curled out of the stone chimney, and an ancient mule stood tied to the front post with its head bent low over dirty piles of snow.

Giti crouched behind a thicket of prickly underbrush and

watched to see who was inside. Her stomach growled. She hadn't eaten since her meal of raw rabbit.

The front door creaked open and an old man appeared. His thick woolen hat and bowed legs reminded Giti of a story about a shifty pirate that she had once read in school. The pirate tale was meant to be a comedy, but there was nothing funny about the desiccated human standing on the porch. He hobbled uneasily down the steps and dragged a pail toward the barn. The mule hardly registered his presence. After a bit, he returned to the house holding the pail with both hands and carrying it with much difficulty. Milk sloshed over the sides as he bumped the pail against the ground to take pressure off of his arthritic hands.

"A cow!" thought Giti, and her mouth watered at the prospect of fresh milk. She winced every time she saw the old man wobble, the contents of the pail splashing over the side and melting the snow underneath. An old woman, equally infirm, and wearing an old-fashioned long skirt and a man's hunting jacket, came out on the porch to help the man bring the milk inside. Giti decided to seize the moment and take a chance. She stepped forward out of the cover of the trees, and stood at the edge of the clearing, holding her arms away from her body.

The woman spied her first. She nudged the man to set down the bucket, and pointed in Giti's direction. Giti waved her hand in response. The woman tipped her head to the side and beckoned her over. Giti moved toward them, bending over and picking up the handle of the pail with her left hand and carrying it into the house.

A pot of potatoes bubbled on the open fireplace, and dried herbs hung from the beams around the dark, cluttered room. Giti set the pail on the small kitchen table and stared at the couple. The old woman shuffled forward. "*Wer bist du*? Who are you?" she asked cautiously. She glanced around the room and back to Giti. The old man shuffled forward and took off his hat. Giti noticed that his eyes were glazed over with opaque lenses. It was a wonder that he could find his way to the barn and back.

Giti's stomach growled, and she motioned to the potatoes and then to the milk. The woman ladled her a cup and set it down along with the heel from a loaf of bread. Giti gulped down everything she was offered and wished for more. She wiped the residue off of her upper lip and forced a smile to signal her appreciation, but the woman looked displeased. She motioned for Giti to go back outside—*schnell!* and once on the porch, she handed Giti the ax and pointed to the woodpile.

"We need firewood," she said tartly, and returned inside, bolting the door behind her.

Giti set down her bag and proceeded to reduce their supply of logs to fireplace-sized pieces. She silently thanked Tomas for teaching her how to do this one-handed, and then she thought of him lying in the snow, food for the wolves. The sun was setting as Giti gathered a load of firewood and carried it to the porch. The woman allowed Giti back in and directed her to stack some logs by the fire. Giti noticed that the potatoes were gone, consumed without an invitation to her. The woman pointed to the barn.

Giti huddled alone that night, burrowing herself into the soiled hay with the cow as her companion. She wondered if the couple would offer her another glass of milk in the morning and fell asleep dreaming of Mutti's and Oma's kitchen, full of fresh milk, soft loaves of bread, pungent cabbage, and buttery potatoes. In her dreams, she and Otto were wrestling over the table, fighting for the last piece of Oma's apple cake, always the biggest treat of the fall. Otto reached around her neck and pulled her down away from the cake, but he wouldn't let her go, pulling and pulling her down.

Giti awoke with a start to see the woman standing over her. She had a long kitchen knife in one hand, pointed toward Giti. Her other hand was on Giti's neck, rooting around under her clothes, pulling at the locket. She was trying to work it around to reach the clasp.

Giti sprung up, pushing the woman back more as a defensive gesture than a desire to hurt her. Just then she heard a click, and she noticed the old man standing behind, hoisting an ancient pistol aimed right for her. Giti's head was foggy with fatigue, and she was cornered by the couple. She gestured that they should stand back, and she pointed to the bag. Curious, the old woman allowed her to unclasp the flap. Giti pretended to reach into the bag, but instead grasped the handles and yanked it up, swinging it at the woman's head. The woman fell back into the man as his pistol tilted up and exploded, the bullet hitting the beams over Giti's head and showering them all with splinters.

As the woman struggled to stand, Giti stepped over them and ran for the door. The man managed to cock the pistol again, and another shot rang out, hitting the roof of the empty chicken coop. Giti charged back into the woods, and when she glanced back to gauge her distance from the couple, her foot caught the edge of something hard. She tumbled to the ground, falling face first into a tangle of roots and knocking the air out of her lungs. She lay still for a few minutes, hearing nothing but the buzzing in her head. She slowly pulled herself upright and felt around her forehead for the source of the blood that now trickled down her nose. Her fingers found and tenderly explored the gash above her left eye. The buzzing in her head grew louder, and the forest floor seemed to tip her from side to side, but she forced herself to press on, trusting proximity to the wolves in the forest over the desperation of people.

At daybreak, having been so afraid that she was hopelessly

lost and heading deeper into Prussia, she was relieved to emerge through the dense cluster of birch trees to see the river not far off in the distance. She scrambled down to the bank and surveyed the frosty landscape. A wave of disappointment washed over her, and she shivered. Why had she expected that this new land would be different, would summon her on?

The river was wide and covered with a layer of ice, a trap really. It was thick in some places, not so sturdy in others. A cruel obstacle course mocking her. As the river curved away from her on the left and toward Königsberg, it met low sloping hills with fir trees and a thick layer of new snow. To her right, across the river, were more flat plains and evidence of a few abandoned farmhouses. Giti concentrated on the ice, taking note of the colors. Blue, gray, and green, it resembled a bruise twisting between the two lands. Tomas had promised that this was the path. She plodded forward to the edge of the ice, her feet planted on the last slivers of East Prussia. She thought of the family left behind and wondered if she would ever return to sit in the cemetery on the hill. Otto's voice came to her. "Be happy, Giti! Have faith."

The sun was rising above the trees, and Giti feared the effect of its warmth on the ice. She contemplated the urgency of her next move. Even in winter's miserly daylight, she could detect the darker areas of thin ice in the middle. A wagon would never make it across, but a cold, skinny girl might have a chance. There were no sounds except for a frigid wind rustling the trees and the occasional groan of cracking ice as the water underneath nudged upwards at its frozen covering. Giti knew that she needed to maneuver carefully around the dangerously brittle sections.

She tested the ice with the toe of Tomas's big boot. The mirrored surface was thick enough here, but slippery. It seemed to push her boot forward, propelling her on. Recentering herself, she got down on her hands and knees and began crawling, stopping when she heard a crack or a pop to lay herself out flat and redistribute her weight. After almost a year of rationing food with Tomas to survive the lean harvest, she didn't weigh much even with all of his heavy clothing on. The river was only a small pasture's width across at this point. By boat, it would be a quick jaunt, but slithering across the scratchy, unreliable surface was an arduously slow task.

Giti made it to the middle with little resistance, but once she was exposed and out in the open, the ice turned dangerously thin. She stopped and peered through the translucent layer, willing it to hold her weight. Frantic fish darted chaotically inches from her nose. She watched them for a minute while her heavy breaths misted the surface and obscured her view. She stayed flat on her stomach and scooted to her left to try to find thicker pockets. Slow and steady progress. All she heard was her ragged breathing and the incessant duet of the ice moaning below and the tree branches whistling overhead, nature's chorus of schism and loss. Using her arms and legs, she slowly pushed herself forward across the gravelly surface. Inch by inch, she scooted, too determined to stop. She was well over halfway now, and the ice decided to fight back with creaks, groans, and the occasional jagged branch thwarting her progress.

Eventually the darker, more uncertain patches gave way to a thicker, whiter covering, and she felt emboldened to pick up her pace. Reaching the opposite shore, she scrambled up onto the frozen grass and watched the rays of the sun glint off the glassy surface. Then she waited. As darkness settled around her, and snow drifted down from the branches overhead, she sat on the shore and bid farewell to the only homeland she had ever known. She used her frozen gloves to wipe away the tears that gathered in the corners of her eyes as she thought of all the family she was leaving behind. If Pappi, Paul, Stefan, or Otto ever made it back, she would be untraceable. The river wasn't very wide, one shore identical to the other, but she was in Lithuania now. She was on her own.

The farmhouse was nestled among a cluster of low hills, smoke curling out of the thick chimney. This one had been built long ago of bold timbers. Angles that were once crisp and square were now rounded with time and weather. The house seemed to welcome the embrace of the land around it, settled as it was into the slight rise of an ancient mound. It was notable for its normalcy, and Giti puzzled over who might live there. The siding was old wood, gray and brittle from years of exposure and the lack of paint. A simple front door was positioned in the middle of the structure, with windows on either side. The covered porch was ample and in good repair, furnished with a bench, a rack for firewood, and a rocking chair for the summer months. In addition to the house, there was a barn and a privy. A dirt road with stiff, icy ruts ran in front of the house before curving into the woods and disappearing behind the copse of fir trees.

Giti was drawn to this place and the warmth it projected, yet experience had taught her to be wary. Her mind raced back to the old couple and their nefarious motives. Questions plagued Giti. Will these people hate me for being German? Would they prefer to turn me in to the authorities than share a bit of bread and a cup of milk? She was wracked with indecision and fear, too desperate to leave and too scared to be discovered.

She hunkered down in the woods and watched. Just before dawn, four people stepped out from behind the wood door, ambled over to the barn for tools, and emerged fully prepared to tackle the chores that kept the enterprise going. It had been years since Giti had seen a farm function with any measure of abundance in the middle of winter. Ever since Pappi and the boys had left, their animals confiscated, and the stored supplies requisitioned, the Binz farm had been barely at subsistence level.

For two days, Giti surveyed the activity around the farm, trying to get the measure of the people she observed. As much as she sought escape from the cold, she stayed rooted to the forest floor, brittle with fear and distrust. She eagerly anticipated the morning routine when the group of four set off into the fields to tend the animals or gather food from the forest. A boisterous dog nipped at their heels and ran circles around the cows. "Rikus!" the young man yelled, and the dog obediently bounded to his side. She watched as a fifth person, a woman, flinty and spare with her apron tied hastily around her thin frame, carried laundry from the barn. While her tasks were ordinary, she projected confidence and authority with every step.

At dusk on the second day, Giti watched the woman come out to the porch and call the family back in. She was as stern as the devout nuns Giti remembered from the village, and Giti was afraid of her the most. The younger women, girls perhaps, were softer and less threatening. They put their arms around each other often. The men, one old and one young, walked together, sharing an easy camaraderie despite the difference in their ages. Yet the woman toiled alone, and there was a briskness to her movements that discouraged tender touches and hugs. Having seen her family making their way back, she turned and walked into the house. The four followed her in, and the door closed. This was the hardest for Giti to bear. She wanted to knock on that door and sit by the fire, but fear was her strongest ally, and she stayed hidden in the woods.

Giti was discovered early in the morning, shortly before

sunrise. She was sleeping in a nest of branches and dead leaves when Rikus leaped out of the brush. Before Giti could react, he was sniffing around her, eagerly flapping his tail, sending snow and leaves swirling up into the air. She scrambled to her feet and grabbed her bag, inching her way back toward the deeper recesses of the thicket. She turned to run and found herself face to face with the old man. He carried a torch, and the dancing flames sent bursts of light and shadows across his face. Giti screamed, and she thrust her hand in her pocket for the hilt of Tomas's knife.

"Steady there," he said, holding out his free hand. "I'm not here to hurt you." He reached down and grabbed the collar around the dog. "Rikus is a fine working dog, but maybe not such a good watchdog, eh?" His words made no sense to Giti. It wasn't German he was speaking, but she recognized the tone of his voice, and it reassured her.

She stared, breathing deep, ragged breaths, unsure of what to do. Rikus strained at his collar, his tail thumping forcefully and sending up more puffs of leaves and new snow. Keeping her eyes on the man, Giti knelt down and ruffled the fur around Rikus's ears. The dog was warm and friendly, and Giti put her good arm around his neck. Rikus responded by licking her face, and she pressed her nose into the soft fur on his flank.

The old man took a step closer to Giti. He noticed the filthy bandages around her hand and the deep shadows under her eyes. She resembled a skeleton wrapped in a scarecrow's clothing. "I'm Dėdė Jonas. Are you hungry? You should come inside with me."

Giti took a step back and regripped the knife.

"No one here will hurt you." He gestured with his hand. "Come with me." And he began walking toward the house, whistling for Rikus to follow. The dog raced ahead, and Giti followed him wordlessly out of the woods and into the open meadow. The surrounding snow crunched underfoot and glowed an iridescent pink in the twilight. Rikus ran in front, zigzagging to sniff at the tracks of night creatures as an owl hooted its last call. Giti could see the lights of the house ahead. Smoke curled out of the chimney and beckoned her forward.

Rikus loped up the stairs and barked as a cat scampered around to the back. Dėdė Jonas followed close behind and stamped the snow off his boots before throwing the door wide open. Giti mimicked his actions and followed him inside. She felt the warmth of the fire and heard voices in the kitchen. The scents and sounds of breakfast washed over her as she collapsed on the floor.

———

She woke up on a mat laid in front of the fire, to find the house quiet but filled with the rich scent of warm yeast bread. She tried to sit up, but her head was pounding once again. The woman she had been watching from the woods shuffled over and shushed her with a gentle but efficient pat on the head. Her name was Loreta Shimkus, and she talked to Giti in a strong, reassuring voice. Although Giti couldn't understand any of what she was saying, she softened toward Loreta in response to the woman's ministrations. Up close, she wasn't nearly so severe, merely weary.

Loreta was tall and lanky. Her face was dominated by narrow-set brown eyes, a prominent chin, and thin black hair. Although her features were pinched and plain, she moved with a strength of purpose that inspired confidence and courage. She said something Giti couldn't understand, and left the room for a few minutes. Giti heard her moving about the kitchen, opening and shutting drawers. When she returned, she had a stack of dry laundry, a bucket of warm water, soap, and a towel. She helped

Giti sit up and began peeling Tomas's old clothes off the girl's birdlike frame. By now Giti's clothes were caked with dried blood, dirt, and leaves. Worse, she smelled like a rotten carcass. Giti was ashamed. Loreta showed no signs of judgment as she talked in a calm and steady banter.

She delicately unwrapped the soiled bandages that Giti had kept on her crushed hand ever since Tomas had fashioned a splint and bound it to her fingers. She gently pried Giti's hand off of the wood and held the brittle and misshapen fingers in her own calloused hands. She reached down into the bucket of warm water and drew out a soft square of flannel that she used to delicately tend to the sores and blisters between Giti's fingers. Giti had not examined her hand closely since the night that Tomas had last wrapped it up, and she watched intently as Loreta cleaned it, then rubbed a thick paste into her joints. The bones that had broken were healed but reset improperly, so the fingers curled tightly toward her palm in haphazard order. The pain was still present but in a dull, detached sort of way, and Giti relaxed into Loreta's care. After a time, Giti's whole body was clean, her spiky hair washed, and ointment applied to the sores and blisters that covered her from head to toe. Loreta slipped a clean but worn white shift over Giti's shoulders and tucked her securely under a wool blanket. She checked the pockets of Tomas's old clothes and pulled out the two crumpled photos. She smoothed them reverently and lay them on the table where Giti could see them. Then she tossed the clothes one by one into the fire.

CHAPTER TWELVE

BRIGIT, 2010

Brigit checked her watch. Her flight would be boarding soon and heading back to the States without her, and she surprised herself with the ease of the decision. She and Milo had spent two hours sorting through Lukas's photographs and maps, and they proved to be a remarkable record of a different time, not so long ago. They chronicled a period of oppression and strife that had ripped apart families—hers and Milos included—and caused festering wounds that were still unhealed. Now that she had seen more of Lukas's work, she needed to decide what she should do next, and returning to Boston was not even an option to consider. The clues lay here, and Brigit was itching to talk to Rachel and get her advice. It would be hours before daybreak in Boston. Brigit assumed that Rachel kept a loose schedule and was rarely at the society before late morning. That gave her a window to patch together a strategy with Milo.

Milo sat on the floor surrounded by Lukas's journals. There were six small leather-bound books in all, and they were filled with names and addresses, lists of expenses, and long narrative passages describing his travels. Some dates were missing, and none of the pages were numbered. Milo was struggling to decipher Lukas's cryptic penmanship. The journals had gotten wet at some point, rendering some of the entries illegible. Adding to the mess the blotches of ink that seem to be from Lukas himself, it was a daunting task. Milo ran his hand through his hair. Whether Lukas was trying to conceal information or was hopelessly disorganized, Milo couldn't tell, but teasing out information from the journals was going to be difficult.

Brigit reached into her bag and pulled out the slip of paper that Mrs. Penworthy had given her. "Here's a thought," she said, passing the paper to Milo. "Rachel gave me the name of an engineering student from here who was in Boston for some time. He used to hang out at the society and translate old documents for them. Peter Mazieka is his name." She laughed. "I think he helped them out because he was homesick. They had the hots for him, and it won him some free meals, but Rachel said that he especially liked the ancient books in their dusty archives. Maybe he can help us out with Lukas's journals."

Milo was intrigued and punched in the number on his mobile phone. To their great surprise, Peter answered on the second ring. Brigit didn't understand any of the conversation as Milo explained the situation to Peter, but she could see him becoming more animated the longer they talked. He walked around the room, gesturing to the piles of paper and photographs that he and Brigit had assembled, then he stopped and listened for long spells during which Peter was apparently responding to Milo's descriptions.

Finally, he hung up the phone and smiled broadly. "Your friend may be an engineer, but he's also something of an amateur sleuth. Turns out that his grandfather and great-uncle were partisans, part of the Forest Brothers. His grandfather was caught and executed, but his great-uncle appears to have escaped. Peter suspects that he made his way to America, but he hasn't found any proof. Peter's been searching for information about his family for years."

According to Milo, Peter was anxious to meet with them and review Milo's documents and photographs. He lived in Kaunas and had invited Milo and Brigit to join him and his family for dinner that evening.

"But you are leaving on your vacation today, right?" Brigit asked.

"Well perhaps I can delay it by a day or two." Milo pointed to the scattered papers. "Vacations are perhaps overrated."

They repacked all of Lukas's papers into the black box and stored it in the trunk of Milo's tiny blue Fiat. Brigit ran back to the hotel to let the desk clerk know that she would need a room for at least another night, then she sent Otto and Margie an email updating them on her plans. Finally, she emailed Rachel alerting her that she would be calling soon with a bold request. As fast as she could grab a few supplies for the day, she was on her way back to Galerija Emilia.

Brigit had not felt this optimistic in ages. She could finally glimpse a possibility that she would meet her aunt and somehow arrange a way for Otto and Giti to talk after so many years.

Otto was an enigma for most of Brigit's childhood. Outwardly, he was jovial and carefree, but in the quiet spaces, he would retreat into himself. He suffered from crippling nightmares and headaches and deflected any opportunity to talk about his past. His job as an officer aboard commercial shipping vessels kept him away from home for months at a time, and for the periods when he returned home, he wanted only peace, happiness, and tranquility.

Brigit learned about Giti the year she married Joe. It was also the year that Otto was first diagnosed with lung cancer. The confluence of events made Otto uncharacteristically wistful. He apologized to Brigit for being gone so much during her childhood, and he seemed eager to open up to her about his family and his history, but terrifying memories buried for years are not easily dredged up. He glossed over details of how he and his family were separated, and Giti became a ghostly anecdote, an elusive aunt who disappeared off a train. Over the years, Brigit thought about Giti occasionally and promised herself that she would tease more out of her father, but she and Joe were consumed with building a life together.

As Otto's health declined, he began to push with a renewed urgency for Brigit to apply her special skills to a search for her aunt. Bridget longed for a connection to her father, and so she wrote the letter to the German Red Cross that yielded the photo by Lukas Galinis.

Now, she found herself in Vilnius with a strange man whose family had a mysterious if tenuous connection to her own. She was unfettered, untethered, and possibly on the cusp of an exciting discovery. For the moment, she had no regrets.

CHAPTER THIRTEEN

GITI, 1946

Loreta's potato pancakes were like a homecoming. With the crusty shell and fluffy interior, they transported Giti back to a world where people cared and loved. Giti ate every one that was set in front of her. She was malnourished and ill from almost a week of exposure to the frigid Lithuanian winter. She was responding well to the food and companionship of the Shimkus family. She was eager to be up and helping out around the house, but Loreta was adamant that she stay on the soft pallet by the fire. She fussed around Giti, bringing her broths and teas to strengthen her and applying great globs of balm to her frostbitten toes, gaping sores, and mangled hand.

Giti's wounds slowly healed, and a healthy pink returned to her cheeks and to the tips of her fingers and toes. The balm eased the raw skin, but it did nothing to untangle her fingers or ease her sorrow. As the family gathered each evening to share stories and make plans, Giti stayed close, willing the care and camaraderie to envelop her. She had only known one other family—her own—and she was intrigued by the Shimkus's relationships and their ways of making do in a harsh post-war world. She realized early on that they were a patchwork quilt kind of family, and she endeavored to piece together their connections. Jonas was Loreta's much older bachelor brother. Loreta's daughters Paulina and Julija were joined by their cousin Matis, who delighted Giti by speaking a bit of heavily-accented German. In charmingly corrupted sentences, Matis explained that Teta Loreta's husband, Dėdė Josef, had been killed early in the war fighting against the Nazis. She and Dėdė Jonas had kept the farm running in the face of fighting, deprivations, the changing face of occupiers, and abuse that Matis alluded to but would not describe to Giti.

Matis was uncharacteristically taciturn when talking about his own family. "My mother and Teta Loreta are sisters. We lived in Kaunas, and I was out one day with my friends setting off homemade bombs at Russian targets. When I got home, my parents were gone. Neighbors said that the Soviets came and took them away. I don't know where they are, but I am sure they are coming home one day." Giti watched him silently, willing him to continue. "I was just fourteen, but this is the only other family I know, so I started walking and have been here ever since." He shrugged and said no more on the subject.

When Giti lay on her pallet at night and watched the embers of the fire slowly die down, she dreamed of what it might be like if Loreta and Jonas were her own *teta* and *dėdė*. She thought of Mutti, Pappi, her brothers and grandparents, and wondered what they might be doing together if the war hadn't happened. Would *they* have taken in a starving child who'd wandered in from the cold one day? Mutti and Pappi's faces were growing ever more indistinct, and she struggled to conjure up their voices in her head. Her memories of Otto remained clear. Her enduring mental remnant was his face, buried in the shadows of the train car, strained with worry.

At sixteen, Matis was closest to her age. It was reassuring that he could speak to her, even though she couldn't bring herself to talk back yet. Paulina, already a grown woman of twenty, fussed with Giti's hair. Juli, the family chatterbox, delighted and irritated Giti with her one-sided incoherent conversations, which were so enthusiastic as to be both spectacularly entertaining and annoying. Jonas and Rikus were her outdoor companions once Loreta deemed it safe enough for Giti to venture beyond the cozy confines of the house.

As the weeks went by and Giti's condition improved, she became Loreta's shadow, seizing each opportunity to lend a hand or take on a chore. Giti was convinced that the family's generosity and hospitality were conditional. She reasoned that they didn't need her as Tomas had, and she was one more mouth to feed using their limited resources. Loreta was not given to displays of affection, but she did what she could to comfort Giti through the silences and in the quiet moments. When Loreta finished her chores and banked the fire in the evening, she watched Giti sleep and wondered what the child had seen and done to bring her all the way to their doorstep.

Late one afternoon on a warm spring day, Giti returned to the house from her chores in the barn and discovered the family gathered together in a heated discussion. It was her worst fear. Surely, she thought, they were arguing about her. She cowered inside the door, anxious to pick up a thread from the discord.

Jonas was doing most of the talking while Loreta stood by the fireplace with her arms crossed resolutely over her chest. Paulina sat on the floor cradling Juli as she cried freely. Matis hovered nearby, leaning in as he challenged his uncle. When he raised his voice, Juli cried harder. Loreta begged them all to calm down. Then Giti heard her name, and she knew. They were trying to find a way to tell her to leave.

She tiptoed back out the door and hid in the woods until the sun went down and the lights dimmed in the house. She heard them calling her name, and although Matis walked nearby trying to find her, she burrowed down beside a fallen log and allowed him to pass by, his voice growing weaker as he searched deeper in the woods. Rikus scampered nearby, but Matis called him off, and he bolted into the woods to accept the treat that he knew Matis kept in his pocket.

Well past dark, Giti tiptoed in the door when she was confident that the house was quiet. She gathered up her bag, making sure that her treasures were safely tucked inside along with a few scraps of bread, a potato, and Tomas's knife. She didn't know where she was going or how she might survive another spell living in the woods. At least the bitter cold had begun to abate in favor of a fickle spring.

She stood on the threshold and soaked in the last bit of family warmth from the home, surprised at how fond she had grown of each of them in such a short time. She would never knowingly put them in danger. She ventured back toward Loreta's kitchen and found a scrap of paper wrapped around some dried herbs. She reached for the pencil that hung from the window by a frayed bit of twine, and in the best handwriting that she could manage with her left hand, she scribbled in German, 'I thank you all so much,' confident that Matis could read it. She left it on the table and backed out toward the door.

"Where are you going, my little friend?" Matis tiptoed through the door, bringing a blast of cold air with him. He picked up Giti's bag. "We've been searching for you all day." His tentative smile masked his concern. Giti was relieved that he was not mad. She stood still and stared back at him, her heart racing, the words rolling around in her head, but none coming to her mouth.

"Teta Loreta is worried sick about you. She believes the soldiers came in the woods and carried you off. Is that what you want her to think?" He set down a package inside the door, and Giti noticed for the first time that the back of his head was bleeding. She walked towards him and reached out to touch his soiled collar. He brushed her off. "I'm fine, a low tree limb, that's all," he murmured, and Giti knew that was a lie. She burst into tears and threw herself into his arms, sobbing with such pain that she woke the whole house.

Loreta rushed out in her worn white nightgown and gathered Giti and Matis together in one big hug. She glared at Matis and gestured toward Giti, the words bubbling out of her mouth. Jonas, Paulina and Julija all tumbled in to see what had happened. As Loreta examined and cleaned the cut on Matis's head, they exchanged a quick, terse volley of words. He explained to Giti. "Paulina spotted soldiers earlier today, and they argued about whether they needed to hide you. They want you to be safe, but they didn't want to scare you. When they went to check on you, you were gone."

Giti scrunched her eyes and summoned the words to explain her actions to Loreta, but her voice wouldn't come. She took Matis's hand, pulled him over to the table and pointed to the note she had left earlier. She grabbed the pencil and added, '*I am so sorry. I am a burden to your family.*' Matis translated while Giti labored over forming the shaky letters using her left hand.

Loreta came to her side and gently teased the pencil out of her hand. She cupped Giti's face with her calloused palms and spoke to her softly but firmly. Matis waited until she was finished and then explained to Giti. "She says you are not a burden. One day, you will be able to tell us your story. You may stay here as long as you need, and we will do our best to protect you."

In her young life, Giti had been a witness both to unspeakable cruelty and abundant kindness from strangers. Others had died protecting her, and she had failed to protect Otto. What would her presence mean to this family? She had misunderstood their discussion and had put herself, and possibly the whole Shimkus family, in jeopardy. She also knew that Matis was not telling her everything, and one thing she had learned was how to recognize danger. She saw it written all over Matis's face.

CHAPTER FOURTEEN

BRIGIT, 2010

Milo drove while Brigit watched the frost-tinged countryside roll by. She tried to imagine how it might have appeared in the years right after the war, when Lukas was on foot, armed with his camera and his sense of justice. She gazed out of the little Fiat, observing the tidy compact houses from the post-Cold War construction boom that dotted the flat plains and low hills. The outskirts of Vilnius soon gave way to small farming communities filled with older structures, which appeared a bit more cobbled together but were no doubt steeped in memories.

Brigit's phone buzzed, and she was excited to see Rachel's number pop up. She was eager to learn about the evening at Galerija Emilia, and was incredulous when Brigit told her about Milo's connection to Lukas Galinis. Rachel asked to speak directly to Milo, so Brigit reluctantly switched to speakerphone and fidgeted while he and Rachel conversed in Lithuanian. When he finally finished his chat, Brigit signed off by promising that she would share Rachel's warmest greetings with Peter. Then she turned to Milo. "So? What happened? What did she say?"

"She might be willing to fund my research into Lukas if we

can make some kind of agreement for a long-term loan of his photographs. I'm supposed to send her a proposal. I was clear that the loan of the photographs would only come with the publication of my book, which I hope she will help me launch— once I write it, of course. She also said to be kind to you because she has friends in high places and will ensure I receive a thorough thrashing if I do not help you properly. You may not have known Rachel long, but you have made a fierce ally." His face broke into a giant grin as he tapped out a jaunty rhythm on the steering wheel.

A fierce ally? Brigit liked the sound of that. Milo merged the car into a busier highway, and Brigit turned her attention back to the view out of her window, noting the road signs pointing the way to discreet villages and reclusive backroads, and wondering what stories each of those journeys held.

Milo soon broke the silence. "You know, Lukas was just a kid, barely out of his teens, but he lived his life with more guts and integrity than most. I hope that I can honor him by discovering more about his work and putting it out there so that he gets the credit he deserves. How is it that he seems to have had such conviction and force of purpose so early on?"

"Well maybe we are on our way to figuring that out," Brigit asserted. "Why do other people's lives seem to have so much clarity, when our own are muddled at best? My relationship with my dad is complicated. Things with my husband were tenuous. I need to try to make things right with my father before it's too late. Maybe Lukas can lead me there too?"

They settled into a companionable silence, each mulling over the possibilities for what they might discover.

CHAPTER FIFTEEN

GITI/GIEDRE, 1946

Giti finished her chores in the barn and hurried back to the house for the evening meal. By now it was midsummer, and the sun sparkled high overhead with hours of daylight still before the short night to come. A brilliant golden hue washed over the somnolent pastures, and insects droned lazily over the tips of the rye stalks basking in the fields. Cowbells clanked pleasantly in the distance.

She took off her straw hat and ruffled her hair, now a riot of short blond curls. She peeled off her heavy work boots, set them gently by the door, and replaced the bucket on the rusted hook in the pantry. She poked her head in, expecting to find Loreta at the sturdy kitchen table, kneading dough or chopping vegetables, but today was different. Though no one was in sight, the state of the house indicated a flurry of activity. Loaves of steaming rye bread cooled at the open window alongside fresh, leaf-shaped kibinas, stuffed with pork or bursting with fresh, hot fruit. Baskets and jars cluttered the table in an uncommon riot of disorder in Loreta's usually pristine kitchen.

Paulina rushed in with a bowl overflowing with berries, still warm from the sun, and tucked them into a commodious basket full of provisions. "Oh, Giedre, you're just in time!" Paulina used Giti's new Lithuanian name, a necessary precaution to hide her Prussian heritage from the authorities. "We've been looking for you. Juli's out front, impatient to leave." Paulina nudged Giti gently from behind and propelled her toward the front door. "Oh dear, no shoes, that won't work." Paulina dashed back to the kitchen to retrieve Giti's boots and tossed them on the floor. "Come on!"

Giti thrust her feet into her boots and took in the scene around her. Juli stood out front, a basket in hand, wearing her best dress. Her hair had been combed carefully and plaited with colorful ribbons. Giti noticed that Paulina too had changed into her special occasion dress. She scrutinized her own attire, an old canvas tunic restyled from one of Juli's old school dresses, and was embarrassed that her legs were covered in bug bites from a day in the fields. Jonas was hitching the mule to the wagon, and he reached out and beckoned toward Giti while Juli crawled in the back and situated herself in the hay.

"Giedre!' Giti heard Loreta call her from inside the house. She ran back up on the porch, pausing only to wipe a smudge of cow dung off her cheek before heading to the kitchen. Loreta was packing up the bread and pies. She tossed Giti a wet towel to clean herself and then thrust baskets of warm food into her arms. They emerged from the house together, stacked the provisions in the wagon, and climbed in for the ride. Jonas urged the mule forward, and they were off.

Loreta and the girls kept up a spirited banter on the route, and Giti strained to hear a familiar word or two. Festival, food, maybe herbs? She was picking up Lithuanian quickly, but the talk was too fast, too excited for Giti to process it all. Matis. Where was he? No one seemed to miss him, so Giti decided not to worry. They took the road around the bend and toward the low hills that circled the village of Stubriai. There ahead Giti spied a collection of wagons, all disgorging families carrying blankets, food, and baskets. This was clearly a celebration.

Jonas pulled the wagon off the road alongside their neighbors' buggies, and waved cheerfully at the men and women assembling in the clearing. Up ahead, stretching over the trail leading into the woods, was a giant gate, constructed just for this celebration. The entire structure was covered in plants. "It's Kupoles, Giedre!" said Juli, as she raced to greet the other girls massing to the side.

Loreta and Paulina hauled baskets of supplies, and Giti eagerly joined in, following them through the archway. Up close, Giti inhaled the scent of the fragrant herbs. She marveled at the abundance of wild garlic, yarrow, horse's shanks, and dandelion, all intertwined with care and precision. She tucked a stray bloom back in, and scurried up the trail to rejoin Loreta and Paulina in a clearing at the top of the rise. A towering cone of logs was arranged in the middle, and families were staking out their spot and assembling their supplies for the feast to come. Giti's stomach growled as she set her basket on the outstretched blanket and arranged herself on a corner to enjoy the meal.

"Silly girl," Paulina reached down and coaxed Giti up. "We've still got work to do." She thrust the basket into Giti's hands and motioned for her to follow.

They retraced their steps back down the trail and entered the woods on the other side of the clearing. All the young women and girls seemed to be doing the same, wading deep into the trees and scanning the forest floor, squealing with delight at finding an elusive bloom.

Paulina breathlessly schooled Giti while searching the undergrowth. "It's St. Jonas's Eve, and on this one night, herbs turn magical. We must make a wreath out of twelve different kinds before midnight! Rue! Come get some, Giedre. This is the best, and we've found it first."

Giti was a skilled scavenger and herbalist. She easily amassed a bounty of herbs in her basket. She found blackberries, blueberries, a patch of fireweed, and a sea buckthorn shrub bursting with clusters of bright yellow fruit. More dandelions, rue, and wild onions appeared as she ventured out of the woods and into another clearing.

She spied Juli sulking on a log and sauntered over to join her, inspecting the contents of Juli's basket. A couple of crushed dandelions and a cluster of pine needles was all that she had managed to collect. Giti tutted and divided her lot, giving Juli enough to fill her quota.

Juli's doldrums evaporated, and she hugged Giti tightly. "Thank you! I wasn't sure how I would manage. Now we make the wreaths, so you can entice your true love!" She drew out several bluish green strands of rue and held the stems as though they were made of glass. She lowered her voice to a whisper. "Now *this* is special. It's a love potion. Whoever brings you back your wreath tonight is your true love!" She winked and giggled.

Giti couldn't quite get the gist, but Juli's girlish laughter got the point across just fine. The two girls rubbed shoulders while they wove their herbs into simple crowns.

"What do you think?" Juli asked as she placed her wreath on her head. "Am I ready to fall in love?"

Giti nodded and placed her own wreath on her fair curls, a thick circle of leaves sprinkled with the yellow sea buckthorn fruits, bright red berries, and abundant sprigs of rue. Juli pulled a small piece of green ribbon out of her pocket and used it to tie the last branch of blueberry bush to Giti's wreath. She stepped back to admire her handiwork. "You're just beautiful!" she announced, and they followed the noise of the crowd to the banks of the gentle creek that gurgled around the reeds and rocks in its path.

As the crowd cheered, each girl stepped up in turn and

tossed her wreath into the gentle current. Giti edged up to the bank last and peered into the lazy water.

"Toss it, Giedre!" Paulina urged, and Giti lifted her wreath off her head and flung it into the water, where it landed with a soft splash before floating gently to join the other circlets languorously wending their way around the bend and toward town. The girls urged them on. The faster the current, the faster their true loves would appear.

Another cheer went up as the last wreath bobbed out of view, and the revelers returned to the feast just as the sun disappeared behind the horizon. They lit the pyre and feasted and sang as the roaring fire flickered and danced, each family sharing their abundance with their neighbors on the eve of the longest day of the year. As last darkness descended, the young men returned from their games, most carrying a wreath plucked from the creek. The girls squealed or shrieked depending on which of the boys offered their crown back to them. Handsome Ricchus produced Paulina's scraggly collection of herbs, and she blushed when he placed the soggy laurel back on her head.

Young Marcus, a boy of barely ten, shyly brought Juli her wreath. She grabbed it out of his hands and tossed it to the edge of the blanket, churlish in her dismissal of the young lad. He was crestfallen, and even though Loreta scolded Juli and apologized to Marcus, Juli was unmoved. Young Marcus retreated to the edge of the crowd where he watched Juli from afar.

Giti watched in anticipation, but no one seemed to have found hers. No matter, she thought with a hint of disappointment, probably none of the boys really wanted to share this night with a stranger anyway. Giti moved to help Loreta dole out the last of the delicious kibinas. With the mystery of the wreaths over and the gloaming fully realized, the crowd turned its attention to the dancing blaze of the giant pyre.

The girls once again ventured off in small groups, two or three together at most.

Loreta motioned for Giti to follow them back into the woods. "You must find the fern flower," she said as she arranged herself so that she could hold Giti's gaze, her intensity both endearing and amusing. "It only blooms at midnight on St. Jonas's Day, and it has special powers of wealth and happiness, but you have to be first. Now scoot!"

Loreta propelled Giti back into the woods, where she inched her way forward alone, her eyes adjusting to the gloom of the trees. The power of the fern blossom seemed too fantastical to be true. Giti was a girl, but she had lived a lifetime of hurt. Folktales held no promise for her. She knew the magic of the forest, and it wasn't a bloom with special powers. For her, it meant solitude and the escape from terror. She ventured to a quiet spot, away from the crowd but still within earshot of the raucous gathering at the fire. She sat on the soft moss covering the forest floor, and leaned against an old log. The novelty of the day had dimmed, and in this quiet moment, she thought again of her parents and Otto. What would they think if they saw her now?

"So, my little forest friend, might this splendid crown belong to you?" Matis stood a few yards away holding a glistening wreath, the yellow fruits glowing in the darkness, and the green ribbon unmistakable. Rikus bounded up next to him and wagged his tail.

Giti smiled and reached out to claim her handiwork. Matis leaned over and placed the wreath on her head as he plopped down next to her and rested his head back on the log.

"Sometimes I wonder about you," Matis teased in German. "You seem almost content deep in the woods, like you're part animal or something."

Giti inched away and crossed her arms tightly over her chest.

"I meant that in a nice way," Matis said. "Most girls wouldn't like to be out here all alone. You're brave, that's all."

As if to prove his point, Rikus stretched out, and laid his head in Giti's lap while she stroked the thick fur around his collar. Matis and Giti sat in silence, and she wondered again about him. If she was brave, as he insisted, then he was an enigma, always disappearing then reappearing at the most unexpected times. Giti noticed Matis's disheveled clothes and the empty rucksack he carried. She longed to ask him where he had been, but the words still would not come, so she sat with him and mulled over her questions.

The joyful songs from the celebration echoed throughout the woods. Suddenly Matis was on his feet, a bundle of unspent energy rousing Rikus and urging Giti to follow. Together, they ran to join the crowd. As they neared the bonfire, dying down to a low mound of embers, a shriek went up as one of the girls raced back to the celebration for confirmation that she had indeed found the fern flower. Matis darted off and was the first of the men to jump high over the pyre. It was a celebration of life and hope, and Giti reclaimed the corner of the family blanket to watch from a distance, for the first time remembering her own family in happier times.

The authorities appeared at their door one day in late summer, stern men bedecked in uniforms studded with signs of power. This was the family's worst fear, and Giti was especially vulnerable. If the police suspected that she was German, she would be deported to Russia, or worse. When the official car pulled off the narrow lane, Giti, along with Paulina and Julija, was whisked down to the cellar to wait out their visit. Giti quivered in the dark, enclosed space. She closed her eyes but couldn't push out the memories of the day she and Otto were captured. Paulina and Julija sat on either side of her, and they all held each other tightly as they listened to Loreta through the floorboards that hovered over their heads.

"It's the Cheka," Paulina hissed. The Soviet secret police. It was the first time Giti heard the dreaded term. It would not be the last.

Giti forced herself to slow her breathing and calm her nerves. She could decipher some of what Loreta was saying. Matis ... farmers ... food. The authorities growled and lashed out, but Loreta's voice was calm, strong, and insistent. Giti struggled to understand, but she thought she heard Loreta insist that Matis was just an innocent boy. That much, Giti thought, was untrue, but she admired Loreta's resolve and steady presence.

The men stomped across the floor, and the girls winced as they heard cabinets and drawers being emptied and the contents being thrown across the floor. Giti wondered what they were searching for. As long as she had been with the family, she had never seen anything suspicious or incriminating, except for the mystery that seemed to accompany Matis's activities. Eventually, the girls heard the boots stomp away, followed by the slam of the door. Giti was too terrified to move until Paulina and Julija coaxed her out.

The house was a mess. Precious food was strewn about, drawers upended, their few cherished books scattered, and beds overturned. As they set about cleaning things up, Paulina whispered to Giti, "Matis is a fox. He's too sly to get caught."

Giti wasn't so confident that Matis could outwit the Cheka, and she worried about what he could be up to. She peeked out the window and saw Loreta with the cluster of men, talking to

Matis and Jonas. Matis, normally so cocky and bold, leaned against the barn with a bowed head and slumped shoulders. Jonas stood to the side with his hands outstretched, placating the demanding visitors. Matis seems meek as a lamb, thought Giti, but still, she had seen people beaten for less.

The sight of the two Cheka officers filled Giti with dread and foreboding, even as young as these two seemed to be. Giti had learned quickly what a whiff of power could do to people, and sometimes the most inexperienced had the most to prove. Her heart pounded as she watched Matis, Jonas, and Loreta disappear with them into the barn. When they emerged a few minutes later, both of the Cheka men held butchered chickens, their still-warm feathered bodies twitching and dripping with blood. Their demeanor became less accusatory, but they still held their free hands over their weapons. Matis and Jonas helped them bag the chickens and toss them in the back of their truck. Then the men climbed in and sped off.

The whole house was unsettled for the next few days. Giti watched Matis carefully. He stayed close to home and worked himself to exhaustion in the fields. He said little, and the family slipped back into a cautious routine.

One evening, when everyone had retired, and the only sounds were the embers crackling in the oven and an owl calling out to claim the night, Giti lay on her mattress, willing herself to sleep to calm her anxious thoughts. Each time she closed her eyes, she replayed the vision of the train hurtling away from her with Otto trapped inside. Where did that train take him? Is he still alive? Would she ever see him again? In the clutches of the night, Giti could only envision the worst.

Her frightful ruminations were disturbed by a sharp creak of the floorboards and a rapid intake of breath. Giti cautiously opened one eye and spied Matis stalling in the middle of the floor, waiting to see if he had woken her up. She closed her eyes and concentrated on breathing in a slow rhythm.

Satisfied that she was still asleep, Matis crept to the kitchen, grabbed an empty flour sack, and exited through the rear door. Giti threw back her covers and pulled on her clothes. Within minutes, she was out in the night, lurking in the shadows of the house. The summer warmth had faded with fall, and the night was turning chilly. Giti clung to the side of the porch. Only the warm vapor from her breath gave evidence of her presence. She surveyed the farmyard, and as her eyes adjusted, she saw nothing out of place. No movement, no lights, no clues to where Matis had gone.

Then she saw him emerge from the barn, a shadowy figure advancing slowly and with purpose. The flour sack was now full, and Matis carried it firmly in front of him. On his back was a large basket. Together, the two parcels bulged with food. Giti's mind raced with possibilities. It occurred to her that Matis was selling on the black market. What other explanation could there be?

A dog barked in the distance. Giti watched Matis hesitate, then take a tentative step. He paused once more, then picked up his pace and crossed the road in front of the house, heading toward the woods beyond. Giti gave him a bit of a head start and then followed behind.

He walked for almost an hour, and Giti managed to stay close. The sound of the bundles jostled by his steps served to mask any noise her slight body made. Giti paused any time he paused, and she stayed near to his path when he resumed. Eventually, he came to the edge of a vast clearing. A brook, half-rimmed with ice, gurgled to one side, and a steep heavily wooded incline bordered on the other. Giti crouched behind a tree and observed as he walked to the edge of the clearing and laid aside his parcels. Then he cupped his hands over his mouth and initiated a muffled version of an owl's hoot. He repeated the call twice more and sat down to wait. Soon, a similar call echoed back from the wooded hillside and two murky figures appeared at the edge of the clearing. Matis stood and moved along the tree line to greet them with hearty handshakes and silent hugs. Giti detected two people, whether men or women, she couldn't tell. They were heavily bundled and carried an empty basket and sack that they exchanged with Matis for the full ones. The greetings were quick, and the parcels were handed back and forth with practiced efficiency before both parties turned to retrace their steps.

A loud pop rang out and a flare exploded in the night sky, illuminating the clearing in a harsh yellow light with traces of acrid smoke. Matis and the two figures broke into a run as shots rang out from across the clearing. Giti could see the flashes of light as the bullets flew. Men in uniform poured out from behind the trees on the opposite side of the expansive field, at least a half dozen with weapons drawn and firing.

The figure with the full sack was struck down, and in the fading light of a flare, Giti watched in horror as his lifeless body hit the ground with a thud. Shots answered from deep in the recesses of the hillside as more of Matis's comrades provided cover. Several other shadowy figures emerged, and under heavy fire, they scooped up the sack of food and pulled their fallen comrade back into the cover of the trees. The uniformed men raced across the clearing in pursuit, but were brought down one after another by sniper fire from up the hill.

Giti stayed crouched behind the tree, but every muscle in her body was tightly wound, and all her senses were finely tuned to her surroundings. Her eyes darted wildly from the rescue scene and gunfire on one side, to Matis crawling his way to safety on the other. Matis took cover behind a tree, shielding himself from the conflict in the clearing within Giti's field of vision. She watched helplessly as he hunkered down in the undergrowth, his breaths foggy, rapid, and irregular. Giti couldn't tell if Matis was injured, but it was clear he was unarmed.

The men in the clearing lay dead or mortally wounded, and Giti could hear Matis's friends scampering up the hillside and away from danger. The area was eerily quiet and dark once more. Matis slowly, shakily stood up and rested his head against the tree. He leaned to the side and held his head in his hands for just a moment before pushing himself back upright and turning toward home.

She didn't want him to see her. As Matis made his way close to Giti's hiding spot, she adjusted her position around the tree to avoid his line of sight, and that was when she caught the flash of movement from the clearing. One of the men who had appeared dead pushed himself to his knees and had his weapon pointed right at Matis's head.

"Matis!" Giti shrieked, and she lunged forward to put her body in his path, causing him to trip and tumble over her. The shot whizzed past and splintered a nearby tree. The man swayed unsteadily, dropped his weapon, and collapsed on the ground once again.

Matis rolled over onto his stomach and grabbed Giti fiercely. "What the devil? How did you get here?" he asked.

She embraced his arms and his face, feeling up and down his chest for blood. "Are you hurt?" she blurted.

Matis clapped his hands over her mouth and swiveled back toward the clearing. He began to stand up, and Giti tried to pull him back down, but he easily brushed her off. He crouched and crawled his way back toward the clearing. There was no more movement, no more noise. The bodies lay in the weak moonlight, an eerily peaceful scene bathed in shadow and thin blue light. Matis walked out of the cover of the trees. He picked up the first weapon that was in his reach, and within a few seconds, he had fired a shot at each of the men on the ground, ensuring that none remained a threat to him or Giti. Only then did he drop the weapon, walk back to Giti, and pull her into a fierce embrace.

"Oh my God!" he said, the words tumbling out. He pulled back and held her face in his hands. "Where did you come from? What the hell are you doing here?"

Giti stared back. Her heart raced and her mind was a jumble of fear and relief. "I followed you. I saw you sneak out, and..." Giti didn't want to tell him that she didn't trust him. "I didn't know what you were doing. It seemed dangerous."

Matis smiled and gently cuffed her shoulder. "Well, you picked a fine time to find your voice!"

They ventured home, retracing their steps and stopping often to make sure they weren't being followed. Neither said a word as they slipped in and out of the shadows, avoiding the small clearings and expertly maneuvering the hidden paths. The leaf-covered ground crackled underfoot, and the owls hooted to mark their passing. Despite the carnage in the clearing, they spied no vehicles on the road. The dead men's failure to return had not yet triggered alarms.

They arrived back at the house to find it still and dark, with only the thin light of the moon glinting off the windows. Rikus emerged out of the shadows, barked once, and then wagged his tail when Matis whistled softly. He loped out to nuzzle them and followed them into the warmth of the family room. Matis stirred up the fire and turned to face Giti. "You can talk."

Giti wrapped her arms across her chest. It had been a long time since she was able to summon her voice. The horror of seeing the soldier take aim at Matis had unlocked something inside her, something that had seized her when she fell off the train, something that had felt protective, but had turned into a prison. She exhaled and smiled weakly. "I don't know what to say," she explained in halting Lithuanian. Her voice came out raspy and strained. She paused for another minute, searching for the right words. "What happened back there?"

Matis sat down next to Giti and started talking in slow, measured tones. "*Zaliukas,*" he said. "It means a person who blends into the trees. In this case, many people, and they rely on our help." He told Giti about the partisans who had disappeared into the boreal forest and who waged a campaign to regain Lithuania's independence during Soviet occupation. They were known as Forest Brothers. Matis recounted for Giti how Jonas arranged for him to deliver food and supplies.

"Jonas?" Giti was surprised. She knew that Matis was involved in something secret, but she never suspected Jonas.

"Aye, he's in it to his eyeballs," laughed Matis, "but he has a heavy foot in the underbrush and that damn dog is always two paces behind. He's worthless as a delivery boy."

Matis fell quiet, and Giti watched him sit with his shoulders humped over, rubbing his hands together to generate warmth and dispel the fear that had settled between them. Finally, he spoke. "They know who I am. Someone gave out the location of our meeting tonight, and those men knew that I was coming." He let that thought settle for a minute, and Giti got a chill thinking about how close Matis came to being killed or arrested. She reached out and put a hand on his shoulder.

"You must be careful."

"No, Giedre, you don't understand. It's more than that now. I have to leave here. Now. Tonight. They will come looking for me, and they will watch for me. It's not safe just to hide. I have to go."

Giti searched around the room, her mind rattling around over ideas to keep him hidden so that he could stay. But she of all people knew that houses don't hold good enough hiding places to escape people bent on evil. Outside the windows, the faintest traces of dawn were inching their way up on the horizon. In an hour, it would be light, and the milking would begin soon.

"Giedre, you must listen." Matis put his hands on her shoulders and turned her to face him. "This is dangerous work, and I don't know anything about your past, but I think you know something about danger and risk and survival." He reached down and held her gnarled hand, using his thumb to gently caress the scarred fingers. "You have a story to tell, and one of these days, I hope you can trust me with it."

He searched her eyes, and she nodded. "Now, I need your help. The brothers and sisters—there are women too—need food and supplies. This living under Stalin's thumb, being slaves to the Soviet system, it's not our future." Matis hesitated, searching for the right words. "Jonas organizes things, but we need a courier. Someone with smarts and strength, who can be invisible to the authorities. Someone who can navigate the forest." He paused to gauge her reaction. "I won't lie. It's dangerous work, and you never really know who you can trust. The Soviets, they're easy enough to know, but it's our neighbors, friends, customers. There are those who would rather take a coin than serve their country. Just like tonight—someone gave me up, and we might never know who that was. You just don't know who you can trust. Can you do it? Can I count on you?"

"How will I know what to do?" Giti said with a stammer, as her mind raced to process his request. "Where? Who? How?" Giti was both ecstatic that he trusted her, and terrified at what he was asking her to do.

"You're naive to agree so quickly, but I trust you," Matis said, and he flashed her an endearing smile. "All I know is I trust you."

Matis squared his shoulders and sighed loudly. Giti

watched him as he disappeared up into the loft that he shared with Jonas, and returned with a bag stuffed with his clothes and a few possessions. Jonas followed him groggily down the ladder. Matis hugged him and gently cuffed Giti on her shoulder. Then he grabbed a loaf of bread that Loreta had set out for breakfast.

"Take care of each other. Tell Teta Loreta that I love her and the girls."

Matis slipped out of the door and was gone. Giti realized too late that she never said goodbye.

CHAPTER SIXTEEN

BRIGIT, 2010

Brigit had pictured Peter as a brooding academic, slight of build, and obsessed with detail, so she was shocked at the burly man who opened the door of the modest duplex and welcomed them with a deep, jocular voice. His height and girth filled the small entrance hall, and his face was framed with a mass of unruly black hair and wiry whiskers. Brigit decided he was an affable giant, and she pictured him comically sitting with the prim Mrs. Penworthy over a dinner that was modest in quantity and formal in presentation.

He ushered them into a compact sitting and dining room and introduced them to his petite wife Agne, and their daughter Eljia, a robust baby with chipmunk cheeks and a mop of her father's extravagant raven hair. He scooped up the infant, and they all sat down at the table. Milo opened the box and began to spread out Lukas's photographs, explaining the groupings that resulted from the numbers on the back. Then he drew out the journals and laid them out alongside.

Peter handed the first one to Agne with a wink. He explained, "Agne and I met when I returned from Boston, and I took my notes from the materials that Rachel collected to a local museum and handed them over to the prettiest archivist in town. She's the one who made sense of the scribblings on the page. I think you'll find she's your key to unlocking Lukas's journals."

Agne laughed. "You should have seen him. This big hulk of a man walking in with a binder, pages spilling out everywhere. It was a mess!" She glanced at Peter with a wry smile. "We figured it out in the end. He had some good leads, but nothing concrete. We're still trying to find out about his uncle." She reached into her pocket, drew on a pair of gloves and carefully opened the journal.

Brigit realized her heart was racing as she watched Agne read and sort through the photographs. She described for them how her family might be connected to Lukas's story, and shared with them the urgency surrounding Otto's need to get information about his sister. She pointed to the photocopy. "This one here is the one I got from the German Red Cross. I am hoping that this woman is my aunt, Giti."

Peter frowned. He stood up and placed Eljia in a playpen, returning to the table with a magnifying glass. "I wish we had the original. It's hard to see the detail here. Hopefully there is something in the journal. I am very curious as to how this photograph ended up in Germany though. Do you think Lukas ever traveled there?"

Milo thought it unlikely. He relayed all that he knew of Lukas's activities—that he had roamed throughout southern Lithuania from 1950 to his arrest in 1952. Based on what little information he had learned from his father, Milo understood that Lukas became involved with the Forest Brothers early in his travels, probably in 1950. He would move about the countryside for a time and then return to Kaunas to his parents' home where most of his prints were stored. He sensed the danger that he was in and gave his parents strict instructions to hide the photographs in the event their house was ever searched by the Cheka, which it was, of course, after his arrest. His parents were told nothing of where he was being detained, and nothing about a trial or conviction.

One day, an older woman showed up at their door carrying Lukas's bag, his journals, and a bundle of his photographs. She had met Lukas on his travels and clearly cared for him a great deal. The Cheka followed just a few days later. Milo's grandparents were aggressively interrogated, but gave nothing away. They never spoke of Lukas again until they were quite old.

After the fall of the Soviet Union and the death of Milo's grandfather, his grandmother took the photographs out of hiding and gave them to Milo's father. It was a window into a world that they had worked hard to keep from him. He tried to track down more information, but vestiges of Soviet control kept the fledgling new Lithuanian government tied in knots for a long time. When Milo opened the Galerija Emilia, it was the perfect venue from which to launch the search anew.

Peter listened carefully and nodded often. His work focused on the specific activities of the Forest Brothers, and he was confident that they all had bits of information that would mean more if they combined what they knew.

"These photographs are not as innocent or spontaneous as they seem," he ventured a guess. "Let's see what Agne can pull out of the journals, but my thought is that these are pictures of fellow partisans and revolutionaries. That must be why they were so valuable. Taken at face value, they appear to be everyday scenes with nothing particularly alarming going on."

Brigit was confused. "What do the factory pictures have to do with the Forest Brothers?"

Peter shrugged. It was a mystery. He added that research into the Forest Brothers was highly controversial and fraught with challenges. On the one hand, it was amazing that the Forest Brothers were not better known outside of the Baltics. They were considered the largest band of resistance fighters in the 20th century. On the other hand, a concerted effort by the Soviet propaganda machine had branded the group as murderers and terrorists, and those biases lingered. The truth, according to Peter, was complex, and scholars who worked to uncover evidence of partisan activity ran the risk of being vilified by supporters on either side of the narrative.

"What we know is that they operated in the rural areas, hiding out in bunkers and attacking Soviet officials in targeted raids. They risked imprisonment and death by defying the Soviet regime. Prior to the Soviet occupation, a few who would later become partisans cooperated with the Nazis and helped facilitate the Holocaust in Lithuania. After the Soviet invasion, some partisans were complicit in trials of Lithuanian collaborators, and in some cases, the families of the accused, including children, were killed." Peter extended both hands out, palms up. "It's a matter of finding the balance in truth-telling, acknowledging the immense contributions of the partisans in the creation of our modern Lithuania, while also recognizing that atrocities were committed. Memories of the survivors are still too fresh for us to have a full accounting."

Peter rubbed his forehead in frustration and continued. "The Forest Brothers, both men and women, depended on their fellow countrymen for survival. Farmers kept them alive by providing food and supplies." The factory pictures and cityscapes were a puzzle for sure. Peter pointed to the journals. "Do you have them all?" he asked Milo. And Milo could only say that he had all that his father had found. "Would your father be willing to talk with us?" Peter inquired.

"My father—his name is Andrydas, by the way—he says he's told me all he knows," Milo said, "but maybe you can jog his memory a bit. If you're willing to try, I'll let him know to expect a call from you." Milo wrote down his father's phone number and handed it to Peter. "Good luck! He's famously reserved, but he'd love to see his brother's work acknowledged. He feels the loss keenly, I believe."

Brigit and Milo left in high spirits. Despite the grim reports of partisan resistance and the deprivations of the area during and after the war, they felt like they had made a solid connection with Peter and Agne, and were eager to follow up on any leads that Agne might find in Lukas's journals. Brigit conducted a quick internet search from her phone and learned a bit more about the Forest Brothers, but nothing that might shed more light on Giti and her whereabouts. She was unsettled. What was she supposed to do while she waited for Peter and Agne? It could be days or weeks.

Brigit speculated out loud. "If that *is* my aunt in the photograph, then the journals have to be our best avenue. Perhaps she was involved in the Forest Brothers, or maybe she was just a person in Lukas's path and her image in his photograph is just one brief intersection of their lives ... or maybe that's not her at all, and this is a wild goose chase."

Milo responded, "Well we absolutely need to follow Lukas's path for now. I hope his journals will eventually lead us to the woman in your picture. He's our best bet."

Brigit stole a quick glance at Milo. His thick copper hair and strong cheekbones were tempered by his soft, hazel eyes and professorial spectacles. Clearly he was a thinker, indifferent to his own ample charms, but he was someone she didn't even know twenty-four hours ago and to whom she was now indebted in her search for Giti. Could she trust him? Brigit was sure that they were on the path to *something*, though just what trail they were following was less clear. One thing was certain, she was not going to invest her whole search for Giti in him.

"Well, what if he doesn't lead us to my aunt?" she challenged. "How can I justify putting all my time and effort into Lukas when that might not lead me anywhere near Giti?"

Milo was taken aback. "Hey, do what you want. I don't want to hold you back."

Brigit retreated. "Of course you don't, and I apologize. I just meant … my dad … there just isn't time, that's all."

As Milo pulled the car to the curb in front of Brigit's hotel, an uncomfortable silence had developed between them. With her destination in sight, Brigit's exhaustion caught up with her, and she failed to suppress a broad yawn. "Well, that's embarrassing!" she said. "In the States, we would say that I've hit a wall. Thank you, Milo, for everything. I mean it. Delaying your trip, helping me get to Kaunas and all."

Milo was gracious. "It's been an eventful day for both of us, and I must admit, I'm glad we went. Maybe Peter and Agne will find something that helps us both. Perhaps you can use the time to find new avenues to search for Giti. Have you thought about going to Kaliningrad? That's what Königsberg is called now. Maybe she made her way back there?"

Brigit considered the suggestion and yawned again. "You know, that makes sense. I'll do that. What will *you* do now?"

Milo thought for a minute and then said, "I think I'll go to Rome tomorrow, if only for a couple of days. Peter and Agne will hopefully have something soon, and I'll let you know if I hear anything from them."

Brigit rooted through her bag for a scrap of paper to give Milo her number.

He laughed. "I have it, remember? The voicemail?"

Brigit climbed out of the car, and Milo wished her well. As she watched him drive away, she pondered briefly how she might get to Kaliningrad, but jet lag was taking over. She headed straight to her room, switched off her phone, and indulged in a long shower, letting the warm water soak over her head and run down her back. She had always diligently straightened her exuberant curls for Joe, and now it felt freeing to embrace her natural hair.

The water turned cold, jolting her from her thoughts. She grabbed a towel and walked straight into the bedroom, dripping water in her path. Still cloaked in the towel, she climbed into bed and nestled into the thick duvet, where she fell into a dreamless sleep.

The room phone trilled. Normally it was a brisk and efficient tone, but in the gauzy weave of Brigit's deep sleep, it was jarring and insistent. Brigit opened her eyes, but it didn't help. She was surrounded by Stygian darkness, and the only light leaked from the hallway under the door. She reached out, knocking her mobile and passport to the floor before she clasped the receiver. Milo's voice reached her before she could form any words of her own.

"Brigit? It's Milo, and I am downstairs. May I come up?"

"What?" Brigit's mind scrambled to glue her thoughts together. "What time is it?"

"Uhm, right, sorry, but it's about 6:00. In the morning. It's important, can I come up to talk?"

Brigit opened the door in time to catch Milo rounding the corner in the narrow hallway. His head was down, and he had clearly just rolled out of bed himself. He was wearing an old pair of trousers under his thick jacket, and he had forgotten to put socks on with his running shoes. He glanced up to see Brigit standing in her bathrobe, her hair still damp and full of errant curls.

"Good morning, sunshine," he said, and handed her a cup of

coffee. "I hope you like it fully loaded. I wasn't sure about the cream and sugar, so I went all in with both." Another crooked smile.

Brigit stepped back to let him in, and she sat on the edge of the bed and sipped the sweet, hot coffee while he settled himself into the desk chair. Suddenly aware of her skimpy robe, she tugged at the hem and tried to cover herself up. Milo pretended not to notice.

"So, you're not on your way to Rome?"

"Agne called. She found something, and she wants us to come back straight away. Honestly, Brigit, I waited as long as I could to disturb you. Sorry to wake you up." He leaned forward and put his arms on his knees. "She says she's found something in Lukas's journals that we need to see. I have an afternoon flight to Rome. Will you go to Kaunas? This morning? I'd like to know what she's found, and I rather suspect you'll want to see it too."

CHAPTER SEVENTEEN

OTTO, 1951

Summer returned to the camp with days and nights of perpetual light and the giant swarms of mosquitoes that buzzed in Otto's ears and savagely feasted on his skin. He batted away the loathsome insects and rubbed his hand over his whiskered chin. Every summer, he was plagued with bites that left his pallid skin with deep welts and oozing blisters. The few summer months were a short part of the year, but the near constant daylight meant longer workdays with fewer breaks, grueling for the prisoners but a festival for the mosquitoes. Shielding his eyes, Otto checked the position of the sun and reckoned that it was getting late. The post-dinner work shift would end soon, and the boys would trudge back to their huts and try to get some sleep despite the sunlight streaming through the cracks in the walls.

For the past two years, Otto had been assigned to a construction crew working to build the town around the camp. When Otto arrived six years ago, there was only the prison and the railroad. Now, as the camp expanded to hold more and more of Stalin's political targets, a whole town had been hastily erected around the stone walls. Roads radiated away from the grim fortress and led to stores, a post office, various professional buildings, and eventually to leafy neighborhoods where the camp administrators lived with their dedicated wives and wholesome children. All of it: the roads, parks, stores, and homes, had been built with prison labor.

Befitting his position as a camp trustee, Otto had been assigned to an engineer, Max Fedoreyev, to help him oversee aspects of the town's design. Max had run afoul of the authorities in Moscow because of his family's aristocratic roots and had been sentenced to fifteen years' hard labor. Judging from the number of engineers, architects, and construction crews who had stumbled off the trains and into the camps over the last two years, it was clear that they had been deliberately targeted for this type of work in the growing network of gulags.

Otto was now eighteen and had lived a third of his life in the camp. He was brought in as a terrified boy and through deprivations, oppression, and loneliness, he had discovered a knack for resourcefulness driven by a strong survival instinct. His fear of Frau Petrov, and her ability to manipulate him, had undercut his parents' stern lessons of right and wrong. He now lived in a world of gray, in which waking up each morning was the goal, regardless of what he had to do to get there. He didn't often think of the boys who disappeared after he spilled their secrets to Frau Petrov. He didn't really care if he had a friend in the camp because experience had taught him that friends were temporary. They either died of disease or were killed by the guards or, more likely, the gangs that were rampant within the camp. Otto artfully avoided being sucked into declaring loyalty to one gang or another, most arranged along patriotic lines. Poles stuck with Poles, Ukrainians with Ukrainians, and Germans with Germans.

Otto was an opportunist. He was a devout German when it suited him, but he was careful to cultivate alliances across gang lines if it better met his needs. What he lacked in a formal education these past long years, he had gained in language acquisition. He could carry on basic conversations in German, Russian, Polish, and Lithuanian, and now that a Ukrainian boy had joined his hut, Otto was mastering a little vocabulary with him as well.

Otto's boyish face and slight build belied his newfound ruthless streak, and his brief stint as Frau Petrov's mole in the barracks had insulated him long enough for him to learn to use his fists and his smarts to defend himself against threats and intimidation. He had lost one of his front teeth and developed a mild case of tinnitus from a blow to the head, but he had inflicted much worse damage on others, and he was generally left alone.

Although Otto had shed much of the influences from his life in Königsberg as a way to harden himself for survival, he held on to one soft spot that grew more important with each passing year—his obsession with Giti. Otto still kept her photograph by his bed. He visited Giti's image every night and tried to imagine where she was and what she looked like now. She would be twenty and a grown woman. Was she married? Did she have children of her own? He was long past praying, but every night, he thought about her and hoped that she was safe and content.

Otto knew what the boys and men did to the women and girls in the camp. He knew that the women had little, if any, say in the matter. They existed as rabbits, low on the food chain and subject to the men's need for possession and domination. The searing memory of his grandmother's and mother's deaths was undiminished by the years. He was appalled that the men would stake out their territory, often to remind themselves that even if they were prisoners, they still had a primitive and obsessive power over someone else. It was Otto's weakness that every time he met a girl in the camp, he wanted to protect her in a way that he hoped someone would help Giti.

Max recognized Otto's usefulness, and being a somewhat shady character himself, he immediately felt a kinship with the gangly boy who had a gap-toothed smile, a savage right hook, and a tenderness for women. Max was a complex character. He was a brilliant engineer and could design elaborate systems for laying roads, running sewers, and constructing an electrical grid. Along the way, he cheerfully extorted the town's merchants and craftsmen for precious supplies and resources that he was able to barter for favors within the camp. Otto was his accomplice and light-fingered helper. With his roaming privileges and abundant charm, Otto was able to run Max's operations with impunity. The guards were some of their most loyal customers.

This evening, at Max's direction, Otto released the work crew of young boys who had been tasked with hauling stones from the quarry. The boys silently filed into place and began the two-mile trek back to the camp with the black cloud of mosquitoes attaching itself to their legion of human flesh. Otto fell in behind, and Max soon joined them. As the boys entered the camp, parading through the massive gate and past the guard tower with the ever-present weapons pointed in their direction, Max pulled Otto aside. They walked along the perimeter of the camp until they reached one of the administration buildings, a squat and utilitarian structure. Max let them in the back door that led directly to Sergeant Kuznetsov's small, cluttered office. The whole building reeked of cabbage and stale cigarette smoke, but it was downright fragrant compared to the prisoners' huts that perpetually smelled of excrement, unwashed bodies, and infection.

"Ah, my able engineer and his fierce sidekick," the sergeant sneered. It was a relationship of mutual benefit if not mutual respect. "I have an errand for you two. Mr. Lebedev has arrived in town, sent by party bosses in Moscow to open a clothing factory. Mr. Lebedev will be using prison labor, women and girls for the most part." He lowered his voice and moved closer to Max and Otto, out of earshot of the other guards. Otto noticed his breath smelled strongly of vodka, the beverage of choice. He continued. "I need you to visit him tonight and help him understand the way commerce works in this camp." Spittle peppered his beard as he spoke, and he gestured erratically with his pudgy fingers. He stepped back and spoke in a louder tone, "The wise authorities hope that this experiment will lead to greater efficiency and productivity." At this he winked, handed Max a piece of paper with Lebedev's information, and both Max and Otto knew their roles from here.

They retraced their steps out of the camp, with Max leading the way. When they reached the guard tower, Max showed the paper to the watch officer, who waved them on without much scrutiny. Max and Otto generally enjoyed free reign as long as the guards had their vodka and their smokes, which Max and Otto provided weekly. But as often happened, two guards slipped out of the watch hut and trailed behind them, making no effort to hide their presence. One was a tall, muscular man, his face riddled with acne scars; the other was short and squat with a perpetual wheeze in his breathing. His short legs pumped double time to keep up with his companion's long stride. Max and Otto kept their gaze forward and their movements predictable and unthreatening.

They found Mr. Lebedev's hut among the lines of temporary housing built for the influx of craftsmen. Max and Otto knocked and were greeted instantly by Anton Lebedev, a towering hulk of a man with a bushy black beard and streaks of gray in his close-cropped hair. The guards loitered menacingly outside. Inside the hut was a sputtering fireplace, oppressive in the heat of the afternoon, a rickety kitchen table and chairs, and a mattress lying directly on the floor. The table was covered with bolts of cloth and a Soviet-made sewing machine.

Otto poked around the tiny space, searching for any evidence of wealth or resources to be exploited, but saw none. The house wasn't much better than the prison huts. *Maybe it smelled better*, Otto thought, but it would be quite inadequate for a family once the ten-month winter set in.

Mr. Lebedev was clearly expecting them and greeted them warmly. "I was told to expect some..." he searched for the right words, "*friends* who would help me with the logistics of setting up shop."

Max didn't bother with formal introductions. He got right to the point. "I am Max Fedoreyev and this is my colleague, Otto Binz. We are your friends as long as you cooperate and do your part. Otherwise, you will find that we can be quite difficult. We have two associates outside that help with the facilitation of our work, if they are needed." In truth, the guards were there to spy on Max and Otto, but Max was more focused on perception than reality. "So, here's the point. I am an engineer, responsible for the layout and critical needs of this city. You will need your factory built and staffed as quickly as possible. I don't know where you're from, and I don't care. Winter comes early here and lasts forever. We can get your factory and," Max gestured around the sad hut, "your accommodations underway as long as you cooperate and help us with our needs." Max paused for emphasis. "Do I make myself clear?"

Lebedev glared at Max and Otto, sizing them up. He was probably bigger than the two of them put together, and he was considerably healthier. He crossed his arms defensively. "And what kind of help do you need?"

"Otto and I here appreciate a bit of food to supplement the fine cuisine we enjoy at the camp, for starters. Once your factory is built and we have your workers delivered and inspected, we will of course expect additional garments that will enable us to make sure your workers are reliable and productive. Other guards too may have needs for coats and trousers so that they may be at your service. Again, we assess needs as the situation warrants. The more successful you hope to be, the more you will be expected to help us."

Lebedev continued to stare at Max and Otto, a grimace forming on his face. Otto generally stayed quiet in these initial discussions. Max liked to establish his superior position first, and it served them well to have Otto's role and talents remain a bit of a mystery. Lebedev grunted and mulled his options. Clearly no one had told him how things actually worked in the service of Stalin's system of camps and gulags. He took note of Otto's soiled shirt, which was several sizes too small. Max's clothing was just as threadbare and ill-fitting. Lebedev rustled through a pile of samples and pulled out two uniform shirts. He deftly removed any insignias and thrust them at the two prisoners in front of him.

"I'll be grateful for your help," he said, "but I won't be strong-armed. You help me, and I'll help you as much as I can, but don't get greedy. I'll be expecting some progress on my factory soon enough."

Max and Otto accepted the offering and tried on their new shirts, pleased to have clean cloth against their skin. The soiled shirts were stuffed under their arms. They never missed an opportunity for a deal. Someone with something worse would be willing to trade up. They spent an hour talking over Lebedev's needs for the factory design, and Max promised Otto would return soon with drafts to discuss. The men parted with terms agreed and distrust established.

The next week, Otto returned to Lebedev's hut to take the draft plan for review. He went alone except for the guard that trailed behind, this time just a boy, younger than Otto. Otto knocked at the door of the hut and then barged in, always mindful to keep his adversaries and accomplices on their toes. Lebedev was hunched over the sewing machine, scraps of fabric in piles on the dirt floor. Startled, he jumped up and grabbed a pair of scissors, lowering them when he realized that Otto was alone.

"Max asked me to bring you these," Otto said, ignoring the scissors and laying the plans on the table. "He wants you to review the plans, and he'll be by tomorrow to talk to you about them."

Lebedev backed down and spread out the plans. After a moment he asked Otto, "What's in this for you? Being Max's errand boy?"

Otto's expression remained impassive. "I don't believe that concerns you, Mr. Lebedev. If I could pass on a piece of advice, I suggest you keep your questions and opinions to yourself."

"Well, what if I could help you get out of here? What would you say to that? I have factories in Kursk and Moscow. Perhaps I could arrange something?"

Otto wasn't interested in working in a factory in Moscow, but the notion of getting closer to East Prussia was intriguing. Still, he distrusted Lebedev's motives. "What's it to you what I do?"

Lebedev held Otto's gaze. "It's really nothing to me, except you seem like the useful sort, and I could benefit from your knowledge of the way things work around here. I'd need someone loyal to me first and foremost, though." Lebedev fished in his pocket and drew out a coin. He handed it to Otto.

Otto clasped the shiny currency. He had no idea of what it was worth and what strings might be attached. He palmed it and turned toward the door. "I'll think about it."

He walked back to the camp pondering the conversation. Max would be furious if he knew Lebedev was planning to undercut him, that much Otto knew, but he wasn't planning to tell Max anything. Best to wait a bit and see what Lebedev might be able to offer. The garment maker had just dangled in front of him the very real possibility of escape. Moscow and Kursk. These were places that existed to Otto only as a fantasy, and the tantalizing prospects began to percolate in his imagination.

Otto checked his enthusiasm. He would not be entirely free. He would be beholden to a new master, he was sure of that, but might there be a third path? Could he use Lebedev to secure release and still avoid a new form of prison? He twirled the coin in his hand, feeling the cool metal and running his fingers over the grooves. This was indeed a dangerous game to play.

Max was waiting for him at the entrance to the camp. "So how did it go?"

Otto shrugged. "He's looking at things. I told him you'd be there tomorrow."

Max regaled Otto with news of their various endeavors as they walked into the prison and stopped to check in with the attending guard. So normal was this routine that Max kept right on talking and giving Otto instructions as they poked their heads inside the watch hut. The guard on duty waved Max through, but he stopped Otto.

"You'll be waiting here for the sergeant, lad," the burly officer demanded.

Max stepped back in. "What's the matter? We've done nothing wrong. Just going over plans for construction, is all." Max crossed his arms and stared at the guard.

"Fedoreyev, this has nothing to do with you," the guard shot back angrily. "You are dismissed. This one," he pointed to Otto, "will stay as requested."

Max looked at Otto and tipped his hat. "Find me," he mouthed, and Otto nodded his head.

Otto sat on a stiff chair, his thoughts churning through all the possibilities of what this confrontation might mean. The coin burned his fingers. What had he done worthy of punishment? Did the guard listen in on his conversation with Lebedev?

"Binz!" thundered the sergeant, and Otto rose to follow the command, walking warily into the sergeant's office. The sergeant closed the door and crossed the room to stand behind his desk.

"You have served your sentence and are hereby released," he announced to a stunned Otto. The sergeant pushed a bag over the desk to Otto. Here are your supplies. You are to leave this camp and go straight to the train station. Your train leaves in an hour and you are to be on it."

Otto stared, unable to process this order. He had long ago abandoned any thoughts of leaving this hellhole. He opened the bag to find Giti's picture, an extra shirt, and two pieces of paper. One authorized the train trip, the other was a set of orders.

"Your talents are needed elsewhere in service of the State. You will be taken to Lithuania, where you have orders to report to a *kolkhoz*," the sergeant bellowed.

"A what?" Otto had never heard the term. "I need to say goodbye. I cannot just leave without letting Max know." Otto realized he was pleading.

The sergeant leaned over the desk. "Here's the truth, you little gap-mouthed flunky. You're leaving here and you're leaving here now. I don't give a shit if you want to get on your knees and pray to the Almighty himself, you're walking out of here and getting on that train. You make the train for Lithuania and you're free. You miss it, and you're on the train to a gulag farther north where you can work in the coal mines for another twenty years or so. So you aren't kissing your precious Max goodbye. One way or another, we're rid of you." He glared, then brought his face nose to nose with Otto. "Now GO!" he screamed. Otto grabbed the bag and hurried for the door.

He walked out of the camp in a stupor. Freedom was unknown and threatening territory, and he was panicked about leaving Max without a word. He had no sense of time, and no plan for his next steps. He paused at the entrance to the camp one last time, and then he ran full speed to the train.

PART 2

CHAPTER EIGHTEEN

LUKAS, 1950

May 1

Today I left Kaunas. Mama and Tėtis waved goodbye from the front door, and I could see the fear on their faces. Andrydas peeked out from behind Mama's skirt. He is such a gentle boy. I will miss him most of all. They do not want me to go. What are my choices? It is not safe to stay or go, and I would rather risk my neck out in the world than hide from danger at home. My camera is my weapon and my lifeline. I want to take pictures and capture the beauty of ordinary Lithuanians, their bravery and their courage—nothing more. I plan to walk to Klaipėda by way of Tauragė and visit the factories there, stopping at farms along the way. So many of the small farms have been turned into ugly Soviet collectives, and I am told that conditions there are grim. I long to see the port at Klaipėda: the vast water, the ships, and the dock workers. I have my camera, precious film, chemicals and developing supplies, and a few books to keep me company. Mama gave me jars of preserved food, but I cannot imagine walking too far with the rattling of bottles in my knapsack. I will share them at my first stop. That is sure to win me a few new friends.

My clanking companions didn't last long. Within the first few hours, I encountered a Soviet checkpoint near Kulautuva. Before that, I had walked in silence, and as soon as I passed the last outskirts of Kaunas, I contented myself listening to the birds and the occasional rumble of thunder in the distance. It is a temperamental spring day, with bouts of weak sunshine interrupted by snarling clouds eager to release their heavy loads. The road wound through the plains for most of the morning, closely following along the river. Lost in my reverie and coming around a particularly sharp bend, I stumbled into a small clutch of officials, all of them leaning against two parked cars. Based on the number of spent cigarettes scattered at their feet, they had been standing there a long time, toeing the dirt aimlessly and looking entirely out of place in their suits and heavy coats. Summoning their sternest expressions and hauling themselves upright, they demanded my papers and my purpose. I must get on my knees tonight and say my prayers for forgiveness for I told them that I was off to tell the story of the glorious Soviet victory in Lithuania, professing a love of Stalin that I do not feel. I managed to assure them that my purpose was golden. My lie was convincing, helped I am sure by my generous gift of jars of Mama's preserves and pickles. They clapped me on my back and wished me well and I, and my much lighter knapsack, proceeded down the road. I assume that this will not be my last lie, but I think it is a small price to pay to keep my camera and film intact. Plus, I learned a valuable lesson to be more alert and learn to avoid these stops.

By late afternoon, I arrived at the yard of a kolkhoz in Stanislava. The main farmhouse was an odd, weathered rectangle with a small porch. The barn and outbuildings sagged, but resemblances to a family farm ended there. It was all industry and purpose. I was curious about the lack of young men on the farm. The crew consisted almost entirely of women and much older men, which made me something of a spectacle. Most were polite, reserved, and bone-thin. I was told that the family who farmed this land had been sent to a labor camp for re-education. The land was incorporated into the local collective for the sole purpose of growing grain. That was clear to me from a quick scan of the early spring fields, but it was confirmed by a grizzled old man who spoke with contempt about the inefficiencies of the system. "This land would have been quite productive back in the day," he spat out, "just the one crop is a poor use. That's for sure."

Shortly, a Mr. Melis emerged from the main house, wiping his hands across his ample belly. He, at least, did not seem to be suffering the loss of food and sustenance that I had been warned about. He was introduced to me as the administrator of the collective, and when I told him that I was a wandering scribe, photographing the 'new' Lithuania, he expanded in great detail on the successes of the Soviet system. The entire region had been joined into a system of collectives, and a detailed plan of mass-scale crop production was well underway. Land was used efficiently so that Lithuanians in the city and in the country could benefit from enhanced food production, an assessment that was quite at odds with that of the old gentleman I had talked with earlier. Based on the ravaged appearance of the workers I encountered, I rather believed the older gentleman was speaking wisdom and truth, and Mr. Melis was mastering the art of Soviet propaganda. I asked about the family who used to own the farm, and he grimaced. "Fools, the lot of them," he snarled. According to Mr. Melis, Lithuanians that resisted the Soviet system were idiots and has-beens. "We are the future," he crowed.

This was a new realization for me. I had written in my head a story of the brave, long-suffering Lithuanian people oppressed by Soviet invaders. I had not created a space in my mind to consider that there were Lithuanians who were participating in and encouraging Stalin's abuses of our homeland. I must think on this and adjust my willingness to trust even my own countrymen.

Mr. Melis gave me a quick tour of the operation, pointing out his special innovations that were sure to bring great prosperity once the workers grasped the concepts. I took several shots, capturing both Mr. Melis's pomposity and the diligent work of the farm hands as they concluded their tasks for the day. We viewed the reorganization of the barn as a processing center in the absence of animals. Women were quietly assembling the supplies needed for the next day's tasks and men strolled in and out to replace and store the tools. My presence with Mr. Melis offered them no basis on which to trust me and my motives, so they kept to themselves. The fields offered little in the way of improvements. Early May is a time of preparation, not abundance, so I only had Mr. Melis's word that the yield would be substantial.

Mr. Melis was quite agreeable to my suggestion that I take a portrait of him and his family the following day. He eagerly paid me half to incentivize me to spend the night in the barn. I found this humorous because I was planning to ask for that privilege, and it surely ended up being to my benefit that he thought that my presence was the result of his largesse and not my need. He departed for the day promising to return in the morning with his wife and two children. That left me to my own devices for the evening. I wandered back to the barn where a man and his daughter remained behind. He introduced himself as the caretaker of the property and treated me with great kindness and a healthy dose of suspicion. How do I break through this barrier of distrust? I realize that I will have to calm the authorities in order to prevent seizure of my person and equipment, but this game also prevents me from establishing a basis of friendship with the people I care to talk to most.

"Have you food for the night?" the old man inquired.

"Well, to be honest, no."

He smiled, displaying a gummy mouth devoid of all but a few teeth. "We have little, but you are welcome to our table. Irina here will enjoy the company of someone other than her old pa."

Irina, who was easily the age of my own mother, bowed her head shyly and hustled off to the house to prepare dinner. Actually, that might be a grand name for the sad collection of hard bread, nuts, and thin cabbage soup that she proudly placed on the worn table. I was grateful for anything to still the rumbles in my stomach, and it occurred to me that she may have prepared more than they reasonably could afford to share in deference to me. Fishing down in my knapsack, I found one extra jar of my mother's pickled beets, and you would have thought I'd given Irina a crown of diamonds judging from her squeal of delight. I was sorry that all the other provisions were in the bellies of the checkpoint men I had met earlier in the day.

Over dinner, the old man and his daughter were gracious if reticent. I told them a bit about me, of my journey, and my encounter with the checkpoint early in my travels. I held back on too many details since I count as my most important lesson of the day the need for discretion and small measures of the truth.

The old man nodded and confirmed that the checkpoints were frequent. "Many a man or woman has disappeared after failing the interrogation," he said. "Best to keep your wits about you and your papers in order." He did not elaborate.

I took a chance and asked about any local resistance to the Soviet authorities and their Lithuanian representatives.

"Why do you ask, lad?" was his immediate response.

I tried to reassure him, but he had long practice deflecting and resisting betrayal and so gave nothing away. This is something I will have to mull over.

The next morning, the workers assembled early. Some live in huts on the property, and others commute from nearby. There seemed to be little discrimination as to how the tasks were assigned. Women picked up the heaviest tools and carted them off to the fields as easily as the men.

Mr. and Mrs. Melis arrived later in the morning with their two well-fed and well-scrubbed children. They were quiet and unremarkable. Considerable interest collected in the group as I began to unpack my equipment and set up the shots. Workers laid down their tools and stood on the fringes as the family, dressed in their Sunday finest, gathered in front of the house and stood ramrod straight, looking outward as if posing for one of the vast propaganda murals. I tried to make small talk to help them relax, but they were posturing as much for the crowd as for me. I need to conserve as much film as possible, so I admit to pretending to take more pictures than I did, but I believe that I will have a successful trio to bring to them on my return trip. Mr. Melis paid me another installment on my small fee, and I made a point of writing out a receipt for him with a copy for me. No doubt, he assumed it was to guarantee the final business transaction, but I saw it as a way to keep paperwork in my possession that would satisfy authorities if I am stopped and questioned again. I packed up my supplies and bid them farewell. I walked down the road and turned back to see Irina. She stood at one of the windows and waved timidly. I returned her kind gesture and proceeded on my way.

CHAPTER NINETEEN

GIEDRE, 1951

"Giedre!" Juli ran around to the back of the barn where Giti was hitching the wagon to the decrepit mule. "Mama found one more bag. Can we get it in?"

Giti exhaled sharply and stood up to see Juli running toward her. "Juli!" she hissed. "You shouldn't draw so much attention to us. Just go away, please. I have work to do."

"Oh, Giedre, you don't have to be such a fussy goose all the time," Juli said in a sulk, out of breath and sucking in air. "I thought you were leaving already, and now that you don't have Paulina's help, I thought I might try." She pouted in a well-practiced way that served her when she needed something from one of the farm workers.

Giti gritted her teeth and took a deep breath. It was hard to believe sometimes that Juli was the older of the two. "Juli, stop pouting. If I need your help, I'll ask for it!"

"Who made you boss? I'm going to spite you for being such a self-important bore." Juli started to hoist herself into the wagon seat and knocked Giti's basket to the ground. She plopped onto the bench and stared at Giti, waiting for a reaction. The bag of supplies remained on the ground.

"Scheiße," Giti swore softly. She took a deep breath and bit her lip. She wanted to reach up and yank Juli off the wagon, but she had to constantly remind herself that she was here courtesy of the whole family, and that included Juli. If not for them, who knows where she would be?

She tried to soften her tone. "Of course you meant well, but we have to be careful, and you need to stay here. You'll be missed if you ride with me."

Now that Paulina was married, Giti and Juli were paired more often in the work teams. Although Giti tried to be fond of Juli, she found that she often had to work hard to be patient. She looked at the bag, at Juli's eager face, and back at the wagon.

"Thanks for the extras. The provisions are so scarce this time, I'm sure we can get it in."

———

It had been four years since Matis had gone underground with the Forest Brothers. He had traveled away from the area around Stubriai, and it was generally thought that he had embedded himself within a group of partisans near Klaipėda, on the coast. Occasionally, word filtered down to them about his activities, but they had not seen him since the night of the ambush, and that was a good thing.

The morning after the shootout in the forest, authorities had shown up at the door of the Shimkus house at first light, with an arrest warrant for Matis. The charge was murder. They savagely searched the house and the barn, but found no clues. Jonas was briefly detained but returned home two days later, after he convinced the authorities of the truth: he had no knowledge of Matis's whereabouts. He had been beaten and still bore the scars.

It never occurred to the authorities to suspect Giti. She was small, female, and visibly handicapped, so they ignored her. In the years that followed, the family talked often about Matis and laughed at their memories of his antics, but as much as they missed him, they did not want him to return. They knew the house was being watched, and the warrant remained in effect.

In her role as liaison with the partisans, Giti demonstrated an impressive ability to think on her feet and move seamlessly throughout the countryside. She was a chameleon and cultivated an aura of being unremarkable and invisible. It left her out of suspicion and allowed her a bit of cover for her trips out in the community to gather and deliver supplies. What Matis had recognized that night in the forest was that in situations when most people might panic, Giti remained clear-headed and self-possessed. In the early days after Matis's departure, she copied his techniques and ran supply lines through the woods to the clearing. She didn't yet have an idea who she could trust, so she worked on her own.

Jonas and Giti had managed a smooth and seamless network until two years ago, in February of 1949, when everything about the Shimkus's world had changed with a knock at the door. While it was not unexpected, it created a new sense of urgency and exposure, for the knock heralded the arrival of a letter on official stationery demanding that Loreta Shimkus surrender her land and operations to the local agricultural collective, effective one week from the letter's date. While the Shimkus farm could hardly be classified as elite, the family were landowners who controlled the production from their small plot, and that was an affront to the Soviet way. The Shimkus property would become a *kolkhoz,* a community-run collective, and their land would be dedicated to farming vegetables and growing feed for livestock.

A few days after the letter arrived, Mr. Grigas visited the farm. He was a Lithuanian who worked with the Soviets as the local administrator for the network of collectives around

Stubriai. He was a large man with an ill-fitting brown suit, a thin mustache running across his sweaty upper lip, and thick, bushy eyebrows that hovered over hooded eyes. He walked into the house without a knock or a warning. His aim was to intimidate and aggravate, yet Loreta was not to be baited. She dutifully wiped her floured hands on her apron and, ignoring his brutish entry, invited him to survey the house.

Mr. Grigas laid down the rules. There would be jobs for all in the family, but they had no claim to the property. Others would be assigned to work here, and the Shimkuses had no priority or authority. All was accomplished at his direction. Mr. Grigas pointed at Giti. "And this is your niece?" Loreta silently nodded her head again. "What can she do? Will she be in the way? If so, I will need to arrange for her to be sent to an institution that can care for her."

"Oh no, Mr. Grigas!" Loreta's eyes widened in alarm. "She can help me in the kitchen or work in the fields. She is strong and dedicated. I think you will find her an earnest worker."

"Hmph," he replied, unconvinced and unconcerned. "See that she knows her place." Giti gripped her knitting needle fiercely and considered plunging it right into his heart. Loreta sensed her frustration and shot her a glance as he turned on his heels and strode out the door.

Slowly, painfully, the Shimkus family adjusted to the loss of their home. In the weeks that followed, Mr. Grigas visited the farm on an erratic schedule to oversee the installation and management of the new expanded workforce. Sometimes he was accompanied by his wiry and stoic wife, and sometimes he was joined by his overfed son, Bruno.

Bruno Grigas was a man about the same age as Giti, with a big temper and a small imagination. Generally, he lurked about the farm, sneering at the workers. He embraced his inherited penchant toward sloth and turned it to more nefarious purposes.

It quickly became apparent that Mr. Grigas was grooming Bruno as a manager despite his visible vindictive and cruel streak. Giti, Paulina, and Juli learned to stay far away from him.

"That man is bad business," remarked Jonas. "One of these days…"

The seizure of the Shimkus farm presented Giti with two significant challenges. One was that with production on the farm under Mr. Grigas's control, there simply wasn't the variety of food and goods to be collected and shared from their farm alone. The family was not allowed to maintain their small vegetable plot, and their herd of milk cows were gone. The fields were devoted to sugar beets, cabbages, and hay. Supplies for the family were available as they were for all the collective, through administrative channels in the village. Their resources were counted and monitored, and it was barely enough to keep them fed. The family set aside what little they could. The remainder was collected through a loose network of neighbors organized by Loreta and Jonas to gather provisions and keep them hidden in the cellar until Giti was able to make a run.

And that was the second challenge. With administrative control tightening over the countryside, Giti could no longer roam freely throughout the forests and fields. In the early days of the collective, Giti and Paulina took an old cart from the barn and asked Jonas to help them fashion a false bottom. Under the faux floor, Giti secreted a weekly stash of supplies to be delivered to her contacts. Rather than traipse through the woods, Giti and Paulina drove the supplies around the long way through the village to various rendezvous locations relayed to them by Jonas.

In the spring of 1950, a little more than a year after the farm was seized, Micha had arrived. As had become commonplace throughout the region, a mud-spattered truck pulled into the yard one afternoon, and several workers piled out. This time they were all young men, but it was not always so. Just as often the truck would disgorge women, children, and the elderly. The men stood in the yard, shielding their eyes from the setting sun as they clutched their thin canvas bags of meager possessions and struggled to adjust their vision from the deep, dark recesses of the truck. Micha was the tallest of the crew with intense eyes, close-cut white-blond hair, and a sprinkling of stubble across his angular jaw.

Bruno stormed off the porch, yelling instructions and forcing the arrivals toward the barn for their brisk introduction to his erratic leadership. Paulina noticed Micha right away. She set down the laundry basket she was carrying and watched as the men paraded past the house. Most of them shuffled, stoop-shouldered and defeated, but Micha stood tall and projected an air of confidence. He held his shoulders back and took measured steps, slowly turning his head to take in the surroundings. He locked eyes briefly with Paulina and gave her a quick nod before following the other men around to the back.

His bearing was clearly threatening to Bruno, who sidled up to him and hissed in his ear. Micha stood still, neither stooping to accommodate nor offering any outward opposition. Bruno seethed at invisible slights and imagined offenses. He reached out and snatched Micha's bag and upended it into the dirt before he stomped off. Micha slowly leaned down and gathered up the few articles of clothing, his shaving kit, and a framed photo and calmly put them back in the bag before he disappeared into the row of huts that had been hastily constructed near the barn.

"Common convicts is what they are."

Paulina spun around to find Bruno lurking behind her. "Just a bunch of losers," he sneered as he picked up the laundry basket and held it out. As Paulina reached for the load of freshly scrubbed clothes, Bruno turned the basket over and used his foot to grind the wet shirts and trousers into the floorboards.

He said, "You best mind your manners and stay away from that lot if you know what's good for you." He walked behind her and patted her bottom. Paulina turned on him and spit in his face. He grabbed her jaw and stuck his fleshy face up against hers. "One of these days, you'll regret that," he said, and he chuckled to himself as he sauntered toward the barn after the men.

On one count at least, Bruno was correct. Micha, whose full name was Michaelis Andris, was a paroled criminal of the state. As with the other men in his group, he had recently been released from a prison camp in eastern Russia, where he had been sentenced to five years' hard labor in the coal mines for the crime of being an engineer and an intellectual in a system that valued subservience and mindless loyalty. But while he was technically a criminal, he was anything but common. He was strong, a tiny bit mischievous, and unflappable. Paulina fell in love at first sight. Micha was equally smitten.

The wedding was a simple affair on a sunny summer afternoon, just after the midday meal and before the final shift of the day. Jonas and Juli served as the official witnesses. Giti, who was assigned to the kitchen and wash duty with Loreta, went out early that morning and fashioned a wreath made of rue and zibutes for Paulina to carry, the bold yellows and periwinkle of the forest flowers providing a bright contrast to Paulina's dusty canvas coveralls. Bruno did not allow the ceremony to disrupt the normal flow of the workday, and he was adamant that no extra food or provisions be used in a feast, so after the brief ceremony everyone returned to work.

Giti watched Paulina and Micha stroll back to the fields hand in hand as wife and husband. She was happy for them, and indeed the wedding had brought a welcome atmosphere of joy to the farm. But for Giti, it was a reminder of the family she had lost. Watching Juli fuss to arrange flowers in Paulina's hair, or Jonas dab at his moist eyes during the vows, made Giti feel like an intruder once again. These people had been so kind to her, but they were not her real family. If Giti ever got married, her mother would not be there to watch, Pappi would not give her away, Otto and Paul and Stefan would not tease her groom. They were lost to her. Were her own brothers alive somewhere, getting married and having children of their own? Their faces flooded her memory, and yet the details were elusive, indistinct.

Giti went into the house and retrieved her two treasured photographs. She traced the faces with her finger and thought of each one. She closed her eyes and listened for their voices. Speaking German for the first time in years, she whispered, "I love you Mutti and Pappi, Oma and Opa, Paul, Stefan, and Otto. I hope the boys are alive. I hope you are happy. I hope I will see you again." And she wept.

The evening of the wedding, as the workers came in from the fields, Micha appeared at their door with the small bag containing all the possessions he owned. He bowed his head to Loreta, hugged Giti and Juli, and shook Jonas's hand. He then whisked Paulina outside and swung her around as he showered her with kisses. It was sad that there was no provision for a honeymoon or even a proper wedding night. Loreta had managed to scrape together the supplies for a simple cake, and Jonas produced a bottle of old wine that they all shared. Then Paulina and Micha took a bedroll out to the barn for one night of privacy.

Now, Giti scanned the yard one more time to make sure she and Juli were safe to finish packing the supplies for this run. She saw Micha striding toward the barn, but no one followed. Giti admired Micha. His quiet confidence and loyalty to Paulina endeared him to the whole family, even if he was prone to playing the occasional prank, but what Giti loved most about him was the way he treated her as an equal. He never pandered to her handicap. He sought her advice and helped her when she asked, but he never assumed that she was incapable of performing the same mental and physical tasks as anyone else.

With Juli's sporadic assistance, Giti loaded the baskets of laundry that she and Loreta had finished the night before, fresh-smelling bundles of shirts and household linens. Despite Bruno's insistence that he control all aspects of the *kolkhoz,* Loreta and Giti had managed to build up a bustling laundry business for the merchants in town. It was not a particularly lucrative enterprise, but that was not the point. It gave Giti a reason to roll the wagon out on a regular basis and make the trip into Stubriai. The fresh laundry on the inbound journey and the dirty laundry carried out concealed the supplies hidden underneath. Loreta was able to convince Mr. Grigas that this was the best use of Giti and the more elderly women's labor and a way to use all the talents and resources of the property. When word spread about the excellent services she provided, Mr. Grigas and Bruno were quick to take credit, which was just fine by Giti.

With all the supplies loaded, the mule properly hitched, and Juli enticed toward more immediate and local tasks, Giti jumped into the driver's seat and grabbed the reins. She silently said a prayer that the mule would stay alive long enough for this journey because with each trip she became a little less confident in the beast's ability to pull the load. Micha whispered encouragement into his oversized ears, Giti clicked the reins, and she was off.

Giti shivered in the late fall chill and peered at the clouds amassing overhead. It would snow soon, and the partisans' needs would turn more desperately to survival through the coming winter. After her escape from Tomas's house, Giti had never abandoned her fear of being lost and cold, and she was deeply empathetic to the partisans, who stayed buried in the woods even in the most punishingly frigid months.

As the wagon bounced off the stubborn ruts in the road, Giti settled into her thoughts. She missed Paulina on these runs. They had used the time to gossip and laugh, free from the leering men on the farm. Now that Paulina was pregnant and due to deliver any day, Micha disapproved of her taking risks by spending hours jostling atop the wagon and engaging in illegal activities. Giti understood, and she agreed with Micha, but she still missed her friend. The time away on the wagon was a welcome relief from the monotony of farm life, even if there was the ever-present tension of their illicit activities.

As Giti crested the rise of a low hill, she spotted the checkpoint ahead. She sat up straight, scanned the scene, and searched out any signs of danger. The checkpoint was not unexpected, but the number of soldiers was significantly greater than usual, and their stances signaled apprehension. Usually, Giti found one or two sentries, and often they were asleep. Not this day. Giti counted twelve men: eight soldiers in uniform and four in suits. They stood around a canvas-covered transport truck and two gleaming sedans. Giti slowed the wagon as she approached and pulled her hat down over her eyes. She always carried a knife in her left boot, but it would do little good with this crowd.

Two of the younger soldiers stepped out into her path as her wagon drew alongside them. One grabbed the reins while a more senior member of the cohort walked slowly around the wagon. Giti sat quietly, watching closely to see if she could determine who was in charge. She used her crippled hand to wipe her forehead, not because she was perspiring but to create an effect. Usually when men saw her hand, they dismissed her ability to pose a threat.

The officer walked around to the side of the wagon and looked up at Giti. "Your papers." Giti made a show out of fumbling for the documents that Jonas had secured for her. They were real, but not hers. They belonged to a girl a few years younger than Giti who had died of pneumonia last winter. The officer made a grand show of reading each line. "Marte, eh? Where are you going today, Marte?"

Giti kept her eyes pointed down. "To Stubriai, sir. I am delivering laundry. This is my job."

"It doesn't say anything here about your job."

"No, sir. This is a new job for me." She produced a list of her deliveries and the items for each. He motioned two soldiers over, and they climbed into the back of the wagon. Giti's heart pounded, and she struggled to keep her breathing steady. She managed to maintain her bland expression until the soldiers began tearing into each pile of carefully bound clothes.

"Stop!" she yelled. "They are destroying my work! I'll have to take these back and clean them all over again!"

The officer smiled and said nothing. The men continued to toss shirts and towels without care.

"Sir, please!" Giti looked the officer in the eye for the first time. "Colonel Pashtov's wife is one of my customers. One of those bundles is her delicates. How will I explain this to him?" She used her right hand to gesture across the mess that the soldiers had made.

The officer said something to the men in Russian, and they

climbed out of the wagon. "Very well, Marte. On your way then. Give Colonel Pashtov's wife our regards."

Several of the men snickered, but they moved out of the way of the wagon. The officer leaned over and picked up a chemise that had fallen into the dirt. He held it up for the other men and made a show of brushing at the stain. "Let us hope that this is not one of hers, or she will be very unhappy with you."

Giti rode away feeling unsettled by the exchange. They were on the alert, searching for someone. Several miles past the checkpoint, just as Giti was beginning to calm her heart from the unsettling stop, she saw the fork in the road that marked her turn for the subversive delivery. The right fork went to Stubriai, the left skirted the forest for a while and then turned in toward the thick trees. Giti would meet her contact there, and this part of the journey was where she was most exposed. There was a prominent sign at the fork, and there was no reason that she should be turning left. If she were stopped, she would have no plausible explanation.

"No point except to stay the course," she said aloud with more confidence than she felt. Her ears were tuned to listen for any sound that was out of place, and she sat straight and tense in the wagon seat. A couple of miles ahead, and she should see the rock on the side of the road that was her signal. If the smooth side faced out, then her contact was there. If the jagged side was visible, she was to turn the cart around and proceed to Stubriai. Catching sight of the smooth side of the rock, she clicked on the reins to spur the mule on, ready to get this exchange complete and be on her way.

Rasa stepped from behind the tree when she saw Giti's wagon lumbering up the bumpy road. Giti smiled and pulled the mule to a halt. She jumped out of the wagon and gave Rasa a quick hug. "I'm happy to see you, my friend," Rasa said with a smile.

Giti and Rasa quickly pulled out the laundry and emptied the contents of the wagon. The supplies were stacked behind a camouflaged barrier for the next detail to pick up. Rasa had a few letters and books to send back with Giti, which they secured in the secret compartment. The two women worked quickly and with little small talk. The less time they took, the less chance of discovery.

"Lord, this is a mess!" Rasa said, and Giti relayed what had happened at the checkpoint. Rasa quickly helped her reassemble the bundles as best as they could. "I must get back and let the boys know. Something is afoot at our end, and I wonder if it's a trap." She lightly kissed Giti's cheek. "Take care, my friend. It may be an eventful night." And with that, she disappeared into the forest, and Giti was back on the wagon heading toward Stubriai.

On her return journey, the checkpoint was still there. More soldiers had joined the group, and they had their weapons out, close at hand. The same two soldiers who had trashed the wagon earlier stepped into the roadway to block her path, and the officer approached once more, this time carrying a fancy walking stick with a distinctively ornate leather handle. It was a fine piece of work, and Giti assumed that it was also quite expensive.

"So, Marte. How goes your visit to Stubriai? You were there a very long time." He clicked his tongue and walked around the wagon, using the walking stick to poke around in the bundles of dirty laundry she had collected in town. "Were your customers very put out by your shoddy delivery?" He said this more to the soldiers than to Giti, and they all laughed together.

Giti sat still and straight, endeavoring to stay calm and not provoke these men.

"Did you not hear me, girl?" The officer walked over to Giti and used the walking stick to lift her chin. "I asked you a question."

"Yes, officer. They were most dissatisfied that their laundry was soiled and not clean. I am to rewash it and return it promptly." Giti kept her eyes straight ahead, willing this interrogation to end.

The officer looked at the men and then back at Giti. He moved the end of the walking stick down her chin, brushing her throat, and settling it on her chest where he poked her breasts and laughed. He said something in Russian to the soldiers, and they responded with more laughter. There was palpable tension as the soldiers watched to see how far the officer would go.

Giti took her eyes off the road and stared defiantly at the officer. He was younger than she had thought, and she noticed his steely blue eyes and crooked nose. It had been broken at some point and ill-repaired. He stared back and subtly arched one brow as if to say, "I dare you." Keeping her eyes locked on his, she lifted her right fist and slowly pushed the end of the walking stick away from her body. Her heart was thumping, and her legs were shaking under the thick canvas pants. She thought about her next moves. If the officer decided to strike her, she would use the knife on him. The soldiers would kill her or worse, but she would have that one moment of satisfaction. She flexed her left fingers and slowly began to move her hand down toward the hiding place in her boot.

The deep-throated horn of a transport truck sounded as the vehicle appeared from around the curve and screeched to a halt. The officer dropped his walking stick and spun around, just as the soldiers along the roadside shouldered their weapons. Giti relaxed her left hand and withdrew it from the vicinity of her knife. She watched as two men dressed in rough linen shirts and sturdy canvas trousers, the ubiquitous uniform of Lithuanian peasantry, climbed out of the back with their hands up. They said something in Russian and approached the officer, slowly lowering their arms but keeping their hands visible.

The soldiers kept their weapons trained on the men, but were clearly intrigued by the interaction between them and their officer. One of the men gestured with his palms up and then reached for a packet of papers, which he handed to the officer and then stepped back. The officer leafed through the packet, smiled broadly, and gestured to his men. He issued a sharply worded order, and all, except for the two oldest, lowered their weapons, rushed to the transport truck, and piled into the back. The two casually dressed men followed, and the driver revved the engine.

The officer turned to Giti. "We were just getting acquainted, no, *devushka*? You come this way often, and we *will* meet again." He slapped the mule on its rump, and sent Giti on her way. As her wagon rumbled off, she swiveled back in the seat to watch the officer climb into the passenger seat of the truck. He slammed the door shut, and the truck jolted ahead, driving in a wide arc and returning the way it came.

Giti urged the mule on. Something was wrong, and she couldn't ride on and leave the forest dwellers at the mercy of the soldiers. At the first possible turn off the main road, Giti steered the wagon as far into the woods as the terrain would allow. She tied the mule to a tree, and armed only with the knife, she set off on foot back toward the rendezvous point with Rasa.

CHAPTER TWENTY

OTTO, 1951

Otto stepped off the train in Vilnius and onto a platform teeming with activity. Harried men in railway uniforms shouted orders. Women pushing prams were jostled to the side by stern-faced soldiers massing for the next train. Families struggled to keep children and battered suitcases together in the swirling crowds. Smoke and steam from the trains mingled with dust mites that glistened in the weak light leaking through opaque windows.

After over six years languishing in the camp and four days on a train from Kursk that stopped and sputtered across vast expanses of Soviet terrain, Otto was disoriented by the frantic pace. He had been told to report to the authorities by 14:00 hours, and he swiveled his head from side to side, searching for any clues to guide him as to how he should accomplish this. He briefly considered what might happen if he just disappeared into the crowd, but his lack of money, clothes, food, and experience in the civilian world seemed to him an insurmountable barrier to success. He had entered the camp as a child and had learned few skills to help him navigate this unknown urban world. He could read the little bit of German that his few years in school had allowed him, but the signs around the station were indecipherable. Best to stay within the system for a while and keep the thoughts of escape at bay until he was better prepared.

He spied the large clock hanging above the platform, but he didn't know how to tell the time. He didn't see the number 14 on the clock face, and he puzzled over that for a bit. Life on the farm and the camp had been governed by the sun. Otto peered upwards, but the roof of the cavernous station was covered in grime-spattered glass, and it wasn't giving away any hints. It could be morning or afternoon. Otto had nothing to guide him. Less than a week ago, he was working with Max at the camp, all rules known and acknowledged. Now came these new sights, new people, new rules. Otto was dizzy with confusion.

Shrill whistles blew as the train wheezed its readiness to depart on the next leg of its journey. Late-arriving passengers scurried across the platform, and Otto was pushed left, then right in the frantic crowd. Determined to take charge, he grasped his canvas bag tightly and plowed his way toward the large hall in the center of the station to ask for assistance. After a few attempts at conversation in his patchwork, camp-taught Lithuanian, he was directed to a gaggle of men who seemed very much like him, as they clustered around an official-looking, but empty, kiosk. Their ratty clothes, meager belongings, and undernourished bodies were the hallmark of camp inmates, and their listless expressions signified that none were expecting jubilant relatives or long-lost sweethearts to emerge from the crowd to claim them and take them home.

Otto sauntered up to the group and learned that indeed this was the muster point for paroled prisoners seeking their work detail. Otto encouraged quick introductions and surmised that most were of German derivation with a few Poles, Lithuanians, and Ukrainians mixed in. Otto started to feel on firmer footing.

He had been living among men like this for years and was savvier than most at reading his fellow inmates. His gregarious entrance was less about his interest in knowing the other men personally; rather years in the camp navigating gang rivalries had taught him the necessity of knowing as soon as possible who your potential enemies and allies might be.

The men continued to stand around for several hours, and as each train pulled in, their group swelled with new arrivals. Otto observed carefully as each new man walked up and made a space for himself in their loose queue. As the group grew, Otto observed that the men began to divide themselves into their country clusters. Soft chatter emerged as the men sought to establish mutual connections or shared experiences.

Eventually a guard, an old, grizzled man missing his left leg, hobbled up with a clipboard. He sized up the group, spit on the floor and rustled through some papers. Speaking in Russian, he began calling out names. "Fritz Biedemeier! Filip Valus! Otto Binz!"

All accounted for, the guard motioned for the group to form a line and march to the entrance to the station. There, they found a large truck with a canvas-covered back and more guards milling around. At the sight of the pitiful group, the guards tossed away their cigarettes and grabbed their weapons, which they used to prod the men into the back of the truck. Otto hopped in last, and the truck roared to life. It pulled out into traffic and headed to an unknown destination. Otto speculated that he had been standing with the men for at least four hours in the station, and he wondered how long of a drive they had. No one had mentioned or offered food, and Otto's stomach was not the only one growling.

Close to midnight, the truck rumbled up a dirt lane and sputtered to a stop in front of a plain wooden building. During the long hours on the road, the guards had left the back flap of the truck open. The men were nauseous from fumes and hunger, but at least they could get their bearings and see the flat Lithuanian countryside rolling past on their way out of town and across the country. The long summer day had accompanied them most of the journey, but for the last hour of the trip, the men had traveled in increasing darkness. The stop was a welcome one, and all the men piled out of the truck and quickly found a spot away from the others to empty their bladders. Then they looked around and took in their surroundings.

The building in front of them was long and low-flung with little embellishment to mark it as anything but administrative. An uncovered wooden walkway extended across the front, and the whole structure was dark with the exception of a single candle burning in the window on the far right. Otto walked around the back. Behind the main building were several barns and a row of long huts, none newer or fancier than the main building. Even in the darkness, Otto could make out that the hub of buildings featured weathered siding, tired rooflines, and nothing but packed dirt underfoot. If this was a farm in summer, Otto hated to think what wintertime was like.

"Hey! What are you doing?" a voice called out, and Otto turned and saw the silhouette of a woman framed in the back doorway. She wore a thin blouse hastily tucked into a pair of men's britches. Her muscular arms and tall, lithe figure hinted at manual labor. The rest of her features were indistinct, but she stood hands on hips in a confident stance, and her voice carried authority.

Caught off guard, Otto stuttered a reply. "We just arrived ... from Vilnius and the train." He gestured to the front. "The rest are there." Another pause, and Otto began to regain his footing. "Where am I?"

She didn't alter her posture, but her voice softened a bit. "You're on a *kolkhoz* near Šilutė. Welcome. Now stop prowling around and get back to the front with the others." She stepped back inside and closed the door.

Otto was intrigued. Šilutė, eh? Where the hell was that? He walked back around to the front, and the woman was now on the walkway speaking with the guards. She stood in the shadows, so Otto still could not make out any more of her features. After a brief chat, the guards gathered the men, and gave them their orders. This was their new assignment: a collective growing barley, wheat, and potatoes. Due west and a short drive away was the Baltic Sea. Otto's heart raced. He didn't know a lot of geography, but he knew that Königsberg and the rest of East Prussia was bordered by the Baltic Sea. He was close to home. He immediately thought of Giti and wondered where she was. Did she find her way back to the farm, or what was left of it? Where could she be? Otto was elated. This was as close as he had been in years to finding her and what was left of his family.

Based on the woman's directions, the guards herded the men to one of the huts near the biggest of the barns out back. Inside, it looked almost like the camps they had all just left behind: a long room with a sagging floor, rows and rows of bunks, and a thick, wheezing stove in the middle. As well as could be determined, however, there were no walls or gates or guard dogs nearby. That alone was a new sensation. Several of the bunks were occupied, and the sleeping men grumbled at this interruption to their rest.

Once all the new arrivals were inside and the men had stumbled around to find an empty bunk, the guards announced breakfast at daybreak, and then they disappeared. Otto fished out the picture of Giti from his pocket and gave her a kiss goodnight. "I will see you soon, Liebchen. Soon, I promise." He tucked the photo under the lumpy pillow, and despite his growling stomach, he fell fast asleep.

The clanging bell roused them all after a too brief sleep, and they stumbled out of the hut into a soft dawn creeping up along the horizon, which bathed the farm in a pale orange glow. The cluster of buildings that appeared so bleak the night before had been transformed. The weathered boards were warmer, more inviting, and the vista beyond the barns was now in full glory. The spring barley and wheat crops had been harvested, and the potato crop was well underway. Long, orderly rows of plants stretched into the distance, and Otto and the other new arrivals reveled not only in the simple beauty of what they saw but also in what they didn't see: guards, walls, fear. People emerged from other huts, and Otto was surprised to see not only men, but women, young and old, and children of all ages.

"Are you waiting for a special invitation?" Otto turned around and saw the woman from last night. She stood with her hands on her hips, dressed in a man's gray shirt with gray canvas trousers and wearing a mischievous grin on her face. She was much younger than Otto had thought last night, and much prettier than he had imagined. She had twinkling soft green eyes and reddish blond hair tied back with a scarf.

"Well, I..." Once again, Otto was at a loss for words. "I'm just not sure how all this works," he said.

"It works like this. You grab a plate, walk up to the table, and help yourself. Then you say 'thank you' to the people who prepared it." She sized him up. "Are you from the camps?"

Otto nodded. "Near Kursk, apparently, although I couldn't have told you that while I was there. I entered when I was eleven. My name is Otto Binz."

"Nice to meet you, Otto. I'm Karin." She didn't react to the rest of his story other than to say, "You don't have to wait to be told here. You do your job on the work detail, and you are free to decide your whereabouts yourself."

Otto thought this over and smiled. "Are you in charge?" he asked.

She laughed at this. "You got a problem with that? Actually, my husband is in charge, but he is in Klaipėda. When he is gone, I am in charge. Eat, Otto. You'll be in the fields soon enough, and you look like you need a good meal."

Life on the collective proceeded at a predictable rhythm. Rising at dawn with long days in the fields followed by simple meals. In the evening, groups gathered for conversation, games, and a bit of music. Gone was the constant life-threatening competition for survival from the camps. The gangs were gone too, replaced by a semblance of communal, cooperative living.

Karin assigned Otto to a group that was clearing stumps to create new fields for crops, and he relished the opportunity to work outside in the sunshine after enduring the long train journey. During his precious free time, he began exploring the surrounding territory, walking down the road, reading road signs, and investigating the patches of forest surrounding the farm. When he was ready, meaning when he knew the terrain and the people, he would leave and make his way back to Königsberg.

Anton, Karin's husband, turned up one morning, and Otto was shocked to see that he was old enough to be Karin's father. He had once been handsome but clearly, the rot in his black soul had worn away any sheen over the years. Now wheezing and unfit, his defining features were his scowl and his anger. He spent most of the days traveling from one work detail to another to rage about laziness, ineptitude, and incompetence. Otto learned quickly to stay out of his way.

Otto settled into his new home and resumed the strategies

that had helped him survive the gulag: be friendly but not too friendly, maintain constant awareness of your surroundings, ask the right questions, and be useful to those who have more power than you.

The closest Otto came to having a friend on the farm was his budding alliance with Fritz based on their shared roots in East Prussia. Fritz was from Heilsberg, which he assured Otto was just south of Königsberg. Though their stories were similar, there was a tacit understanding that their partnership was one of strategy. Emotions and painful memories were topics both rigorously avoided.

On a particularly warm day soon after their arrival, Fritz and Otto were in the fields, part of a crew clearing stumps after the trees had been felled. Most were pines or birch with a few aspens mixed in, so they were making good progress, beginning with picks and shovels and finishing with mule labor. Karin worked nearby. She often joined in on the most labor-intensive tasks and easily pulled her own weight with the men. Fritz stood up to stretch his back and watched her as she secured heavy chains around the stumps.

"She's a puzzle, that one," he said to Otto.

Otto swung his pick and split the pine stump they were chopping. He wiped his brow with the hem of his shirt and glanced over to observe Karin. "In what way?"

"I mean, she's young and she's definitely pretty. And she's strong." Fritz hesitated and then said what was on his mind. "What the hell is she doing married to him?" Fritz nodded his head in the direction of the path leading back to the farm. Anton was plodding his way toward them. Even from this distance, the two men could see that his neck was bright red from overexertion and his breathing labored. Sweat poured down his face.

Otto shrugged. He didn't want to admit even to Fritz that he had been pondering the same, curious and a bit concerned about Karin's story. He put his head down and swung his pick one more time. The stump cleaved in two.

Fritz abandoned his musings and was leaning down to attach the chains when they heard Karin yell out. The men snapped their heads up and watched as Anton jerked Karin away from the crew. He wrenched her arm behind her back and pulled her to the ground. Standing over her, he put his face in hers and whispered menacingly.

She whipped her head to the side, but Anton used his hand to jerk her chin back so that she was forced to look at him. Otto slowly laid his pick on the ground and balled his hands into tight fists. He took one step forward, and Fritz reached out and grabbed his arm.

"Steady there, Kumpel. You don't want to get in the middle of a spat."

Otto wavered and relaxed his fingers, but his heart was pounding, and his jaw was clenched. Then Anton raised his hand and slapped Karin across the cheek. He began dragging her from the field, and Otto sprang forward. He crossed the bottom part of the work area, leaping over stumps to stand on the path, blocking their exit. Anton continued to hold Karin by the upper arm, and Otto could see the red finger marks on her cheek and the bruising already developing on her arm.

"Let her go," Otto said with controlled anger.

"I'll do with my wife as I wish." Anton spat as he spoke. He pulled Karin forward and inched his face right up to Otto's. "Get out of our way. This is none of your business."

"Let her go," Otto repeated, standing firm. "You argue as you wish, but you need to let her go."

The other men in the crew had dropped their tools and were making their way toward the trio. Either out of curiosity, gallantry, or bloodlust, each had their own interest in the dispute. Otto remained in the path, saying nothing but blocking Anton's way.

Anton turned back and saw the crowd that was gathering. He dropped Karin's arm and kicked at her backside. Karin slowly pulled herself up and dusted off her knees before she gently lay her hand on the welts forming on her face. She locked eyes with Otto, but her emotions were unreadable. She stomped past both men and left the work area. Anton glared at Otto and followed his wife off the field.

Fritz confronted Otto. "I don't know what just happened there, but you've either won her admiration or her hatred. You're *definitely* on the wrong side of him. Better watch your back, Kumpel."

Karin missed the evening meal. Otto went about his business, but shortly before sunset, he saw Anton climb into his battered truck. When the truck rounded the curve and disappeared from view, Otto walked up to the main building and lightly tapped on the door. It swung open, and he peered inside. Karin was seated next to the far window, huddled under a blanket, which was odd in the warm summer evening.

"What do you want?" she asked.

"Just to check on you. Are you all right?"

She grunted. "I'm alive, thank you. Please leave me alone." She turned her back on him and wrapped her arms around her chest. Otto could see the fresh bruises on her arms and wondered which were inflicted after the pair returned from the field.

"I don't mean to bother you," Otto said. "Just let me know if I can help." He watched for a few more minutes, but Karin didn't reply. Her head stayed down and she kept her back to him. Otto backed out and closed the door gently.

Anton's truck was still gone the next morning. Karin didn't come to breakfast and was missing when the work crews went out. Around noon, as Otto and Fritz were breaking up more of the stumps, the handle to Otto's ax snapped.

"Scheiße!" he shouted as he brushed splinters off his arm.

Joachim, who was generally the foreman of the group, came over to examine the mess. "Head back to the barn, there's likely extras there. Bring another back in case Fritz there busts his up, too. The way you two are swinging, it's a wonder you haven't broken one until now."

The area around the main building was quiet, and Otto was deep in thought when he entered the barn. He poked around for the most likely spot to store extra handles and was startled by a noise overhead. He stopped and glanced up toward the loft. Bits of hay floated in the air above his head, but the noise had been fleeting, perhaps a mouse or maybe a cat. Otto crept over to the ladder and slowly climbed up each rung. When his head was just about level with the loft floor, Karin's face popped up into view.

Otto was so shocked that he almost fell off the ladder. He regained his footing faster than he regained his composure. "Damn you! What are you doing scaring me like that?"

"I could ask the same of you. What the hell are you doing in the barn in the middle of the day? You scared the daylights out of me." She gently nudged his shoulder, and they both laughed.

Otto explained about his broken handle, and Karin came down to help him find replacements. As Otto shouldered the two handles and bid Karin farewell, she turned into the light, and he noticed that her face was clotted with bruises.

"My God, Karin! What did he do to you?"

She sunk down into the soft hay and put her head in her hands. "He's under such pressure, Otto."

"That doesn't make it right."

"No, but there'll be worse if I can't stop the stealing."

Otto sat on the dirt floor, facing her. "What stealing?"

Karin explained that the stores of winter wheat and barley had been counted and bundled for the main administrative unit in Klaipėda, but when Anton delivered it, there were bundles missing. "Anton may lose his position if he cannot find the culprit. We all know what's going on, of course, but who is helping them here? I cannot figure it out. Anton has been accused of selling on the black market."

"Is he?" Otto asked. "Selling on the black market, I mean."

"God, no. He's not brave enough or clever enough for that. It's the partisans. The food is going to them. We just don't know who here is helping them. Anton will be back in three days, and I must have a name for him by then."

Otto reached out and gently touched the bruises on her face. Karin brushed his hand aside. "What can I do?" he asked. "Tell me how I can help."

"You want to help? Gain their trust, Otto, and root out the thieves."

Otto wasn't worried about right or wrong, good or bad. He felt a chivalrous urge to help Karin and recognized the glimmer of a path toward home.

CHAPTER TWENTY-ONE

LUKAS, 1950

June 6

Tauragė. It took me five days to get here, and one day to get robbed of my possessions. I am defeated and must return back to Kaunas to restock my supplies. I lasted only one week from home before I was forced to halt my journey. Fortunately, my camera remains around my neck, and the canisters of film with my photographs are in my pocket, but my developing chemicals and extra rolls of film are gone, snatched off my back by an unknown assailant.

Tauragė is a bustling center of industry, quite a change from the rural roads I have seen for the past week. I visited ironworks, brick factories, and paper mills that spill a foul mess into the River Jura as it winds its way through town. Many of the factories were family-owned before the war and are now under the control of the local Soviet authorities. Most were designed for the production of household supplies, but under Soviet rule, they have been transitioned to the production of military or construction supplies. I was taking photographs of a metal working factory when I was approached by a man just a few years older than I. Emil, he is called, and he was eager to chat. His family is from the area near Klaipėda, but he was separated from them during the war. He now lives with his teta in Tauragė but yearns for more information, particularly of his older brother Filip, who was jailed in Siberia, but whom he believes to be living on a farm in the vicinity of Šilutė. One thing Emil said intrigued me. He alluded to partisan activity in the countryside—freedom fighters who are being supported by the farmers in the area. Emil has heard that they are making successful attacks against those who support the Soviet regime. I asked him how he had come by this information, and he refused to tell me more.

There is so much that I want to know. So many questions and mysteries to solve, and such is my frustration now that I find myself out of money and supplies. Emil has offered to shelter me at his teta's house for a night or two. I will photograph them with the remaining film in my camera and make some studies of the factories before I leave. Perhaps I can learn more about Emil's brother. When I can get back on the road, I will venture to Šilutė to see what I can find out about Filip Valus. It is a great tragedy of the times that family members are separated and lost to each other, despite possibly living in close proximity.

CHAPTER TWENTY-TWO

GIEDRE, 1951

Giti trekked deep into the woods, the terrain by now intimately familiar to her. Until now, her travels had generally been at night, yet now the waning daylight cast the forest in unexpected brilliance. The leaves were a riot of yellows, reds, oranges, and greens, and the late afternoon sun created vibrant spots of warm hues balanced by the gray palette of the old growth birch and aspen bark. The only sounds were the crunching of the brittle leaves under her feet, squirrels skittering up among the branches, and the occasional chatter of a bird. As she hastened through the woods, she mourned yet again how evil men subverted the refuge of the forest into a nefarious trap.

The distance back to the meeting point was much shorter than the truck would have to take on the road, and Giti knew every stream, trail, and hiding place along the route. The truck was traveling much faster, though, and the men on board knew what they were seeking. They were following specific intelligence that Giti could only speculate about. She didn't know what Rasa meant by an eventful night or where the Forest Brothers might be hiding. She was nearing the spot where the road forked and one branch petered into a trail that plunged back into the woods at the place where she had met Rasa earlier. She paused for a moment and listened intently for any sounds from the road or from within the woods.

Closing her eyes, she mulled over every detail of the encounter at the checkpoint. She concentrated on the two men who had arrived in the truck and created such a stir. They were Lithuanian, she was confident of that, yet they were not treated as prisoners. Could they be informants? She thought back to their defining features. One was tall with long, lanky black hair and a distinctive goatee, the other shorter, fairer, with a pronounced slope to his shoulders. She would describe them to Jonas and see if they were locals.

Giti emerged from the trail and approached the rendezvous point. She crept carefully and clung to the cover of the trees as she neared the dirt road. The truck was there, but she couldn't see any of the soldiers. She didn't hear anything either, so the men had already advanced into the cover of the trees along the trail. She reached the truck and carefully laid her hand on the hood. Still warm. They hadn't been gone long. She could see the footprints in the dirt where the men had piled out of the back and stormed into the forest. Seeing nothing else amiss, she pursued the tracks into the woods.

The men were easy to follow. The size of the group and their eagerness in the mission was evident in the way they blundered through the forest, breaking branches and disturbing the cover of the forest floor. Some idiot had tied twine to random branches, apparently in an effort to mark their path. *What fools*, Giti thought.

After about fifteen minutes of steady walking, she came to a gurgling creek where the cold water flowed vigorously around the remains of an old beaver dam, sluicing through sticks, leaves, and rocks. She stopped to cup her left hand into the stream and take a long drink.

She heard the twig snap just before she felt the cold steel of the pistol against her temple.

"Well, if it isn't our luscious laundry maid."

Giti stiffened and moved her left hand down to the top of her boot.

"No, no. You'll be keeping that one good hand where I can see it. Now stand up and turn around very slowly."

Giti raised both her hands over her head and stood up slowly, turning at the same time to confront her assailant. It was one of the two soldiers who had searched the wagon at the checkpoint, the skinny one with the pockmarked face. Giti figured that he was about the same age as her. Standing this close, she could smell him and his foul tobacco-fueled breath.

"Now what's a little laundry lady doing walking in the woods so close to dark? Are you looking for anyone?" He sneered, and Giti noticed that he was missing several teeth. He reached down and fished the knife out of her boot. He twisted it in his hand and then tossed it behind him. He towered over her, and he had the advantage of his weapon. Giti could not overpower him, and now she didn't have her knife. Her brains were her only advantage, and right now, she couldn't think of much to thwart him.

"My wagon broke down shortly after I left you," Giti said meekly. She looked at the ground and tried to summon up a false tear. "I came to find help, but I was afraid of going to the checkpoint again. I'm afraid I'm lost."

The soldier snickered. "Lost, eh? I don't believe you. I think you know who we're looking for, and I think you're going to tell me where they are."

Then he raised his free hand and slapped her sharply across the cheek. Giti cried out and brought her right hand up to quell the sting. The soldier grabbed her twisted fingers and squeezed, and she screamed again.

"Where are the partisans?" he demanded.

Giti was resolute. "I have no idea what you're talking about."

He lowered his face to Giti's and added pressure to the pistol at her temple. "Now!" he screamed.

The shot rang out clear and crisp, and the soldier pitched forward on top of Giti, his blood soaking into Giti's scarf. She was pinned to the ground by his weight before she was able to roll his body away. Rasa stood over her, holding a pistol and Giti's knife.

"Bastard!" was all Rasa said. She reached out her hand and tried to help Giti to her feet. Giti swooned, unsteady and nauseous. Rasa turned her toward the creek and splashed water in her mouth and across her face. The water had bits of ice in it and the cold shocked Giti out of her panic.

"Rasa! Where did you come from? God, I thought I was done for." Giti was panting and struggling to get her heart to settle back down.

"I've been tracking the soldiers, and I heard you scream." Rasa gently touched Giti's cheek. "Are you all right? Did he hurt you anywhere else?"

"No, I'm fine." Giti stiffened her back and tried to shake off her fear.

"We've got spies in the group, Giedre. We were beginning to get suspicious, but we didn't have any evidence. At least not until you made the delivery today and told us about the checkpoint." Rasa paused, unsure how much information to divulge. Considering that she had witnessed her friend trying to deflect the soldier to protect the partisans, she assumed she could tell her more. "There was a gathering of several regiments today. They are planning a coordinated attack on Soviet sympathizers in the area, so some of the men most wanted by the authorities are here."

"So where are the soldiers now? I saw their truck at our meeting point."

"Based on what you told me, we were able to get everyone moved and dispersed in time. By the time the soldiers arrive, everyone will be gone." Rasa leaned over and kissed Giti's cheek. "It was you, Giedre. You gave us the time to get away. The soldiers are likely discovering that they were outsmarted just about now. This guy," Rasa pointed to the body on the ground, "probably stopped to take a piss and got lost. He just lucked out to find you."

Giti could barely look at the body. She swallowed hard and said, "We need to get rid of him."

Rasa nodded. "You grab his feet, and I'll take the bastard's head. We better move fast. I'm sure someone heard that shot."

Giti and Rasa hoisted the body up off the ground. They managed to pick up his feet and head and half carry and half drag him behind a fallen tree, where they covered him up with branches and leaves.

Rasa stood up and stretched her back. "The wolves will find him soon enough." She brushed at the front of her trousers where there were long smears of the man's blood. "We need to get out of here. The soldiers will be back at some point. There's just one problem, though. We still don't know who the spies are."

Giti put her hand on Rasa's shoulder. "I do. I saw them at the checkpoint, and I'd know them if I ever saw them again."

Rasa gave Giti a crushing hug. "You have to come with me then. Let's see if we can get you in front of the traitors."

Rasa and Giti headed deeper into the forest as the sun dipped below the horizon. Giti was more comfortable traveling in the darkness, but she still couldn't shake the feeling that there was a sinister agent behind every tree. After about an hour, they came to a clearing, and Rasa stopped at the edges. She motioned for Giti to crouch down where they waited, quietly hunkered in the brush. Giti was familiar with the tactic, but tonight, she had not planned to be out in the elements after sundown, and she shivered in her too-thin jacket. Her left hand hovered over her boot where she could feel her knife. After a long wait, Rasa fished a mirror out of her pocket and used it to reflect back the light of the bold moon that shone through the cloudless night. Only a few minutes later, a similar spark flashed from the other side of the clearing. Rasa motioned Giti ahead.

They walked around the edges of the field until they came to a small shack, an elfin-sized wooden structure that was once a diminutive someone's hunting cabin. It leaned precariously against a cluster of aspen trees. The door opened as they approached. Rasa bundled Giti in ahead of her and closed the door. A match was lit and put to a candle, and the outline of an old man appeared just in front of them. The three of them nearly filled the space, it was so small, and Giti could feel the breaths of her companions. As her eyes adjusted to the darkness, she noticed a trap door in the floor.

Rasa made hasty introductions. "Giedre, we go by code names here. It's an extra layer of protection in case any of us is arrested. I'm Doe, and this is Gopher." Turning to the old man, Rasa whispered, "Gopher, I need to get Giedre in to see the Captain. It's important."

The old man nodded and tugged at the trap door. He held it up for the two women, and Giti could detect a small shaft of light escaping from somewhere below. The reassuring scent of damp earth seeped up and the warmth enveloped them in a humid embrace. Giti used her left hand and her right elbow to steady herself as she navigated the rickety ladder into the pungent hole below. Rasa followed with the old man's candle. Giti could tell by the sounds that they were descending into a much larger space. As her foot touched the dirt floor below, a pair of hands reached out to steady her progress, and with both feet on firm ground, she turned and found herself staring right into Matis's startling blue eyes.

"Giti!" he breathed. "God, what are you doing here?"

Before she could even register her surprise, he had grabbed her by the shoulders and turned her back toward the stairs. Rasa quickly chimed in, speaking urgently to Matis. "Fox, she knows who the spies are. She saw them at the checkpoint, and she can identify them."

Matis spun Giti back to face him. "Is this true? You're sure?" He searched her face for confirmation. "God, Giti, wait! You're covered with blood. Are you hurt?"

"No, no, not hurt." Giti's mind was racing. "Mat ... what do I call you? Fox?" Matis nodded impatiently and pressed her to continue. "I can explain, but there's something else. I left the wagon and the mule tied up by the road, not far from the checkpoint. The wagon has a false bottom, and there are letters there that Ra ... Doe gave me. We need to get it back to the farm before anyone finds it. And I need to get word to Teta Loreta that I am all right. I should have been back hours ago. Bruno will make trouble if he finds out I'm gone."

Matis disappeared behind a wall of sorts and returned with a young man. It was hard to tell in the shadowy subterranean light, but he appeared to be a teenager, and a young one at that. Giti wondered if he had a family and if they knew this young man was holed up under the ground. Matis addressed Giti and pointed to the boy. "This is Badger. Have you ever seen Badger before?"

Giti shook her head no. Matis sighed with relief. After checking for details from Giti about the location of the wagon, Matis sent Badger up the stairs and into the night.

"He's so young," Giti said. "Will he be all right?"

199

Matis waved her off. "You were out living on your own when you were younger than that."

Giti challenged his dismissiveness. "That doesn't make it right! What's your problem? I came here to help."

Matis advanced on Giti so suddenly that she backed into the wall and hit her head. He pressed his face right up to hers. "My problem is that this is a war with serious consequences. My problem is that you could have been killed. My problem is that you and I are going into that next room, and if you see the traitors, it won't be pretty, and I would just as soon Badger be away. He's just a kid."

Matis stepped back. He continued to glare at Giti, breathing heavily. She stared back defiantly, and after a moment, the rage began to melt from his face, leaving only a hard, impenetrable mask. Pointing beyond a makeshift doorway that separated them from the rest of the people in the bunker, Matis asked, "Are you prepared for what might happen? This is a dangerous business we are in, and there are consequences for betrayal."

Giti swallowed hard and jutted out her chin. "I'll do what I need to do to keep you safe."

Matis led Giti and Rasa through the opening that partially concealed an underground chamber. Although the earthen ceiling was low, it was an impressive space carved out underneath the forest floor. The walls and ceiling were supported by thick timbers, and tree roots erupted at odd intervals. The not-unpleasant smell of decayed leaves grew more intense and mingled with a strong odor of tobacco. There were rough wooden shelves around the walls and stools made of overturned crates. Men stood or sat in small groups, conversing quietly. An anxious hush fell over the space when Matis brought Giti into their midst.

Matis, Rasa, and Giti stopped inside the door, and Matis whispered, "Do you recognize anyone?" Rasa looked at Giti with trepidation. These were her friends and perhaps even her family.

Giti took her time searching from one face to another. They ranged from teenagers to old men, yet they all shared an air of battle-weary warriors. Most had expressions that revealed a thin veil of fear wrapped in resignation. Every man was bone-thin and wore dirty, patched clothes.

Giti shook her head. The tall man with the goatee and his shorter, fair-haired companion were not in the room. She realized that she had been holding her breath and exhaled audibly.

In the middle of the space was a rough table on which a large, well-worn map was spread. Six men crowded around the table, peering at the paper, and gesturing to various points. Matis approached the man at the head of the table. He had thick, gray hair tucked into his cap, and he was so tall that he had to stoop under the low ceiling. His broad shoulders strained at the rough canvas shirt he was wearing. Like most of the other men in the space, he had a gun belt around his waist with a pistol at his hip. Matis whispered in his ear, and he listened intently until Matis finished. Then he slowly turned and looked at Giti. She noticed that his right eye was covered by a patch.

Matis announced, "Captain, this is my friend, Giedre Shimkus. Giedre, this is our commander. He is very interested in hearing about your day."

The Captain extended his large right hand to shake Giti's, and she blushed. Holding up her fist, she said, "Captain, I'm afraid that we have something in common. We are no strangers to injury, it would seem."

He dropped his hand, momentarily nonplussed, then he broke out in a broad admiring smile. "So it would seem, Fräulein. I can tell from your accent that you are not one of us, eh? Please tell me, Giedre, how have you come by the information that has been so helpful to us today, and," he paused, "why should we trust you?"

The Captain, Matis, and Giti huddled in the corner, and Giti told him how she had followed Matis into the woods that night and had, as a result, become involved as a courier for the partisans. She explained her methods and shared every detail of her experiences at the checkpoint. She also told them about being attacked by the soldier in the woods.

The Captain listened intently and allowed her to finish her story before he began his questions. Giti knew that he was trying to find inconsistencies in her story, and she was honest and forthcoming in her responses. He wanted to know how an obviously German woman was now attempting to pass with a Lithuanian name, how she had come by her association with the Shimkuses, and why she was interested in helping the partisans. Giti told him her story. It was the first time since she was taken from her home that she had told anyone what had happened to her, but she was careful not to reveal too many details. She was deliberately vague with names and locations, and, for the moment, the men didn't press her for specifics.

Matis listened with a bowed head. Giti could see him clench his fists when she talked about what the Russian soldiers had done to her mother and grandmother. When she described how she had killed the Russian soldier at Tomas's house, she saw he had tears in his eyes.

Giti finished her story, dry-eyed and resolute. She could not bring her family back. One day, she would find Otto again, and she would try to find out what happened to her other brothers. But on this day, she could do something to repay the Russians for her losses, and she was going to do whatever the Captain needed her to do.

"So, Fräulein, now you must tell me every detail about these men who came to the checkpoint. Spare nothing. We need everything you can remember."

Giti remembered it all. She described the men: their clothes, their voices, the way they walked, the way they talked. The Captain and Matis listened. There was no need to ask questions. She had given them abundant details about the two men they suspected.

The Captain gave her a patronizing pat on the shoulder. "Now, Fräulein, we must get you back home."

"No!" said Giti, taken aback. "I want to help, to see this through. I can identify them if I see them again."

"Oh, I have no doubt about that," the Captain said. "But you must realize that your absence from the farm is probably causing quite a stir right now. If you want to keep helping us, we need to get you back. If you see or hear anything we need to know, you must get word to Doe. We will handle the rest."

Giti was not so easily fobbed off. "My cover is probably already blown, Captain. Please allow me to stay."

He bent down and kissed Giti on her cheek, then he exchanged a knowing glance with Matis before he walked away. Conversation over.

"Giti, move along," ordered Matis, brusquely. "We need to get you back. Teta Loreta and Dédé Jonas will be upset, and you're more help to us there than here." Matis put his hand on her back and propelled her toward the makeshift door. A dozen pairs of eyes were trained on her as she passed by, and her face burning with frustration and humiliation.

Matis gestured at the ladder, and Giti reluctantly began the steep climb back to the surface with Matis close behind her. When they reached the top, Gopher was gone. He had melted back into the woods.

Giti and Matis stood alone near the top of the ladder. The moonlight through the sole window cast a blue glow over

Matis's blond hair, uncut for months. His face was set in a scowl, unreadable and aloof.

"It's time to go. Be careful in the woods; there are sure to be soldiers out looking for their comrade."

Giti grabbed the front of Matis's shirt. "As if you care. I took a great risk coming here tonight, and you are so ungrateful."

A loud clatter erupted behind them, and Rasa emerged through the trap door with a rusty lantern. Giti noticed that Rasa was wearing an extra pistol at her hip. She put her arm around Giti and whispered urgently, "We have to go. The Captain wants you home and in bed by morning. I am to take you, and I intend to get you there safely." Rasa turned to Matis. "And I suggest that when we're in the presence of the others, we are to call her Vixen."

Matis stepped back and crossed his arms over his chest. "No, Doe, we call her Wolf."

He opened the door and, with an exaggerated flourish, pointed both women outside. Giti and Rasa slipped back out into the moonlight. As soon as they were out of sight, he closed the door and whispered, "Safety and speed, Giti. I'd never forgive myself if something happened to you."

Giti awoke in her bed the next morning to see the bright autumn sun streaming in through the window. Bits of lint wafted in the air, and the old cat in the window slept soundly. She heard Loreta kneading bread in the kitchen and the chatter of the women doing the washing out back.

After giving a hasty explanation to Loreta and receiving a fierce hug in return, Giti darted outside to search for the wagon. She found it parked by the barn and tilted precariously toward the rear axle. Micha was using a board to prop up the undercarriage so that he could install the fresh wheel that lay on the ground at his feet. He heard her approach and set down his tools.

"It's a shame that your wheel broke yesterday. I heard you had to walk home." He looked at her and then winked. Giti nodded. She wondered how much he knew and how much she should explain. "Come on, Giedre, help me hoist this thing up. We'll have you back on laundry duty in no time." When Giti got closer and bent down to help wedge the board under the wagon, Micha whispered, "We were worried about you. Jonas went to search. He just got back."

"Oh God, Micha. I'm so sorry. He shouldn't have gone out after me. Loreta must be furious. Does Bruno suspect anything?"

"Not yet, but things are a little unsettled. Bruno hasn't arrived yet, so we need to get this wagon fixed and out of the way." Giti helped Micha roll the wagon into the barn, and then they parted, each heading to their normal work duty.

Giti was elbow deep in soap suds when she heard the horn of Bruno's car blaring from the road. Everyone within earshot looked to the front of the house to see the black sedan speeding down the dirt lane. He pulled off the road, slammed on the brakes, and sent chunks of dirt and gravel flying into the crowd. He stormed out of the car, his face red and twisted with rage.

A companion, a man Giti had never seen before, climbed out of the front passenger side. He was thickly built and moved in a way that made villainy a reasonable inference of his occupation. She noted his face was set in a grimace. It was obvious that his nose had been broken more than once, and Giti reckoned that he had broken his share of other people's noses, and worse. The laundry women huddled together, too afraid to approach and too curious to back away. Giti stood at the back of the crowd.

Bruno and the man went to the rear of the car and opened the trunk. Together, they leaned in, and after a lot of heavy breathing and loud swearing, they pulled out the body of a man, his dark hair falling limply over his face. They dumped him on the ground, and Bruno kicked the body until the man's face was visible. Giti spied the distinctive goatee. The men once again reached into the trunk and after much commotion, they pulled out a second man, this one fairer and smaller with sloping shoulders. Both had nooses around their necks and gunshot wounds to their chests.

By this time, Jonas, Micha, and several of the other men had run to the house, alerted by the squealing tires and loud cursing. Bruno walked up to Micha and grabbed him by the front of his shirt. He put his face as close as he was able to Micha's nose and snarled, "Bury them!" Spit sprayed into Micha's eyes, and he resisted the urge to punch Bruno in the gut. Bruno and his companion stormed back to the car, reclaimed their seats, and sped off in the direction from which they had come.

Micha and Jonas looked at Giti, and she nodded once. They knew, and they were all in danger.

CHAPTER TWENTY-THREE

OTTO, 1951

Otto mulled over Karin's dilemma and quickly hatched a plan to find out who was stealing from the *kolkhoz*. If nothing else was gained from his time in the gulag, he had learned to be devious, and ferreting out information just happened to be his specialty.

He returned to the worksite with the new handles and attacked stumps with renewed vigor. At dusk, as the men were piling up the wood from the felled trees, Otto grabbed a handful of logs and tossed them in the wagon. "Damn Soviet dogs," he said under his breath, but loud enough to be overheard. Several of the men glanced quickly in his direction and then distanced themselves.

Fritz pulled at his arm, and then leaned in close to Otto's ear. "What do you think you are doing, Kumpel, trying to get us sent back to prison? Shut your goddamn Prussian mouth."

"Why should I shut my mouth?" Otto said, a bit louder this time. "Karin's face is like a punching bag. She didn't deserve that."

"Maybe no, maybe yes, but it's not our concern. You hear me?"

"Apparently, she's being blamed for missing supplies. Do I need to remind you of all people that I enjoyed the Soviets' hospitality for several years after they killed my family? I am not exactly going to sit by while they destroy a woman's face for nothing. It's just brutality."

Fritz held on to Otto's elbow. "Her *husband* is destroying her face, and you best understand that. Whether you like it or not, she belongs to him and there's nothing you can do about it."

Otto shrugged off Fritz's hand and stormed back to the huts. He stayed apart from the men during the evening meal, and they were happy to give him a wide berth. Karin made a brief appearance, grabbing a plate of food and then disappearing inside the main building without speaking to anyone. Only the most recent arrivals seemed to notice, which told Otto that the beatings had happened before.

That night, after the camp had gone quiet and the hut was silent except for the persistent snores and wheezes of the men, Otto slipped out of the cabin. The bright moon pitched everything about the farm in sharp relief, and the silences of the night gave the landscape a sinister air. He snuck into the barn and hauled himself up the ladder to the loft. If he stayed on his stomach, he could perch unseen at the edge and still have a view of the crates of supplies stacked in the shadows along the far wall. Ilsa the tabby cat, arguably the farm's best mouser, padded softly up to him and rubbed her head against his leg. Otto smiled and stroked her fur, eliciting quiet purrs of approval as she curled up in the warm spot next to his chest. Otto drifted off into a shallow slumber.

Deep in the night, Ilsa hissed and pulled herself up, her muscles coiled and her body poised to attack. Her abrupt reaction jostled Otto into sudden, disorienting alertness, and he rubbed his eyes and peered over the edge of the loft. The barn's interior was washed in inky darkness—it would be hours yet before the farm woke to another workday—but Otto detected two figures creeping below. They sidled up to the crates and pulled out rough linen bags, which they began to stuff with produce. Otto noticed that they were careful not to remove too much from each carton. As they worked, they exchanged rapid hand signals. Clearly, they had practiced this routine before.

Otto blinked his eyes and squinted to focus, but he couldn't identify the intruders. He wondered if they were part of the collective, or thieves from outside the community. He leaned ever so slightly to try to get a better view, and a rotten board under his knee popped. The intruders' heads whipped up in the direction of the loft, but they calmed as Ilsa jumped down and warily approached them. One of the intruders stuck out his hand with a small treat, which Ilsa accepted gratefully. She relaxed and rubbed herself against his boots. Insiders, then. Ilsa was notoriously prickly with strangers.

As the men moved to access more of the crates, a cloud drifted away from the moon, and a crack in the barn wall lit up. The men walked right into the natural spotlight. Otto smiled. It was Joachim and Arni.

Otto hadn't expected his task to be so easy, and he made a strategic decision. He could save Karin by exposing this little bit of knowledge, but what if he knew more? Could he stall any more of the abuse she suffered, while perhaps trading a bigger chunk of intelligence for a greater reward? Worth trying. He could handle Anton. He lay flat and still on the loft floor until he was sure that Joachim and Arni were gone.

The next day, Otto made sure to approach Arni on the worksite during a brief water break. The two were friendly, but rarely interacted beyond greetings and pleasantries. Otto gulped his water loudly and wiped his mouth with the back of his hand. "Where are you from?"

Arni kept his eyes lowered and replaced the lid on his canteen. "Why do you want to know?"

"Just curious, I guess. You don't seem like one of the damn Russians, is all. I'm guessing that you're Lithuanian. Didn't mean to cause offense. My apologies."

"None taken. It's just that you don't know who you can trust. Yes, I grew up near here. My family was deported to the Soviet Union several years ago while I served in their godforsaken army. I left the army, and here I am."

Otto nodded companionably. "Russian bastards killed my family. My sympathies to you." He stood up and went back to work.

Anton drove the truck up the lane at dusk and parked in front of the main building. Otto watched from the hut as the portly administrator climbed awkwardly out of the driver's side door, wiped the sweat from his high forehead, and disappeared into the barn. Otto waited a beat and then followed.

Anton was busy pulling down crates and counting out the supplies. He didn't hear Otto approach. Idiot, thought Otto, as Anton tossed the crates aside. No finesse, just a brute.

Otto stepped out of the shadows. "I know what you're up to." He reached down and picked up a cabbage that had rolled across the packed dirt floor.

Anton was caught off-guard, and it took a second for him to focus before he charged toward Otto. "Thief!" he yelled, before he threw an errant punch. Otto ducked easily as Anton's fist flailed and missed its mark.

Otto laughed as Anton stumbled. He tossed the cabbage from hand to hand, taunting the older man. "I'm not your thief, and I'm pretty sure I could figure out who is, but that's not the point. You're busy thieving yourself, and I can prove it. What's more, you're beating your wife to cover up what you're doing, you bastard. That's the lowest of the low."

Otto had no proof of any wrongdoing on Anton's part, and he was pretty sure that Anton was not helping the partisans, but he didn't care. Max had taught him that anyone with any degree of authority was up to no good in Stalin's Russia. The trick was making them believe that you knew more than you actually did.

Anton reached behind the crates and produced a crowbar. He barreled toward Otto and took a wild swing. Otto raised his arm and deflected the weak thrust. The crowbar dropped to the floor with a loud clatter. Anton, thoroughly enraged, lunged again, wrapping his arms around Otto's waist and trying to knock him down. He was out of breath and no match for Otto's youth and strength. Otto easily tripped Anton and pushed him onto his back in the dirt. He retrieved the crowbar and held it an inch above Anton's nose.

"This is the way it's going to be, you cowardly bastard."

Anton wiggled and squirmed, and Otto laughed. He was sure that Anton would not call for help. He would do anything to avoid being seen in such a vulnerable position. Otto poked him in the face with the crowbar and leaned in close. "You better listen to me and listen well. You're going to leave your pretty wife alone, and I mean alone, as in you're never touching her again." Otto used the crowbar to jab Anton in the crotch to make his point. Anton winced and whimpered. "I'll help you figure out who is stealing your shitty little vegetables and who they are giving them to, and in return, you're going to help me find information about my family. Are we clear?" Otto took the crowbar and wedged it back up under Anton's chin. The man tried to push the metal away from his face, but Otto held firm. "I said, are we clear?"

Anton spit at Otto's face and missed. "What makes you

think I can get you any information about your family?" Anton asked with a sneer.

"I'm pretty sure that you and your Stalin-loving buddies can get whatever you want if you're motivated," Otto replied. He shoved the crowbar harder against Anton's chin. The man was struggling to breathe. "So, I'll ask you again. Are we clear?"

Anton spit out phlegm and coughed. He managed with great difficulty to say, "You leave my wife alone."

Otto smirked. "I have no interest in your wife, you old goat, except to make sure you never hurt her again. She deserves a fine husband, that's for sure. Not you and not me. Someone who will take care of her. You and I have a partnership based on mutual interests. I'm interested in finding my family, and you're interested in staying out of the Cheka's basement. But let's be clear—you touch your wife or you double-cross me, and I'll report you for all the sneaky business you have been carrying on here for God knows how long." Otto leaned in, putting his face right up against Anton's nose. "I have proof." He waited for a reaction and Anton nodded his head.

Otto stood up and cast aside the crowbar. "Stay away from Karin and leave me alone. I'll have some information for you soon enough." Then he walked out of the barn without looking back. Karin stood on the porch, the bruises on her face still visible as angry black and purple patches. Otto nodded to her and walked on by.

Otto spent several weeks keeping an eye on Joachim and Arni. They all worked on the same crew, and so they spent their days together, but he couldn't discern any indication that the two men were in cahoots. They socialized with all the laborers and were rarely seen together in conversation. Otto suspected that the circle of thieves was bigger than just the two men, but they were all well-schooled in the fine art of deception. Impressed with their savvy, Otto knew that patience was its own reward. His diligence paid off when a summer storm roiled up out of the east one afternoon.

The men had been preparing the fields ahead of the approaching winter when the weather quickly turned sour. Steel gray clouds congealed to obscure what had been a sunny day. Soon, clusters of loose leaves and weeds spiraled up in the sharpening wind, dense drops of rain fell, and cracks of thunder were followed instantly by daggers of lightning. The men gathered their tools and ran for the cover of the trees lined up along the margins of the field.

The air was charged with electricity from the storm. The men's hair stood on end, and their skin sizzled with the crackling power. Trapped under the canopy of swaying trees, the men huddled together and watched the rain fall in heavy curtains. Before they could react, a loud crack of thunder and a blinding bolt of lightning burst in tandem. They had barely heard the deafening crack when they were jolted off their feet. The smell of burned wood and singed flesh was overpowering.

Otto discovered he had been knocked backwards. He wiped rain and leaves away from his face when he looked over and spied Joachim lying on the ground next to a tree that was engulfed in flames. The raw wound of a lightning strike snaked up the trunk beside him. Otto heard a second crack, this time of wood, not thunder. He glanced up to see a burning branch split off of the main trunk directly overhead. Otto pushed himself up despite a searing pain in his arm.

In a rush of adrenaline, he leaped over the smaller branches scattered in his path and reached Joachim just as a giant branch snapped overhead. Otto bent over and screamed as he shoved his arms under Joachim's shoulders, hoisting him up and

213

dragging him away. The flaming limb fell, landing on Joachim's ankles. Otto dropped Joachim's shoulders and lurched toward the branch. He grabbed the larger end and pulled it off of Joachim's legs. Joachim screamed as the flames caught on the ends of his trousers. Just before Otto blacked out, he fell across Joachim's legs and smothered the flames.

A week later, Otto was standing with the crowd that gathered on the porch to welcome Joachim back from the clinic in Klaipėda. He clapped along with the others as Joachim emerged slowly from Anton's truck and hobbled unsteadily toward his friends. He stopped long enough to doff his cap to Karin and then nod to Otto, himself bandaged and recovering.

"You returned uglier than you left, comrade,' Otto teased. "Welcome back."

"True, all true, Otto, my friend. I am told that thanks are in order."

Otto waved him away and watched as Joachim was hugged and helped by the men who were able to stop their chores and fuss over their friend. Anton tolerated a few minutes of celebration and then ordered everyone back to their posts. Otto accompanied Joachim to the hut, where the two men sat on their bunks and compared injuries.

After a brief round of pleasantries and a few lighthearted jabs, Joachim turned serious. He stared at his feet and used his crutch to sketch lines on the dusty floor. Otto sat quietly, hoping to gauge Joachim's thoughts.

Joachim said softly, "I am trying to figure you out, Otto."

"Figure me out how?"

"Whose side you are on. Do you have loyalties to anyone but yourself?"

"Should I?"

"It seems a matter of honor in our present situation to at least pretend to have loyalties. You're either an ardent enthusiast of our Stalinist friends, or you feel a passionate tug toward the oppressed Lithuanians."

"I feel a passionate tug for staying alive, and I would like to find my family, but I suppose if there is a group that inspires me, it's generally the underdogs," Otto replied.

Joachim nodded thoughtfully. "And if I were able to present a compelling case for the underdogs, might you be willing to help?"

Otto leaned down, put his elbows on his knees, and tapped his bandaged hands together. "Just tell me when and where, my friend. You can count on me."

Otto heard no more for several days. He visited Joachim often, but there were always others around, alternately jockeying for Joachim's attention or teasing him for his temporary assignment working with the cooks, peeling vegetables and turning the roasting spit. When Otto's hands recovered enough, he eagerly returned to duty despite the onset of cold weather. He hated to be idle, and he was losing valuable time with his information gathering. Anton had resumed making threats against Karin. Otto needed to make a move—and soon.

It was a relief when one evening, Arni sought him out. They were walking back from the fields at the end of the day when he fell into step alongside Otto. They acknowledged each other's presence but walked in silence until the rest of the men had peeled away to return to their friends and families.

"Joachim suggested I talk to you," Arni said.

"Oh," Otto asked, "about what?"

"Assistance for an underdog was the way Joachim phrased it."

"Ah yes." Otto nodded his head. "He mentioned something like that to me once. How can I be of service?"

Arni stopped walking and stared at Otto. "To be honest, I am not sure that we can trust you, and I told Joachim that. He is willing to take a chance, but I am still unconvinced. You are something of…" Arni searched for the right word, "a mystery."

Otto stopped and faced Arni. "A mystery? I am a German who was taken from my home by the Soviets. I was sent to a camp in the middle of God-knows-where to languish for years. Suddenly, and for no particular reason that I can tell, I was freed and put on a train for here, where I now stand with you. I have no country, no family, and no close friends. So, I ask you, where should my loyalties lie?"

Arni pondered the question briefly and then asked, "So you have no special arrangement with the Russians? No deal, no attachments?"

"If I did, would I be standing here with you? I am small potatoes to them, Arni. I am useful only for the labor I provide, and as long as I give more than I take, I figure they will leave me well enough alone."

Otto took a step closer to Arni so that they stood face to face. "And I have known for weeks that you and Joachim are stealing from the *kolkhoz,* yet here you stand, unaccused and unblemished. Draw your own conclusions." Otto walked away.

"Otto!" Arni called out. "Wait!"

He hastened to rejoin Otto on the walk back. It was decided then that Otto would take Joachim's place to help the partisans hiding in the woods. Arni described in the vaguest of terms what they needed to do in the coming days. "It is not your fight, but we all have a common enemy," Arni explained, and Otto agreed eagerly.

After midnight, when the *kolkhoz* was desolate save the skittering mice with the owls in pursuit, and the hut was animated only by the men's nocturnal chorus, Arni nudged Otto awake and gestured for him to dress and follow. They bundled up in their jackets and scarves and crept out of the hut, keeping to the shadows. They stopped first at the barn, where Arni produced sacks, which they filled with cabbages and potatoes. Ilsa peered over the edge and purred, which to Otto sounded like an admonishment.

Once the bags were full, they wordlessly filed out of the barn, slowly making their way into the woods beyond the fields. Otto followed Arni stealthily, shifting the lumpy bag from hand to hand while making mental notes of landmarks and clues that might help him find his way back. In this way, they walked for about an hour. The waxing moon shone through the prickly canopy of naked tree branches, casting eerily sharp shadows.

Eventually they arrived at an abandoned farm, the roof of the house sagging inwards, and the walls listing dangerously to one side. Arni and Otto stopped at the side of the barn, and Arni stuck out his arm as a signal to Otto that he should crouch and wait. Then he grabbed both bags, snuck around the corner and disappeared from Otto's view.

Otto rested his back against the wall in a manner that gave him the most expansive view of the house and barn. Moonlight glinted off slick patches in the worn metal roof, illuminating the barn door and casting the porch in deep shadows. Otto noticed various farm tools and parts strewn about the property, decayed and abandoned. If they had to leave suddenly, this would be like a minefield to maneuver. It felt sinister, and Otto, who was generally not given to worrying, shivered with unease.

Arni reemerged at Otto's left, catching him off-guard and causing Otto to gasp in surprise. Arni slapped his hand over his mouth to prevent him from making more noise, and Otto glowered at him. He despised not being in control.

Arni raised his eyebrows as if to say, "Are you all right now?" and Otto nodded, prompting Arni to remove his hand and motion him to follow him.

They circled the barn, entering through a loose board in the back, and Otto was shocked to see a half dozen men already inside. Most he had never seen before, but he recognized Filip and acknowledged him with a slight nod. Arni and Otto took their places in the circle, and Arni pointed to a tall man at the opposite side. The man had a scruffy growth of whiskers and wore a soldier's jacket. His shoulder-length blond hair was tied back under a military cap. He stepped forward and took in the measure of the group before speaking softly.

"Thank you for being here. As far as we can tell, we weren't followed, but we need to work quickly and quietly. Beaver, is the house checked and clear?"

"Yes, Fox, we checked it twice. It's clear."

The man called Fox then addressed Arni. "Possum? Anything out of the ordinary to report?"

"No, Fox, no signs of anyone else at the perimeter." Arni shoved Otto forward. "He is filling in for Goose."

Fox assessed Otto and glowered at the men. "We have good intelligence that there are German weapons and ammunition stored in this barn, courtesy of the Nazis who used to live here."

"So how do you know about the weapons?" One of the men challenged Fox.

"You don't need to know that," Fox said tersely. "There is a trap door in the floor somewhere. Let's find it and get the weapons out. We'll carry them to a rendezvous point about a mile from here, and another crew will take over from there. Do I need to clarify anything?" It was a rhetorical question—no answer was expected or welcomed.

The men fanned out and set to work inspecting the floor. Soon they heard a hollow thump, followed by a soft whistle. They gathered around while straw was brushed away, exposing a makeshift wooden cover. Fox brought out a torch and stood over the spot while two men pried it open with crowbars. Fox pointed his light down, and the glint of metal flashed back at him.

"Christ!" One of the men blurted out. "There must be dozens of weapons down there."

Fox called to a young man who hustled to his side. "Badger, get down there and make a quick count. Then we'll send Possum to help you lift everything out."

A young man scampered down a rickety ladder, and in a few minutes, he handed Fox a list. Fox whistled low and slow. "All right, Possum, let's move it all out."

The men quickly organized themselves, and the small hideaway under the barn was soon emptied of pristine German-made Karabiner rifles, an assortment of Mauser pistols, and ammunition. Then a few of the men began ferrying the weapons to the rendezvous point in the woods, a place to which Otto was not invited. Arni and Otto trudged back the way they came.

"Possum, eh?" Otto teased. "Will I get a code name?"

"Perhaps," was Arni's curt reply.

Otto had to admit that he felt considerable admiration for the men he had encountered in the barn. Fox was young, but clearly a capable and credible leader, and he accepted Otto and his assistance readily. It had been a long time since someone had believed in him enough to trust him, and he had enjoyed being a part of something so noble. Yet, he swiftly tamped down any thoughts of regret over double-crossing them. He would use anyone or anything to get back to Giti.

At breakfast the following morning, Otto rubbed his eyes

and fought fatigue as he grabbed a hard roll and a boiled egg. It was going to be tough if there were too many nights like this, working all night only to return and work all day. He stifled a yawn and looked around for Karin, but she had not come out of the main building yet.

Otto watched with a sense of dread as Anton emerged from the barn. He wore a rancid scowl and charged back toward the house without offering any commands or pleasantries. Did they take too much and trigger Anton's suspicion? Judging from the hard set of the old man's mouth, and the red flush creeping up his neck, Otto had to believe that the theft had been detected. He followed Anton toward the building and slipped unnoticed through the door.

Anton's voice, an assault of accusations wrapped in barely controlled rage, boomed against the bare walls. He punctuated every word with venom. "You are worthless!"

Karin pleaded. "Anton, I had no idea. I was there for hours and saw nothing! Nothing!" Silence, then a scuffle. Karin screamed.

Otto barged in through the door to see Anton standing over Karin. She was sprawled on the hard wooden floor in her nightgown, and Anton was holding her up by her hair. A bright red mark crossed her cheek.

"Let her go, Anton." Otto balled his fists and prepared to lunge toward the corpulent man.

"You have no business here," Anton shot back, holding fast to Karin's hair. She whimpered softly.

"Otto, go!" Karin begged. "You'll just make it worse."

Otto slowly walked toward Anton and forcefully pried his hand off of Karin's hair. "Anton, you made a deal with me, and we have business to discuss. That's why I came in. To give you some news."

Anton hesitated for just a moment, debating whether he

could believe Otto, then he dropped his arm and released Karin's hair. "Let's go in my office, shall we?"

Otto nodded and Anton motioned for him to go first. As Otto turned toward the office door, Anton gave Karin a swift kick. She doubled over and coughed. Otto felt the color drain from his face, but he kept moving.

CHAPTER TWENTY-FOUR

LUKAS, 1951

July 12

Jurbarkas

I have been in this town for one month today, and although I suspect that I wore out my welcome long ago, I am loath to leave. I did not intend to stay so long, but an unfortunate accident on the road involving an ill-tempered runaway horse left me with a sprained ankle. The local doctor and his wife have been most kind to take me in. They lost their son in the war, and I think it gives them a small measure of normalcy to have a young man under their roof. They were kind enough to allow me to turn their shed into a makeshift darkroom to develop the rolls of film collecting in my knapsack. Some are quite good.

Mrs. Laukaitis called me Ado twice today. That was her nickname for her son, whose full name was Adonis. Both times, she seemed completely unaware of what she had said. The first time I corrected her, and it clearly caused her much distress, so I did not say anything the second time. I feel deceptive, but perhaps it brings her a measure of peace. I will ask Dr. Laukaitis about it when the time is right.

The doctor allowed me to accompany him on his rounds once I was able to put some weight on my foot, and it was during one of these visits that we had the most amazing encounter. Dr. Laukaitis had been called to the home of an elderly woman who complained of boils. Before we reached the woman's house, we stopped at the market, and a man rushed out and demanded to speak to Dr. Laukaitis. They disappeared for a few minutes, and then Dr. Laukaitis returned to the wagon and spurred the horse on. Soon we had reached the patient's house, but the doctor stayed on the road, keeping a brisk speed on the bumpy dirt road.

"Aren't we expected back at that house?" I asked, confused at this change in plans.

"We have an emergency, and I find that I must trust you," he replied. He was determined, and I could tell that he was scared.

"Of course you may trust me," I reassured him.

The horse picked up its pace in response to Dr. Laukaitis's repeated prodding, and soon we were out of town and heading toward a kolkhoz. But once again, when we reached it, we kept on going. I felt in my bag, relieved to know that my camera was there with some film. Eventually, we came to a concealed lane that led off the main road. The lane disappeared into the woods, where it narrowed to the width of a small footpath. The doctor drove his wagon as far into the lane as possible, and once the path petered out, we disembarked and tied the horse to a tree.

The doctor said that our destination lay ahead on about a twenty-minute walk. Could I make it? I assured him that I would keep up, and I did, although it hurt like the devil and I knew I was setting my recovery back by days if not weeks.

At one point on the path, the doctor stopped and whistled. At first nothing happened, and then a young man came out from behind the trees. He was wearing a uniform of sorts and carried a German-made pistol. He and the doctor exchanged hushed greetings, and then he pointed to me. The doctor nodded. I followed his lead and nodded to the man too, although I had no idea what I was promising.

We walked a bit more and soon stumbled across a small opening in the forest floor, a square entrance reinforced by timbers, just wide enough for a man to squeeze through. Inside the hole was a crude ladder leading down, which we all took in turn to a cramped chamber underneath. Inside there were at least a dozen men, most sitting with their backs against the earthen walls. One lay on the dirt floor, blood blooming on improvised bandages, and another sat unsteadily with a large bandage wrapped around his head. The men were relieved to see the doctor and alarmed in equal measure at my presence.

The doctor leaned down to check the man lying on the ground. He groaned as the doctor came near, and when the bandages were pulled away, we saw a ragged wound. The doctor fished out a syringe from his bag and injected it into the man's upper leg. Presently, he calmed down, and the doctor replaced the bandage, shaking his head. He then went to the other man and examined his head. It appeared that a bullet had grazed his temple, leaving a stripe in his close-cropped hair. The doctor was able to clean and dress the wound. By the time he had finished his work with the second man, the first man was dead.

As we walked back to the wagon, I asked the doctor what had just happened. He replied, "Forest Brothers, son. Fighting back against the invaders with everything they have. Heroes, the lot of them."

I thought back to the faces of the men we had met that

day. Young, serious, determined, almost feral. I admired them fiercely and promised myself that I would do anything to help them. I am in awe of their sacrifices and their dedication. From that moment on, my mission became clear. I want to be one of them.

CHAPTER TWENTY-FIVE

BRIGIT, 2010

Milo and Brigit were in the car before the sun breached the horizon. As the sky struggled to lighten, it promised to be a raw day. Low-slung clouds lurked overhead, and frigid gusts of icy wind rocked the traffic lights. Milo's little car soldiered unsteadily through each sudden gust, and the headlights flickered fitfully as debris blew across the highway.

He drove with intense concentration. Brigit shivered in the gloom while she stared out the window at the same tidy cottages and gentle countryside that she had observed the day before. Yesterday, the passing vista of prim cottages was a comforting sight, but today Brigit viewed the same landscape with foreboding. What could Agne's news possibly be?

"So, you're flying to Rome today? In this weather?" she asked, curious about Milo's trip.

Milo peered up at the sky. "It's not looking good, is it? I've taken off in worse weather, but I can't say it makes for a pleasant trip. It'll just be that much sweeter when I'm finally sitting in a bar in the Piazza Campo de' Fiori, sipping coffee and watching the activity in the market."

Icy blasts buffeted the car again. Milo quietened to

concentrate on his driving, and Brigit watched the road ahead. In her mind, she was far away, imagining Milo in Rome, dining casually in an Italian square and sipping rich wine while the afternoon sun bathed the warm ochre stones. He would be content and unhurried. She smiled at the thought.

As they pulled in front of Peter and Agne's house, she allowed herself a sigh of relief and realized that she had been clenching her fists. She stretched her fingers and rubbed her knuckles. "Well done, Captain," she said as she tipped an imaginary cap in Milo's direction.

Milo exhaled and offered her a weary smile. The wind continued to howl, mixed with tiny snowflakes and ice crystals.

When Agne saw their car approaching, she raced to the front door. Peter appeared in his pajamas, his hair an explosion in all directions.

Agne ran up to the car and waved as Brigit and Milo got out. She was wearing a skimpy pair of pajamas that barely covered her midriff, and she seemed oblivious both to the plummeting temperatures and to her indecorous attire.

Brigit gave her a hug. "Let me guess, you've been up all night." She motioned to Milo, who was trying hard not to get caught staring at Agne. "We couldn't wait to get here."

Peter stuck his head out of the front door and said something to Agne. She glanced at her pajamas and laughed. "Oops! Come on in," she said with an embarrassed smile. "I made a breakthrough with Lukas's diary, and it consumed me. I forgot what I was wearing."

Brigit was buoyed by Agne's excitement, and she sincerely hoped that there was a clue about Giti.

Agne returned wearing a more modest outfit of baggy trousers and one of Peter's T-shirts. She moved to the table where Lukas's journal pages were spread out and made room for Brigit and Milo to sit down. Peter stood up and made four cups of coffee. He brought them to the table on a tray with cream and sugar and sat back down to finish feeding Eljia.

"Thank you kindly for your hospitality. Has Agne shared what she found with you?" Milo asked him.

Peter smirked. "I'd be surprised if half the neighborhood doesn't know. Agne shrieked at about, oh, must have been 2:30 this morning. Eljia went back to sleep, but I've been awake and going over the journals with her since. I think she's found a tangible clue. I managed to keep her from calling you for a couple of hours, but she couldn't wait beyond that."

Brigit fidgeted and squirmed. She leaned over the table, staring at the pages of indecipherable scribbles, and tapped her foot impatiently as the men exchanged pleasantries. Agne gave her a wink. "Let's get started, shall we?"

Agne and Peter pulled a large map of Lithuania off the floor and spread it out on the table over the journal pages. Agne explained, "Now I've only managed to get through a portion of the diary entries, but we can see something of the route Lukas took and how he came to be involved with the Forest Brothers."

She pointed to the map and showed them how she had plotted what she knew. Agne had drawn out the first journey in red. "Journey number one, he makes it as far as Tauragė. He starts in Kaunas and walks to Tauragė in about a week. Here he gets robbed, so he has to return back to Kaunas, very disappointed and with lots of questions." Agne pulled out the final journal entry from Lukas's first trip and handed it to Milo. She pointed out specific passages, and Milo read the entries while Brigit peered over his shoulder.

Then Agne picked up another journal entry and handed it to Milo. "This is from his second journey in 1951. Take a look."

Milo scanned the page. "I can't make sense of this. The earlier one is hard to read because of his terrible handwriting, but you can eventually make it out. But this," Milo picked up the second sheet, "is gibberish."

"Not gibberish," beamed Agne.

Peter interrupted. "It's in code!" Agne swatted at his arm, and he added sheepishly, "Sorry. Agne solved the code. I'll shut up now."

Agne picked up a sheet of paper with her writing on it. "It's a simple code, but we have to assume that from the time that Lukas left Tauragė to the time he went back on the road, he became concerned that his journals might somehow incriminate him or the people he meets. Let me rephrase that—he always knew there would be problems if his journals were scrutinized by the wrong people, but after Tauragė, there's a new urgency to his precautions. It's as if he knows of a specific threat, or a threat to specific people."

She set down her notes and showed Milo and Brigit her translation. "See, he has used the most basic code—switching out one letter for another. I tried to find patterns by comparing his writing from the first trip to the second, and worked my way back from there. His code is rather unsophisticated, and a professional code breaker would crack this in seconds. But I'm not a professional code breaker, so I'm pretty proud of myself."

Brigit picked up the map. Agne had identified at least three separate journeys from June 1950 to the final, unfinished trip in 1952, and she had color-coded the map to show how Lukas had traveled west from his home in Kaunas. The first journey was more of a meandering path when compared to the later routes, which showed that by 1951, Lukas was leaving Kaunas with a more set mission. He traveled more directly and spent less time on points closer to home.

"How much detail does Lukas share in his journals?" Brigit asked.

"Some days he shares more than others, and there are gaps.

Honestly, his notes are a mess. In a few of the entries, he provides very detailed information about the photographs he's taken and the people he has met. Most of his notes sadly are random bits of information, and the pages aren't numbered. They *are* dated, so that helps. We just don't know what's been lost.

"Basically, Lukas is a big idealistic kid, and he develops a rather naive desire to give life and limb in support of the partisans. On his second trip, he leaves Kaunas in July and seems to be making a beeline for Klaipėda. Unfortunately, he is injured and gets waylaid in Jurbarkas. He finally makes it to Šilutė on the third trip, in the dead of winter, in 1952. He goes missing shortly after that."

Brigit couldn't hold back any longer. "Agne, forgive my bluntness, but I am busting to know if any of your discoveries in Lukas's journals involve my Aunt Giti."

"Remember that I still have about a third of the journals to go through, so I am not done by any means, but no. There is nothing so far about a Giti Binz."

Brigit's shiny anticipation soured. She crossed her arms over her chest and bit her lip, trying to be gracious in the face of Agne's efforts. Why were she and Milo summoned here so suddenly?

If Agne noticed Brigit's disappointment, she gave no indication. She ruffled through the journal pages until she found one in particular. She picked it up and put it in front of Brigit. "Nothing about Giti," she repeated, "but you'll be interested in this."

Agne put the yellowed page in front of Brigit, who stared at the coded writing while Agne fished out a second sheet, this one in her own handwriting. Agne set her translation next to the original, and Brigit could see only that it indicated that the original was dated January 1952 and the location was Šilutė.

Agne moved her finger down to the bottom of the page, where Lukas listed the photographs he had taken, and there it was: *34 Fritz Biedemeier ir Otto Binz*.

Brigit started. "There must be some kind of mistake. My father was never in Lithuania. Is Otto Binz a common name?" She looked from Agne, to Peter, to Milo.

Agne reached on top of the china cabinet, pulled down photograph 34 and placed it in front of Brigit. Two men stood in a clearing, facing the camera. In the background was a dilapidated shed buried in piles of fresh snow, and behind that, an impenetrable mass of frosted trees festooned with icicles. One man was tall and dark-haired, his cap tilted rakishly to the side and his hand resting on a shovel. The other was just a wee bit shorter and of slighter build, his blond curls visible under his cap. He was motioning toward the photographer and sharing a lopsided grin. Brigit gasped as she stared into the youthful face of her father.

CHAPTER TWENTY-SIX

GIEDRE, 1952

Giti met Rasa in town after the last load of laundry was delivered. Rasa hopped up into the wagon, and Giti spurred the mule back toward the *kolkhoz*. The cold January air sliced through their lungs, but the women huddled together and made no effort to hurry. Giti treasured this time with her friend, and they slipped easily into conversation. Although Rasa was a few years older, the two women had bonded quickly, and they eagerly anticipated any chance to meet.

Giti had been taken off delivery duty for the time being. The Captain was not convinced that all the traitors had been exposed, and he was concerned that Giti was under surveillance. She was frustrated by her inability to help, but maintained her laundry routines to avoid suspicion when she was allowed back to more dangerous duties.

"Hello, Wolf. You'll never believe what happened," Rasa said with a twinkle in her eye.

"I can't imagine," Giti exclaimed, "but let me try to guess."

Rasa beamed. "You'll never guess. I shot a wild boar last week, all by myself!"

"What? Were you stalking it, or did it surprise you?"

"Surprised me, and I had my gun strapped to my back. I heard a noise and turned to see it barreling toward me. I swear, Giedre, I looked it right in the eye as I drew my gun out, and it looked right back at me. I knew one of us was going down. I hit it right between the eyes." Rasa mimicked firing her gun with a loud. "Pow!"

"Oh my God. That sounds terrifying. What did you do with it?"

"I ran back to the farm and got a mule and a rope. Trussed it up and let the mule drag it. It lost half its hide, but the meat was still good when I got it back." She pulled out a packet and thrust it into Giti's lap. "Bacon, for you. It's delicious!'

They took the fork that led to Rasa's collective. As Rasa prepared to jump down from the wagon, Giti reached over and gave her a hug. "Thank you and be safe, my friend. Keep your gun handy. Next time, you might run into a more sinister boar, one that speaks Russian."

Rasa winked. "I'm charmed like one of your magical fairy-tale creatures. Enjoy the bacon and remember who is watching over you!" She trotted away down the lane, turning twice to wave before she rounded the bend and was out of sight.

Giti flicked the reins to set off once again, but noticed an envelope sitting on the wagon bench beside her. *Giedre* was scrawled in Matis's handwriting. Rasa must have left it as a surprise. Giti grabbed the envelope and stuffed it inside her jacket. She was partly excited, but mostly terrified to open it. She remembered the surly way he had dismissed her before, and she had no desire to deal with another patronizing encounter, in person or with ink and pen.

As soon as Giti arrived back at the farm and was able to steal away by herself, she retrieved the envelope, which was warm and damp from clinging to her skin. She held it up to the light and rolled it between her fingers. Her annoyance with Matis grew as she anticipated his gruff instructions, and she finally worked up the gumption to slit open the thin paper. She pulled out two notes. One was addressed to the whole family. The other to Giti alone.

> *Giti,*
>
> *Doe tells me that you are well. I am glad that you are friends. I know it has been difficult for you, and Doe promises me that you and she laugh often. It makes me happy to know that you can smile. We have missed your gifts of Teta Loreta's bread and treats. Doe tells me that you have been doing quite a bit of mending for us, and we are very grateful for all your efforts.*
>
> *I have thought often of our last conversation, and I am sure that you are quite irritated with me. I meant no disrespect, actually quite the opposite; I was so worried for you that I lashed out. I failed to properly thank you for your kindness and your bravery, and for that I beg your forgiveness.*
>
> *I have missed being at the house with you and the family. I know that I am where I need to be right now, but it doesn't mean that I miss you any less. I want you to know that I think you are very brave. I always knew that you had a story to tell, but hearing it from you that night made me want to comfort you, and it grieves me that I am unable to do so. I hope that one day soon, I can see you again and perhaps we can begin finding out what happened to your brother.*
>
> *In the meantime, know that I think of you in the highest regard: my friend, my angel, and my she-wolf.*

The note was unsigned, but it did not need to be. Giti

clutched his words and held them tightly against her heart. *Matis.* When would she see him again?

Giti refolded the other sheet and returned it to the envelope. She took it into the kitchen and slipped it into the pocket of Loreta's apron, where Giti was sure she would be delighted to find it.

Giti didn't mind laundry duty in the summer. There was a pleasant rhythm to it and a sense of accomplishment that she rather enjoyed. After spending weeks alone in the forest in filthy clothes, she would always regard the ability to have clean garments as a luxury, and the repetitive nature of the job left her mind free to wander to other matters. She often pondered where Otto might be, and what he was doing. He would be close to nineteen by now. Giti pictured him tall and handsome, like their pappi, with blond hair and sparkling blue eyes. She often wondered if he had a girlfriend, or if he had learned a trade.

Laundry duty in January was an entirely different matter. The women took the wash tubs into the barn to escape the biting wind, and they managed to keep the water warm using a giant kettle over a flame in the yard. Once the clothes were rinsed, however, it was almost impossible to get them dried before they froze solid. The women's hands were always chapped and bleeding from being wet in the frigid outside air. Giti's right hand was particularly prone to cracking, even with Loreta's insistence that she use the leftover udder cream from their dairy days. On this particular afternoon, she bled on three different shirts before Anna, the girl helping her with the wash, insisted that she go inside and help Loreta. Giti wrapped her right hand in bandages and picked up the basket of just-rinsed shirts to carry them into the house for ironing. She pushed open the barn door just in time to see Bruno's car pull off the lane and park in front of the house.

Giti put her head down and continued on toward the back of the house. It was always best to stay out of Bruno's way and avoid attracting his attention.

"Hey, stupid girl," Bruno yelled.

Giti stopped and stared at Bruno.

"Yes, you. How many stupid girls do you think we have around here?" Bruno was nastier than usual today. Ever since he had discovered the bodies of the informants, he had been on a single-minded quest to find the culprits behind their deaths.

"Tell the others that I need to see them," he said, and when Giti calmly resumed walking to the back door, he added, "NOW!"

Giti hurriedly set the basket inside the door and returned to the barn. The women had overheard the commotion and suspended the laundry in anxious anticipation. Giti then ran toward the fields, where most of the men were mending fences. Soon a small crowd had gathered in front of the house. Loreta walked out onto the front porch, calmly wiping her flour-covered hands on a towel.

Giti examined the car. There were other people inside, but just how many she could not determine. Bruno paced nervously in the brown winter grass, smoking cigarettes and tossing the butts into the yard before rolling and lighting another one. The other occupants of the vehicle remained firmly inside, their breath fogging up the windows and obscuring any further identification.

Once Bruno determined that a satisfactory crowd had been assembled, he banged on the side of the car, the whole time watching the people gathered, daring them to challenge him.

One of the back doors of the sedan opened, and Bruno's

companion emerged. He wore a fedora on his thick head complemented by a dark wool overcoat, but he still resembled a venomous prison guard, regardless of his attire. The man stood briefly and stared down the crowd before reaching back into the car and pulling out a young man. The prisoner's hands were tied in front of him using a rope that also extended around his waist. He whimpered and doubled over in pain. As soon as Bruno's companion jerked him free of the car, the young man collapsed on the ground, and the crowd gasped.

"Ivan!" Bruno screamed. "Make this traitor stand and face his countrymen."

The man called Ivan reached down and with one hand, pulled his prisoner upright. He was a ghastly sight. His nose was broken and his eyes were swollen shut. His pants were soaked where he had soiled himself.

Several of the women whimpered, and while the expressions on the men's faces were more subdued, they were appalled by the sight of the broken man, still a boy really. None were more horrified than Giti. She immediately recognized the boy as Badger, the brave courier for Matis's team of fighters. Giti felt the bile rising in her throat.

"So, Domus, you little traitor, do you recognize any of these people?" Bruno asked.

Domus dropped his head. Bruno motioned to Ivan, who grabbed a handful of Domus's hair and forced him to look back up. Giti wanted to run and hide. She imagined herself floating free in the woods, safe from these evil men and the gut-wrenching sight, but she stayed rooted to the spot, willing her feet not to move. She was terrified of calling attention to herself.

Domus struggled to open one of his eyes, and when he did, his head moved ever so slowly as he scanned the faces in front of him. Giti very casually moved her right hand to rest behind her back in the hopes that it would not register any recognition with

Domus, the boy she knew as Badger. His one eye continued to move slowly as he struggled to breathe. At one point, his knees buckled, and the crowd gasped again, but Ivan hauled him upright. Soon, he locked eyes with Giti. He stared at her long and hard as her heart pounded, and nausea roiled her stomach.

Eventually, Domus dropped his head again and said quietly, "No."

"What's that?" Bruno bellowed. He crouched down and put his nose right in Domus's face. "Do you mean for me to believe that none of these people have been to your little hideout to help you and your band of terrorists?"

"No," Domus replied again, so softly that none of the people in the yard could quite make out what he was saying.

"No what?" Bruno spit as he yelled. "No you don't recognize anyone, or no, you refuse to cooperate?"

"No!" Domus stammered. "No recognize." He lifted his head ever so slightly and looked at Giti again. "No one here helped."

Bruno nodded to Ivan, and the man nodded back. He reached under his coat and pulled out a gun. The crowd began to murmur, and Loreta yelled at Bruno.

"Stop this nonsense, Bruno. He is only a boy!'

Jonas and Micha walked forward with their hands held out.

"Bruno, what are you doing?" Jonas asked. "Loreta's right, he is just a boy, and he answered your questions. Leave him here. Please."

Bruno pulled out his own weapon and pointed it at Jonas's head. "Step back, you old goat, or you're next."

Jonas and Bruno glared at each other, then Jonas and Micha stepped back. They continued to reach out with their hands.

"Bruno, you've made your point," Micha said, "let the boy be."

Bruno fired a warning shot into the air. Ivan held his gun

steady, pressing it to Badger's head. The boy was sobbing now. Bruno looked at Jonas, his face twisted into a malevolent grin. He raised his hand, then dropped it quickly, and Ivan fired. Badger's body crumpled to the ground. Giti was overcome by nausea and grief. Jonas put his head in his hands and sobbed. Micha stood ramrod straight, his jaw clenched with pain and anger.

As the crowd watched, terrorized, Bruno turned his gun on two young men in the crowd. He forced them to string Badger's body up and hang it from a branch of the tall elm tree that loomed over the house.

Bruno walked back toward the car and faced the crowd. "He stays. Anyone who tries to cut him down will find themselves in his place. Anyone here who helps the traitors hiding out in the woods will get the same treatment. You've been warned." He and Ivan returned to the car and drove off, leaving the horrified crowd in shock.

Giti forced herself to walk around to the back of the house and once inside, she collapsed in the kitchen, her convulsive sobs raw and primal. Loreta pulled her up by the shoulders and led her into the sitting room, where the family held each other in a tight embrace. Domus's body was just outside the window sending fleeting ripples of shadows across the floor. Giti fled back to the kitchen, unable to look.

Loreta followed and knelt beside her. "Giedre, my darling. It's a nightmare, but Domus is at peace now. The pain is gone."

Giti heaved and struggled for breath. "But you don't understand! He knew me! The night I was attacked, it was Domus that brought you word. He looked right at us and said nothing. NOTHING!" Giti was screaming and thrashing about with her arms. She wanted to hurt someone, but mostly she wanted to hurt herself.

Loreta sat quietly. "He knew all of us, and we knew him. He was young but so very brave."

"But we just stood there and watched him die! He protected us and didn't deserve our indifference!" Giti's rage was dwindling and in its place was a deep well of sorrow, a collection of all the pain of the losses she had witnessed in her young life.

"We weren't indifferent, Giti." Jonas stood in the door, his hands on his hips and his eyes red from crying. "Nothing we could have done would have changed the outcome. Once Bruno had him, he was as good as dead. The only thing we can do now is carry on the fight and make his death mean something."

Paulina reached down and gathered Giti in a tight embrace. Baby Justina was swaddled and strapped to her back, and she began to squirm. "Life must go on, Giti. Domus was fighting for a better world for children like Justina, and it ended for him today. We are all in danger of being in his place, and we either accept that and press on, or we let them win and keep our beautiful country in their clutches." She lifted Giti's chin and stared directly into her eyes. "Our fight goes on, Wolf."

Giti was astonished. "You know?"

Paulina smiled sadly. "Of course we know. You've won our love and our admiration. You've also won something of a reputation for your bravery and your grace. Domus knew that. He had the privilege of doing what any of us would do—protecting you with his life."

For the first time in years, Giti was speechless. She reached up and stroked Paulina's cheek just as Justina let out a piercing wail. "We all have our lots in life now, Giti, and we have come to depend on you to help us fight this fight. Matis needs to know what happened, and it would be better for him to hear it from you."

Giti stood and used the back of her right hand to wipe

away her tears. Loreta was busy spreading out a cloth and placing some bread, cheese, and dried figs inside. She wrapped it all up and gave it to Giti. Micha brought her hat, coat, mittens and scarf, and Jonas slipped a knife into her left boot.

Once she was properly bundled, she kissed each of them in turn and walked out the back door and toward the far fields. Anyone watching would assume that she was taking supplies to the workers who had resumed their work, but right before she got to the back fence line, she took a sharp left into the woods and disappeared.

All through the forest, she alternately cried then raged about Domus's grisly death. By the time she reached her usual meeting place with Rasa, she was spent. She had no more tears, and instead of pity or regret, she was filled with anger over how brazenly Bruno had victimized such a promising young man. She walked on numbly, her feet leading her along this familiar path. She cleared her mind of distracting thoughts and concentrated on honing her senses to be aware of any danger that might lie in her path.

Giti arrived at the clearing in mid-afternoon, with only a few hours of weak sunlight left. In the dead of winter, it was more difficult to find a spot to conceal herself so she chose instead to make herself visible. If a soldier happened by, she would claim ignorance and then kill him.

Giti waited on the edges of the field for about an hour. She unwrapped Loreta's package and, once she started eating, she realized how hungry she was. She forced herself to save most of the food for later, and as the cold seeped into her feet and hands, she stood up to stretch her legs and move around for warmth. She walked around the edges of the field toward the sound of water. She found a creek, mostly frozen over, but a tree had fallen recently, gouging a hole in the ice. Water gurgled freely around the branch, and Giti slipped off her left glove just long enough to scoop up a sip.

"Be careful, I hear the swimming is a bit rough this time of year."

Giti slowly cupped her hand and dipped it back in the water before flinging it in the direction of the intruder. It hit Matis square in the face.

"Ouch! That's cold!" he said.

"Serves you right for sneaking up on a girl. I thought you had better manners than that." Giti stood and faced him. "Oh, but that's right—you don't have any manners." Her bravado slipped and the tears welled up again.

Matis reached out his hand. "Come on, Giti; let's get you out of the cold. I've been watching you for a while to make sure you were safe and not followed. We can't go into the cave right now, but I know somewhere that we can talk."

Giti crossed her arms.

Matis held up both hands in mock surrender. "Fine. Just follow me."

They walked about a half mile to the site of a former farm. The large stone house and various outbuildings were ghostly quiet and had been vacant for a long time, but it clearly had once been a very prosperous operation. Vicious scorch marks marred the face of the stone, and as they approached, Giti could see that most of the windows were blown out and the front doors were missing. The outbuildings were in the same shape.

Matis said solemnly, "They were Jewish, and the Nazis seized them. They stole anything worth taking and burned their home."

They ventured around the house, past the barn, and Giti saw where they were heading. An elaborate dovecote stood to the side of what was once a grand garden. Other than a swastika, painted in angry, threatening strokes, the facade was largely undisturbed. Matis pushed on the door several times with his shoulder, and it yielded in stubborn increments.

Giti walked inside and stared up into the height of the circular building. A wooden staircase wound its way around the mottled walls to a platform at the top, which sat directly under a stone roof. The roof was held up by walls punctuated by windows that were remarkably intact. Dust motes floated aimlessly in the weak light. When Giti lowered her gaze, she saw that everything at ground level was covered in ancient piles of bird droppings.

"I know," Matis said, reading her mind. "It's disgusting down here, but much better up there. Come on." He took her hand and led her up to the platform at the top.

"How many girls have you brought here?" she asked, only half teasing.

He blushed. "Trust me, you're the first. We use this place as a supply drop during the winter. I'm surprised the Russians haven't done something with the property yet, but for now, it's as warm and safe as any place." He squeezed her hand.

True to his word, it was much improved up on the platform, and there were a few blankets, empty tins of food, and broken baskets piled to one side. Matis gathered the blankets, shook them out, and arranged them so the two of them could sit down.

Giti's throat was tight, and she didn't know where to begin telling Matis about the awful events of the day. She got straight to the point. "Domus, our Badger, is dead."

"I know."

"You do? When did you find out?"

"Well, we hadn't gotten confirmation yet, but we heard yesterday that he had been caught running messages into Stubriai. The Cheka had been tipped off that he was coming, and they were waiting for him. Your boss Bruno and his goon

Ivan were just part of the group that took him away. We knew then that he wouldn't make it."

"Oh, Matis, it was awful. His body is hanging from the elm tree by the house, and Bruno won't let us cut him down."

Matis assured Giti that Jonas would take care of Domus and return his body to his family. Giti interrupted and told Matis about Bruno's threats, but Matis put his finger on her lips and shushed her.

"All taken care of, Wolf. Bruno and Ivan will be picked up tonight. The Captain is counting on him telling us who else is involved. That's why you can't go to the cave tonight. You're safer here."

"Matis, there's something important that you should know. They brought him to the house and made everyone crowd around. Bruno asked him if anyone had helped him. He looked right at me and said that he didn't recognize anyone." Giti choked up again and shivered.

Matis replied softly, "Domus was young but very brave. He knew that he would be killed regardless. He would've protected you under any circumstances." Giti nodded, and Matis reached for her. "I would love to light you a fire, but we can't risk the light or the smoke. Will you be all right?" She allowed him to pull her into an embrace, and she nuzzled her head onto his chest for warmth. Soon she was asleep.

The dream was persistent, and frighteningly real. Giti was in the dovecote, but Matis was gone. There was banging below. Once, twice, and then Domus's voice. "Let me in! Let me in!" Giti raced down the circular stairs and pulled at the stubborn door, finally yanking it open and letting the cold air rush in. There was no one there. She wandered out into the garden, which was remarkably lush and manicured. She picked several flowers and tucked them in her hair. As she rounded the corner, she heard Matis calling out to her. "Giti! Wolf! Come here!"

She dropped the flowers and raced toward the sound of his voice. As she rounded the corner, she saw him, hanging from the tree, his body lifeless.

"No!" she screamed and sat up suddenly.

"It's all right, Giti. I'm here." Matis reached out for her and drew her to him.

Giti felt his face, stubbly from lack of a razor but warm, vital, and full of life. "Matis, I dreamed that you were dead. It was awful." She dissolved into tears. "I don't know what I would do if anything happened to you."

"You'd go on and survive, but hopefully you won't have to find out." Matis sat up straight and cupped his hands around Giti's face. "We don't know what is going to happen, but we know we are together here. Right now."

Matis swallowed hard. "Here's the thing. I love you, Giti. I think of you every night when I go to sleep, and your face is the first thing on my mind each morning. I love that you find joy in everyday things. I love your tenacity, your brazenness. I love that you get scared, but you don't back down. I love that after all you've been through, you can still trust and love and fight for what is right."

Giti's eyes teared up and she felt a lump forming in her throat. "I love you too, and I wake up every day wondering when I will see you again and when you can move back and live with us on the farm. But, Matis, I am not brave. I'm scared all the time, and I miss you."

Matis stroked her cheek. "I know you're scared, but you keep going. You never allowed them to take your dignity or your sense of honor. That's pretty incredible. Bravery doesn't mean that you don't get scared. It means that you hold fast to what is right, regardless of the consequences."

Matis leaned down and kissed her softly. His lips were chapped and cracked, and his beard was rough and unkempt, but Giti thought that his kisses were the most luxurious feeling she had ever experienced. She leaned into him, and he wrapped his arms around her, his kisses becoming more urgent. He kissed the tip of her nose, her forehead, her ears, and her cheeks before drawing back and looking into her eyes. "You're beautiful, Giti, extraordinary and beautiful." He kissed her again, long and slow. He released the fastener holding together her thick braid and ran his hands through her curly hair. His fingers reached the chain around her neck, and he drew out her locket. It was warm from lying against her throat. "Is there a story here?" he asked.

"It belonged to my mother," Giti said. She opened her locket to display the photos of her parents. "Mutti and Pappi, meet Matis," she said wistfully.

Matis gently held the locket and peered at the photos, which were impossible to see in the dark. "Mr. and Mrs. Binz, you raised an extraordinary daughter, and I am desperately in love with her. I ask for your permission to marry her." Matis put his ear next to the necklace, then he kissed Giti again. He sat back and smiled. "They said yes."

She returned his smile and reached out to take his hand. She kissed his palm and laid it against her cheek. Then she began to unbutton her coat. Matis put his hand over hers and said, "No, Giti. Not now. It's not that I don't want to—God knows I want to—but I will honor you and do this right. I want to marry you, and I want it to be when we can be together. Not like this, but properly and respectfully. Do you understand?"

Giti nodded, but she was glum and embarrassed. He seemed to sense her discomfort. "You have no idea how hard it is for me to disappoint you. Will you marry me when I can come home?"

Giti said, "Will you stay alive long enough to marry me? I

don't trust time or circumstance. I just want to feel you close and have you back with me now."

Matis pulled her to him once again. "Soon, my love. Soon. I promise that I will do everything I can to return to you soon."

Giti stirred when she heard the owl screech. Snow had fallen throughout the night, muffling the normal noises and lending a brightness to the otherwise muted winter dawn. Pale morning light was creeping into the dovecote, giving the gloomy interior a soft, pink glow. Giti shivered in the cold. Matis was gone, and in his place was a note.

> *My dearest Giti,*
>
> *You made me the happiest man alive last night when you said that you loved me. I can hardly believe that I have the gift of your love and admiration, and I will do everything I can to remain worthy of your affections. One day this war will be over, and you and I will be able to walk openly down the street, holding hands, and making everyone around us jealous. Until then, please know that I am doing what I must, and I know you are doing what you must. We will be together soon. Domus's death will be avenged, and I must tend to that now. Trust me that what has happened in this war, and what must happen in the coming days, is no indication of my character or my honor. These grim times call for horrible decisions. You are my rock. Travel back to the farm safely, and I will get word to you as often as I can.*
>
> *All my love*
> *M*

CHAPTER TWENTY-SEVEN

OTTO, 1952

Otto went about his chores in a stupor, distracted to the point of incompetence. In order to buy himself some time and provide Karin some cover, he had told Anton about the farm with the stash of weapons. Otto hoped that there were no partisans left nosing around the property now that the cache had been cleaned out, but he couldn't be sure. The unknowns kept him on edge.

Otto's fragile security rested only on Anton's false belief that Otto had incriminating evidence against him. If the old man knew the truth, he would deliver Otto to the Cheka within the hour. Otto navigated this dangerous game of pitting men against each other with trepidation. Unlike in the gulag, he now had more than his sorry life to lose.

Otto stewed over the worst-case scenario, which was that he would implicate Arni, Filip, or Joachim, and so he had been intentionally vague regarding all details but the location of the weapons cache. Surprisingly, Anton hadn't pressed him for more. Not yet. He had driven off immediately after their conversation, leaving Otto consumed with worry over what he might find. In this fractured state of mind, he attacked his chores recklessly. He swung for the log and landed the ax dangerously close to Fritz's leg.

"Christ Kumpel, watch what you're doing! What is up with you today? You're more fidgety than a hog on slaughter day."

"Sorry, Fritz," Otto said earnestly. "Just not myself today." He moved over and started on a woodpile away from the others.

"Well, watch yourself. I'm not the only one wondering what you're up to, and I suspect it's no good, Kumpel."

Otto shot back angrily, "You don't know anything about anything. If I am up to something, it's trying to survive, which is something you would know about as well."

Fritz was undeterred. "Well I have the good sense not to get involved with other men's wives. If you want to cozy up to Karin, that's your business, but I advise you to stay away from Anton. That man has connections and is a force to be reckoned with." Fritz lowered his voice. "He hates you, and your interest in Karin isn't helping matters. Let it go, Kumpel, and you might increase your chances for survival."

The next morning, Anton was waiting for Otto at breakfast. Before he had a chance to sit, Anton grabbed him and, without a word, pulled him into the office. Otto could tell he was seething. Anton pushed him into a chair and loomed overhead, pinning his arms. "You made me out to be a fool! There was nothing there, do you hear me? *Nothing!*" He spit as he yelled, and Otto was forced to let the spittle slide down his cheeks.

Otto inhaled deeply to steady his nerves. "My sources told me that there is a trapdoor in the barn, and beneath it, a hollowed-out cellar where the weapons were stored. There was no mistaking the information. Are you sure you went to the right place?"

"What do you take me for? Of course we went to the right place. There was no trapdoor, no cavern. The barn floor appeared to have new straw, so there's a chance that they were able to cover their tracks, but it remains that you gave me nothing useful."

Anton stood up and retreated to the chair behind his desk. Otto wiped his face and flexed his fingers to get the blood flowing again. Anton watched him warily, then lit a cigarette and spoke slowly. "You have one more chance, do you hear me? One more chance to give me information about who on this farm is involved and what they are doing."

He opened his top desk drawer and pulled out an envelope. Otto could see German writing. "I have information about what little family you have left. Get me something that I can use, and you get two prizes. I will leave Karin out of this, and you will have knowledge of your family. Fail me again, and you will be delivered to the Cheka. You have one week. I advise you to make good choices." Anton folded the envelope and tucked it in his shirt pocket, then he dismissed Otto with a wave of his hand.

Seven days. Otto had not talked to Joachim or Arni about any more partisan activities, and no one had approached him. He decided to wait two days and, if he had heard nothing by then, he would strike out on his own and try to find the partisans himself.

Otto returned to breakfast and filled his bowl with hot porridge. The only seat at the table was next to Alfred, a harmless old man with a reliably sour outlook. As Otto sat down, Alfred reached out to block his access. "No room," he taunted.

Otto took his spoon and rammed the handle into the wooden table, barely missing Alfred's little finger. "There's room if I say there's room, Alfred," Otto snarled. He was spoiling for a fight, but Alfred simply scooted over with a grunt.

Joachim and Arni exchanged brief glances, both clearly wondering what had transpired in Anton's office. They sought Otto out as soon as the meal was finished and the work crews were preparing for their tasks. Joachim limped up to Otto and put his arm around his shoulders.

Otto shrugged him off. "Leave me be, Joachim."

"You have me worried, Otto. What is going on with you and Anton?"

Otto looked Joachim right in the eye. "You want to know? He wants me to spy on you, well not you specifically, all of you." Otto gestured to the men picking up tools and supplies for the day's work. "And I won't do it, so there, are you happy?"

Joachim watched Otto closely for a minute and then replied, "So I think it's best if we cut you out for a bit. Anton and his cronies can be, shall we say, persuasive."

"After what I have done for you? That's a low blow, Joachim. Listen, I am in—all in—and if you think I can't take it, then you know nothing of what I have been through."

Joachim lifted his hands in surrender. "Fair enough, my young friend. I apologize for questioning your loyalty." But as Otto stormed away, Joachim shook his head.

⸻

For two days, Otto watched Joachim, Arni, and Filip closely, but none of them seemed to be doing anything out of the ordinary. The weather had turned unbearably cold and fierce, which was to be expected in January, but it left the men with little to do. They played cards in the barn and swapped stories. Otto could taste his own desperation. He *had* to find something to give to Anton.

Snow began falling in earnest the next day, and the men hunkered down in their cabin and wagered cigarettes over a game of dice until gradually all had fallen asleep. All, it seemed, but Otto. He lay on his bunk and held the photo of young Giti. He couldn't see it in the dark, but he didn't need to. He had her image memorized. He tried to envision the determined little girl as a grown woman. She would be twenty-one now, certainly without the blond plaits he remembered. He wondered if he would even recognize her. He set the photo by his pillow and rolled over, but couldn't summon sleep. As he burrowed under his blanket, he heard the creak of floorboards and detected movement in the room. He tried to keep his breathing steady as he shifted his position to better see who was moving around.

Arni. He was sitting on the floor, pulling on his boots and donning a thick sweater. Joachim sat on the bed beside him, fully dressed in his heavy boots and a coat. His cane was propped beside him. Slowly and wordlessly, the two men stood up and slipped out of the cabin. Only a quick flurry of snow and a swoosh of cold air marked their departure.

Otto waited a few minutes to see if they would return. When no one stirred, he slithered out of bed and silently pulled on his warmest clothes. He opened the door and scooted out as quickly as he could, the cold air hitting his lungs and leaving him momentarily breathless. Arni and Joachim were easy to follow. Their footprints led in the general direction that Otto had anticipated, and the snow was not falling hard enough yet to obscure their tracks.

Joachim hobbled over the icy terrain with difficulty, and Otto quickly caught up with them. He remained far enough behind to avoid detection, but they were rarely out of his sight as they led him for miles through the forest. The snow was persistent, and Otto became less sure of their direction the longer they walked. Visibility deteriorated quickly, forcing him to close the distance between them.

At daybreak, the snowstorm blew itself out, and the brilliant pink glow emerging on the horizon reflected across the pristine whiteness left in the storm's wake. The day remained bitterly cold, and Otto shivered despite the exertions of the long hike through the night. Joachim and Arni had led him to a clearing, and Otto was surprised to see a crowd gathered. There were dozens of men and women standing in quiet clusters. Otto found a hiding place behind a fallen tree that gave him a view of the group massing below.

Joachim and Arni mingled with the people for a few minutes until the man Otto recognized as Fox strode to the middle of the clearing. With him was a tall man with a patch covering one eye and another young man of middling height with unruly copper-colored hair and wire-rimmed glasses. The young man had a large camera in his hands, and as soon as the crowd trained their attention on the tall man with the patch, the redhead stepped off to the side and began taking pictures.

The tall man signaled behind him, and on his cue, the crowd parted. Four people were dragged out of the woods. Otto could see that the prisoners were three defiant men and one sobbing woman, all with their hands tied behind their backs and their eyes covered by blindfolds. They were led to a fallen log in the center of the clearing where they were seated and their blindfolds removed. Their hands remained tied, and the four teetered awkwardly, jostling against each other to secure a dignified perch. Otto recognized that the men's attempts at bravado were futile. They knew their circumstances were dire, and there was no escaping this mob.

The man with the patch addressed the crowd, and his voice carried across the snowy field. He named each of the prisoners—Bruno Grigas, Dovydas Kairus, Ivan Chomsky, Mari Pisula—and charged them with the kidnapping and murder of Domus Arnold, a young man and sacred son of Lithuania. He called several witnesses who testified that the boy was in Stubriai, where he was lured by the woman, Mari Pisula. He was then bound and taken to a house on the outskirts of town where he was interrogated by Chomsky and

Kairus. During this interrogation, he was tortured. The witness to the interrogation confirmed that she had it on good authority that the boy divulged nothing to Chomsky and Kairus.

Others came forward to confirm that the young lad was then bundled into a car with Grigas and Chomsky and driven to Kolkhoz Number 152, where he was asked to view a collection of people and identify anyone who might be working with the partisans. The witness asserted that despite his pain, the young man refused to break.

Otto watched as the final witness, an old man they called Jonas, emerged from the crowd followed by a large dog. Otto could see that Jonas was hampered by a pronounced limp and needed a cane. The dog approached Grigas and growled, prompting Jonas to issue a stern command. The dog obediently took his place beside his master. Jonas then began to describe how Domus Arnold was killed. He pointed to Grigas and explained how the crowd had been subjected to the horror of the murder and desecration of Domus's body. Jonas yielded to the large patch-eyed man before he and the dog blended back into the crowd. The woman, Mari, began crying anew.

The tall man with the patch consulted with Fox and several older men. Otto watched as they huddled in earnest conversation, gesturing and pointing to the prisoners. At length, the discussion broke up and the tall man with the patch walked to the middle of the group to address the prisoners. One by one they were forced to stand. Bruno Grigas, Ivan Chomsky, and Dovydas Kairus were found guilty of the kidnapping, torture, and murder of Domus Arnold and sentenced to death. Otto observed that upon hearing the verdict, the man called Bruno broke down and pleaded for his life, alleging that it was Chomsky and not he who was responsible for Arnold's death. In response, Jonas lurched forward out of the crowd. The man with the patch held up his hand, and the crowd restrained Jonas and pulled him back.

Mari Pisula was found guilty of kidnapping. She was sentenced to a public shaming followed by abandonment in the forest. She resumed her crying and fell to her knees, pleading for mercy.

Otto watched carefully and was shocked by the speed of what followed. Without a word, Fox raised his pistol and shot Chomsky and Kairus. Men from the crowd advanced and quickly removed their bodies from the clearing to load them in a wagon.

Bruno crumpled to the snow and resumed his pleading. Fox consulted the man with the patch, and after only a few words between them, the tall man motioned to Jonas. The old man came forward, followed by his dog, and Fox offered him his gun.

Jonas took the weapon and faced Bruno. "Take your punishment like a man, Grigas!"

Bruno slowly lifted his tear-stained face. "Don't do this, old man."

Jonas looked Bruno in the eye. "For Domus!" he yelled as he fired.

Only Mari was left. She had finally gone quiet, and Otto, peering out from his hiding place, decided she was in shock. The tall man signaled to the crowd one last time, and two women emerged, both brandishing knives. They stood on either side of Mari and used the weapons to hack away at her hair using crude chops. Mari remained hunched over until her head was completely shorn. Blood trickled from a cut in her scalp and ran down her cheeks, mingling with her tears. Otto watched as the blindfold was replaced, and Mari, stripped of her coat and shoes, was marched out of the clearing. The log was empty now, surrounded only by stained snow.

The photographer stepped forward and snapped several

pictures of the tall man, Fox, and some of the others in the crowd. The mood of the men was somber, and they stared at the camera sternly. Otto absorbed it all with disgust, sickened by the crisp brutality of it all. As the crowd began to disperse, he crept backwards and retraced his path to the collective, praying that he would be able to find his way.

Otto made it back to the *kolkhoz* before sunset and went immediately to Anton's office. He passed Karin and was relieved to see that she had no new bruises. She barely registered his presence. Otto knocked at Anton's door and let himself in.

"I have news."

"And?" Anton leaned back in his chair and waited.

"And I want that letter you have first."

"Oh no, my comrade," Anton said. "I need a report that I can verify before we complete our partnership."

"I just witnessed the trial and conviction of four people in the forest. It was a horrifying display of violence."

Anton sat up and dropped his cigarette in the ashtray. Otto had his full attention. Anton prompted him. "Names, Otto. I need names."

Otto happily complied, naming the four victims.

"Yes," Anton said, "I am aware of that incident, but just how did you happen to be in just the right spot to witness this spectacle?"

Otto shook his head. "No dice, Anton. I just gave you credible information. You can probably go out and find that woman stumbling across the forest floor right now."

"That may be true," Anton said, "but if you're going to get this..." he fished the letter out of his pocket and waved it at Otto, "then you must give me names of the traitors involved." Anton stood up and leaned over the desk. "I need to know who I can turn over to the Cheka."

"Well, one of the leaders was named Fox. The other leader, the one ultimately in charge, was a tall man wearing military fatigues and an eye patch. And there was a Jonas."

"Binz, I'll say this once. I need full names, not fancy descriptions. There must be a thousand Jonases in this district alone. Get me a name—a full name—by Monday, and you'll have this." Anton slammed the envelope down so that Otto could see the return address from Berlin.

Joachim and Arni returned after dark. Otto quizzed them about where they had been, and they were evasive in their explanations. It irked Otto that he had been closed out of the group. He had to find a way back in. Observing things wasn't helpful anymore. Otto was loath to betray any of the other men that he considered family. He needed to be told at least one name by someone on the inside. Knowing the identity of Fox would be golden, but Otto wasn't holding out for that. The name of any one of the men at the clearing would get Otto the coveted envelope from Anton. Otto continued to get the same dismissive treatment over the next few days. He vowed to bring the matter to a head as he, Fritz, and Arni gathered their tools and set off to repair a shed that had collapsed under the weight of a heavy snowfall. It wasn't a difficult assignment, at best a companionable errand, but it seemed that all the men were ill-tempered and on edge. He suspected that another event was looming, and he was determined to get to the root of their unease. He tried to lighten the mood and weasel his way back into their good graces as they made their way to the worksite. Trudging across the snowdrifts, he kept up a constant banter of lighthearted chatter, but was unable to break through the tension. He managed only to goad Fritz into joining him in a round of German folk tunes, much to Arni's irritation.

As the three men neared the shed, Otto spied a man approaching them on the road. He walked purposefully and carried a bag on his back. As he drew closer, Otto's heart began to thump. Good fortune was indeed smiling, because right in front of him stood the photographer from the clearing. His wire glasses and bright red, curly hair were instantly recognizable. As he drew closer, the man locked eyes briefly with Arni and then addressed Otto and Fritz.

"Good afternoon, gentleman!" the photographer said jovially. "I wonder if you can help me. I am searching for the brother of a friend, and this man is rumored to be living nearby. By any chance do you know someone named Filip Valus?"

"Of course!" Otto and Fritz chimed in together. Fritz continued. "We can take you to him as soon as we finish this repair job, especially if you lend a hand. It'll get us back to camp to meet Filip that much faster."

The young man accepted enthusiastically. The four men proceeded to the shed, and before they were able to get started on repairs, the photographer asked Fritz and Otto to pose in front of the snowy landscape. Awed by the novelty of the request, they stood side by side and stared into the camera lens. As the photographer adjusted his lens, Otto leaned forward and said, "My name is Otto Binz and this is my friend, Fritz Biedemeier. What might your name be?"

Click! The shutter closed the minute Otto reached out to shake the photographer's hand. They all had a quick laugh, and then the photographer offered his hand in friendship.

"Nice to meet you Fritz, Otto, and?"

"Arni," Otto volunteered.

"And Arni," the young man repeated. "I am Lukas Galinis."

CHAPTER TWENTY-EIGHT

BRIGIT, 2010

Milo and Brigit were back in the car driving toward Vilnius, their fourth time in two days on this particular stretch of highway. Low clouds were spitting snow in earnest, and the heater of the little car struggled to produce enough warm air.

Brigit shifted restlessly in her seat, adjusted her seatbelt, and checked her phone one more time. She was reeling from the sight of Otto's picture. Milo reached out and gently laid his hand on her arm, but she jerked it away.

"I'm so confused and disappointed. First of all, in myself—how could I have missed seeing a picture of my own father when we went through the photographs together? And then there's the fact that my father lied to me. Why?" Brigit's eyes filled with tears, but she pressed on. "Why all these years, when he was regaling us with stories of his grand escape from East Germany, did it never occur to him to tell me that he used to live in Lithuania?"

The more Brigit gave voice to her thoughts, the angrier she became. "He knows I am here, looking for a photographer that *he has met*! You would think that he would mention it."

Milo said, "Look, don't be too hard on yourself. You weren't expecting to find your father, and so you wouldn't have scrutinized every man's face. As far as his being a liar, I've never met your dad, so what do I know, right? But maybe there's another way to think about it. How do you even know that he knew Lukas's name? Or maybe he knew it and forgot it. I'm terrible with names! He's also really sick and old. Who knows what he remembers?"

Brigit had to concede Milo's point, but she wasn't ready to give up on her anger just yet. "Okay, so he might not know your uncle's name, but he clearly knew he was in Lithuania."

Brigit thought back to her conversation with her father just a few days ago. "You know, when I first mentioned your uncle's name to my father, he cried inconsolably. I thought it was his fragility, his fear of dying without finding Giti, but could it be that he *did* recognize the name? Where is Šilutė, anyway?" Brigit exhaled in frustration. "I just want to call him, but it's too early in the morning there. I have to wait until I am sure my mom is in the room."

Milo said, "I think that's a blessing in disguise. There are other ways to follow up on this besides unloading on your dad. What about your contact at the German Red Cross? The one you got the copy of the picture from? Let's see what they know about your dad and how they acquired their picture, so that when you finally do talk to him, you know fact from fiction. I mean, think of this Brigit, your dad met my uncle! That's pretty incredible, you have to..."

The car swerved sharply to the right and fishtailed on the icy road. Milo cursed and put both hands on the wheel to try to get it under control. A delivery van skidded by, narrowly missing them. Milo pulled off onto the shoulder and put the car in park. Brigit put her hands in her lap and sat quietly as Milo took a deep breath and settled his nerves. When the highway was clear of traffic, he edged the car back onto the road. He said under his breath, "We're close, let's get you back to your hotel, and we'll make plans from there. Deal?"

By the time they arrived back in Vilnius, the wind had picked up and the snow was coming down in masses of tiny flakes that were likely to fall throughout the day and into the evening. Milo could barely see to pull the car up to the curb. He shifted into park and sighed loudly. "Whew, that was a beast." He held out his hands, and they were shaking. "I think we can safely say that I won't be drinking coffee in Rome anytime soon."

Brigit clasped his hands in hers. "Milo, you haven't slept much in two days, we have been processing some shocking news, and you just drove through a snowstorm. Come in with me, and ride out this storm. Get some sleep."

Milo started to protest, but Brigit reached down, switched off the car, and pocketed the keys. They both opened their doors and headed into the snow, sliding along the sidewalk until they reached the hotel door.

Brigit left Milo in the room to take a nap and carried her computer and notes down to the lobby. She settled into the overstuffed chair and nodded toward the desk clerk who was likely trapped on duty until the storm quieted. On impulse, Brigit slipped into the hotel cafe and purchased two coffees, taking one back to her chair and carrying one over to the clerk. The young woman smiled gratefully.

Brigit fired up her computer. Once her emails had loaded, she was relieved to see a new message from Agne. She had used her phone to snap an image of Lukas's photo of Otto and his companion Fritz, and she had also sent an image of her translation of Lukas's journal. Brigit forwarded the message to Rachel with a brief explanation. *Please call me when you wake up,* she wrote.

Brigit searched for the messages she had originally sent to

the German Red Cross and added to the chain by attaching the photo of Otto and Fritz. She shared Otto's and Fritz's names to her request for good measure. Best to cover all bases. She pushed 'send,' watched her email disappear, and then she stared at her inbox, willing a response to pop up and dispel all her worries. She tapped her foot against the chair and hit the refresh button several times. She couldn't conjure an instant response and was frustrated that the ball was now in their court. It could be next month before she received a reply.

She pulled out her phone and searched her emails once again for the number of the Red Cross. A courteous woman answered on the second ring, and Brigit stumbled over a choppy request in German to speak with Ilse Schneider. The receptionist graciously responded in flawless English that Frau Schneider was, unfortunately, unavailable at the moment. She promised to highlight the email and relay the message as soon as possible. Brigit offered profuse thanks and hung up. There was nothing more she could do on that front.

She sent Margie an email describing briefly what she knew, and asking for her help getting information from Otto. This was a long shot. Brigit had set up an email account for Margie so that they could correspond easier between Boston and Charleston, but Margie rarely checked her messages. She continued to insist on handwritten notes, favoring cursive on embossed stationery. Every time Brigit visited home, she had to reteach her mother how to log in.

As a last resort, Brigit searched Otto's name. She wondered why she had never thought of that before. Considering all she had learned in the last few weeks, she was astounded at her lack of curiosity growing up. She was relieved that internet hits were sparse because at least that meant he didn't have an extensive criminal past for her to mourn.

Most of the entries referenced a late 19th century German

painter. Definitely not her father. Further down though, there was a link to a story about her father's escape from East Germany. A grainy photograph from *Der Spiegel* appeared with an accompanying article about Otto's daring swim across the canal. In it, Otto is pulled from the water by bystanders and wrapped in blankets. The picture was taken from a distance, and it was hard to say if she would have identified Otto if she didn't know the photo was of him.

The article also featured a photograph of Otto in Hamburg as a young sailor. Brigit smiled at the image of her dad, the same curly hair, piercing blue eyes, and lopsided, gap-toothed grin. *He was a handsome man*, she thought to herself, as she traced the outline of his face with her finger. She never could stay mad at him for long, and she had to admit that she was relieved to see that the account in the magazine lined up with the stories that her father had told her all these years.

Her inbox dinged, and Brigit's heart skipped a beat to see that it was from the Red Cross.

Hallo Brigit,

Ingrid tells me that you called with an urgent request. I am glad to know that the package we sent you earlier has been helpful to you. We have two researchers on staff who are more familiar than I with our records from the time period you are requesting, 1945 - 1975. They will be most interested in this photograph of your father and Herr Biedemeier. Please allow me to consult with them, and we will send you whatever information we can find about your father and Fritz Biedemeier as quickly as possible. I will also inquire about the original of the Lukas Galinas photograph number 73. I understand from your request that your father's health is failing and I am so sorry to hear of your worries. We will do our best to respond promptly.

We appreciate your interest.

Regards,

Ilsa Schneider

"Well, that's a start," said Brigit out loud, to no one in particular. She closed her computer, gathered her things, and checked her watch. 4:30pm, and her stomach was growling. It should be a good time to try to call Otto and get some answers, but Brigit was starting to get cold feet. She was nervous about what her father's reaction would be, and she was scared of upsetting him. She also had to admit that she was worried about what he might tell her.

The phone at the reception desk rang and the desk clerk answered. After a brief conversation, she hung up and called over to Brigit.

"Excuse me, madam, but your friend just called and requested some toiletries. Perhaps if you are going to your room, you can deliver?" The clerk's expression was appropriately neutral.

Brigit smiled sheepishly. "Thank you, I'll happily carry his requests upstairs." Brigit collected the bag and then purchased two boxed meals and some hot tea from the cafe. Juggling the precarious load, she made her way to the room and tapped on the door with her foot, her key unreachable.

Milo opened the door wearing the complimentary terrycloth bathrobe, and Brigit laughed out loud. They both recalled how she'd answered the door that morning in a similar fashion.

Milo blushed and reached down to adjust the belt. The robe barely wrapped around his waist and fell dangerously short of decent coverage. "I hope you don't mind, but I helped myself to a shower. I dashed out so quickly this morning after Agne's call, and well, I thought it would be best to clean up a bit."

Brigit smiled. "Of course. Here are your supplies from reception, and a bit to eat and drink."

She walked over to the window and drew the curtains back

just enough to show Milo the cascading snowflakes that were falling unabated in the late afternoon dusk. "You will be here for a while at least. No one is moving around out there. The woman at the desk says we have several more hours of snow, and the wind isn't letting up just yet."

Milo gratefully cradled the steaming cup of tea as he stood with Brigit and surveyed the storm swirling outside the window.

Brigit's email pinged at the same time there was a knock at the door. She sat on one of the beds and opened her computer while Milo went to the door. He returned with a bottle of wine.

"Well look what the clerk at reception sent up. This is awfully kind."

Milo noticed that the color had drained from her face. He put down the wine and sat next to her on the bed. She was clutching her computer, and Milo could see that the email was from the Red Cross. He reached over and clasped her hand while he read over her shoulder.

```
Sehr geehrte Frau Lewin,
    My colleague Ilsa forwarded me your
request for more information about Otto
Binz, your father, and an associate of
his, Fritz Biedemeier. She also
indicated that your father is alive but
quite ill. For this reason, we have
given your request a high priority.
Please forgive the length of this email.
I want you to have all the leads we
could find. As it is getting late, we
are unable to confirm the provenance of
the photograph just yet, but we will
inquire into how the original of Mr.
```

Galinis's picture of the woman came to be in our possession.

We are fortunate to have some of the records of the East German police who were involved in repatriation of German citizens trapped in Soviet territories after the war in the 1940s and 1950s. This subject happens to be of special interest to me, particularly the fate of hundreds of ethnic German children orphaned in Soviet territories during the war, sometimes referred to as Wolfskinder. I believe that your father and Herr Biedermeier were two of these orphans.

First, Mr. Biedemeier. We have a request from a family member in Bonn who began searching for him in 1948. He was eventually located living in a Soviet collective in Šilutė, Lithuania, in 1958 and at the time was married and had two children. It appears that Mr. Biedemeier chose to stay in Šilutė, but remained in contact with his family. A quick phone call to his cousin this afternoon confirmed that Mr. Biedemeier, while advanced in age, is still alive and living with his wife Karin in Šilutė.

Now your father, Otto Binz. Our records indicate that your father was found in 1952 living in a Soviet collective in Šilutė, apparently on the same farm as Mr. Biedemeier.

Interestingly, a request that originated with Anton Pavlis was routed through the Cheka to the Stasi at that time, seeking information about your father's family. It only requests information about Mr. Binz's family and does not mention Mr. Biedemeier or any other Germans who may have been working at that site. It can be inferred from the nature of the request that Mr. Pavlis was an informant or associated in some other capacity with the Cheka. There is no indication in the request as to why Mr. Pavlis would be seeking information specifically for your father.

The Stasi were able to connect your father to Stefan Binz, his older brother and your uncle. Your uncle had previously submitted requests in search of Otto and another sibling, Brigit or Giti Binz. No information about your aunt was ever found, but Mr. Pavlis's request was matched up to that of your uncle Stefan. In 1952, your father was allowed to relocate to East Berlin and was shortly thereafter employed at a factory there.

I hope that this information brings you and your family peace. Please allow me to ask for one favor. It would mean a great deal to my research to be able to interview your father and to learn more about his experiences at the end of the

war. As you can imagine, there are still
many families who are seeking information
about relatives who were lost in the
final days of the conflict. Many have
died, but there is a chance that some of
the Wolfskinder, many of whom found their
way to Lithuania, may still be alive. It
is important that we record their stories
while we can. I await your call at your
earliest convenience.

Mit freundlichen Grüßen,
Josef Keppels

Brigit felt her throat tighten as the tears welled in her eyes.
She cried so hard that she could barely catch her breath. Milo
reached over and drew her into an embrace, and they remained
that way until Brigit slowly became too exhausted to weep.
Finally, she broke the silence, her voice raw from crying. "The
Cheka? My father was involved with the Soviet secret police?"

"We don't know that," Milo said. "I know it's hard, but try
not to jump to conclusions. There could be an explanation."

"Like what?"

"I don't know, but we're not a judge and jury. It was a
difficult time, and people had to make awful choices. We
shouldn't assume anything about your father other than he was
orphaned as a kid and had to grow up and survive under the
worst circumstances.

Let's think about next steps. Agne is still working on Lukas's
journals. If I had to make a guess, Peter is still in charge of
watching Eljia, and Agne hasn't even changed her clothes. She
is glued to the journals. Next, we know that Fritz Biedemeier is
still alive and living in Šilutė." Milo pulled out his phone and

searched a map. "It's near the coast, maybe three or four hours from here. We can go and visit him when the weather breaks. And then you can talk with your dad."

Brigit took a deep breath and nodded. Milo made a lot of sense. She went into the bathroom to splash cold water on her face, and as soon as she turned on the tap, she heard her phone ring. Milo picked it up and brought it to her, but with her face dripping into the sink, she asked Milo to answer the call. She quickly toweled off and waited for him to hang up.

Before she could ask him anything, Milo encouraged her to sit and joined her on the settee.

"It was Agne. She's skimmed through all of Lukas's journals." He hesitated, and it annoyed Brigit.

"What?!"

"Lukas wrote down the name of the woman in photograph number 73. It was taken in Stubriai, which is only about 30 kilometers from Šilutė. Her name is Giedre Shimkus."

Brigit stared at Milo blankly, trying to process the news. "Shimkus? That doesn't sound right. It's probably another dead end."

"No, Brigit! Let's look at it another way. This really might be it! Giedre, Giti, they're so close. She may very well have changed her name. If this is your aunt, then she also knew my uncle."

"But, Milo, I'm terrified now. I don't think I want to know more. It's all gotten so complicated, and I'm afraid that I will just end up being disappointed in what I find out."

Her phone beeped and she reached over to see an incoming call from Rachel. She declined the call, too worn out to speak, emailing Rachel instead to explain all the revelations about Brigit's family that had developed over the day. Rachel emailed back that she would check her sources to see if any of her contacts could run down any information about a Giedre Shimkus from Stubriai.

Brigit silenced her phone and pushed it under her pillow as she snuggled into one of the twin beds. Milo had already climbed into the other.

She was awakened by the vibrations of her phone. Brigit checked the clock—3:30 in the morning. She slipped out of bed, careful not to disturb Milo, and took the phone into the bathroom. She was alarmed to see that the number was her mother's rarely used cellphone, and the message icon signaled a new entry. Brigit trembled as she held the phone to her ear and played the voicemail.

"Mrs. Lewin, this is Inez calling on your mama's phone. Your daddy has taken a turn for the worse, and your mama is asking for you. She wants to know if you can come home. I'm on duty for a couple more hours, so when you get this message, please call me. I'll keep your mama's phone close." Inez signed off by leaving her direct line.

Brigit's hand was shaking so much that it took two tries to key in the proper number for Inez. The phone went straight to voicemail, and Brigit left a quick message.

"Inez, this is Brigit Lewin. Tell my mother that I am on the way and will be there as fast as possible. Thank you for taking care of my father. Please tell him to hang on."

She quickly brushed her teeth and threw her toiletries into her bag. She turned off the bathroom light and carefully opened the door. Milo slept peacefully, curled on his side. Brigit dressed in a haphazard rush and jammed her clothes into her bag. Then she drew a piece of stationery out of the room desk and tiptoed into the hallway, gingerly shutting the door behind her. She checked to make sure she had her phone and passport in her bag, then she pulled out a pen and scribbled a note.

Dear Milo,

*I came to Vilnius to search for answers for my father
and found so much more. I am not sure what to make of the
information that Agne has gleaned from Lukas's journals,
but regardless of the outcome of my search for Giti, I know I
have found kindness, caring, and generosity. Two days ago,
we had not met, and now you are a cherished friend to me.
Thank you for delaying your plans and sharing your family
history with me. Perhaps our families met and cared for
each other long ago. I hope that is the case.*

*I have been called home. My father is failing, and I
need to get back as fast as I am able. You need to get to
Rome and drink coffee in the market square and celebrate
your memories. I hope that you find the inspiration to start
your life anew.*

*You have my number. Please let me know if you hear
any new information from Agne, and I promise to share
anything I learn about Lukas from my father's past.*

With deep respect and appreciation,
Brigit

She folded the note and slipped it under the door. Then she
dashed to the lobby to settle the room charge and make
arrangements to get to the airport. She was relieved to see that
the snow had stopped and the plows were already at work
scraping the street outside. She added a breakfast order for Milo
to her bill and asked that it be delivered in a few hours, then she
scurried outside to catch the taxi that pulled up to the door. Her
ride took her past Galerija Emilia, its windows dark and lonely
in the predawn hours, the final remnants of the shop piled in
bins out front and covered in a pristine blanket of snow.

CHAPTER TWENTY-NINE

LUKAS, 1952

January 15

Jurbarkas

I returned to visit Dr. and Mrs. Laukaitis. They have been extraordinarily kind to me. Occasionally, I fear that I am taking advantage of them, but the doctor assures me that Mrs. Laukaitis is much improved when I am under their roof. Her grief over the loss of her son is oftentimes unbearable, and having a younger man in her care seems to provide her with some solace. I brought them back some photographs that I had taken last summer, and it is remarkable how much Mrs. Laukaitis has diminished just in the last few months. She is, I believe, unaware of her husband's activities with the Forest Brothers. If anything were to happen to him (or me if I am to be honest), I fear she would not recover from the loss. My mother sent me with small gifts to share, and I believe that they were most appreciated, although I do not think Mrs. Laukaitis likes to think that I have a mother who enjoys my loyalty and affection too. The doctor has become my most able assistant in the dark room, and we have had many enjoyable evenings together developing film and sharing stories about the people I have met.

I have made this my base as I learned more about partisan activity in the area. I am constantly reminded of the perils and sacrifices that these brave warriors face in their quest for independence. This time of year is especially difficult for them because they depend on the locals to provide them with food and clothing. The bleak winter months of cold and darkness provide few opportunities for joy or sustenance.

20 January

Location secret.

My hands are still shaking as I write this, and I fear that I cannot divulge most of what I experienced today. I was sent on a mission yesterday to deliver food and the most basic medical supplies to a group of partisans who had made camp little more than ten kilometers from here. As I was in their camp, word came of the arrest of one of their own, a young man who was much loved by all. From what I could learn, he had gone to Stubriai to deliver a message and was arrested. He was tortured and then taken to a local farm where he was murdered in front of the farm workers. His death was too horrifying to recount here, but I am shaken to the core from what I learned of the incident, and yet I am also astounded to hear of his bravery.

News of his murder swiftly reached this camp, and the identities of his kidnappers, torturers, and murderers was revealed. A search party was sent to apprehend them, and this morning, they were forcefully brought to this camp, bound and blindfolded, to face justice for their crimes. The trial was swift and the ordeal was difficult to watch, but I thought of the courage of the young man who gave his life for the cause, and it helped me maintain my composure.

The trial was conducted by the military commander of this region, known only as the Captain. He has distinctive physical features and is quite imposing. While the partisans are existing on the bare minimum of supplies, they display an impressive culture of military discipline. Much of this I assume is owed to the charisma and skill of their leader.

A young lieutenant codenamed Fox was instrumental in the proceedings as well. He is also quite young, but has much responsibility. He is well respected by the men and has earned their loyalty. I had the chance to spend some time with Fox after the trial was over, and he displayed a grave sense of anguish at the necessity of the proceedings, but no regrets. He is an intelligent man who feels called to a higher purpose, but I sense that his role in history comes at a great cost to him personally. He has given me a letter to deliver to a woman near Stubriai, and I consider it a privilege to assist him in this small task. I decided that I will take her picture and bring it back to him.

It is gratifying to see that these men and women operate according to a code of honor and justice. In town, there is much talk of their cruelty and ruthlessness, and while I assume there are always villainous creatures in the mix, I have found the Forest Brothers to be men and women of principle and courage.

23 January

Šilutė.

I finally made the trek here as I promised Emil I would so many months ago. The roads remained covered in snow and ice from the recent storm, and I had difficulty finding the collective. Fortunately, I stumbled on a work crew repairing a shed that had fallen under the weight of the snow. I recognized one of the men immediately as someone who had attended the trial just a few days earlier. He seemed to be a quiet, rather sullen fellow who was introduced as Arni. Not wanting to compromise him, I did not allude to any previous connection, and he gave no indication of having met me at any time.

The other two men were much jollier. In fact, I actually heard them before I saw them on the road. They were singing some form of German songs. I asked if I could take their picture and they happily complied. I also inquired about Emil's brother, and they promised to lead me to him, which they did.

In exchange for their assistance locating Filip, I agreed to help them rebuild the shed. It was a tedious task, but one of the men, Otto, was determined to make the chore less onerous with stories and jokes. We got the structure righted and restored quickly, and were on our way back in no time.

I met Filip and easily recognized him as Emil's brother. They look like twins. I showed him a photograph of Emil at the factory, and he proudly displayed it for his comrades on the farm. I gave him a letter from Emil, which I was embarrassed to admit was over a year old, but he did not seem distressed by the time or distance. He wrote a quick note back and asked me to deliver it along with his picture. I plan to return to Kaunas by way of Tauragė to deliver these greetings.

The administrator of the kolkhoz, Mr. Pavlis, was not pleased to see me chatting with his men. I offered to take a photograph of him and his wife in order to placate him. He is a gruff, miserly man, and one wonders how he managed to marry such a lovely young bride. There is a story there. Perhaps when I return, Filip will enlighten me.

January 31

Stubria

I am running low on supplies and must retreat soon to Kaunas, thus there are few pictures as evidence of this leg of my journey. I am eager to see my parents and young Alvydas. I miss them when I am away, and I know that my mother worries for me. Watching Mrs. Laukaitis react to her own son's death has given me a window into the depths of a mother's love. My own mother admits to finding it increasingly difficult to watch me leave on my journeys.

I traveled back by way of Stubriai, to deliver the letter from Fox to Giedre Shimkus. She bears the scars of a brutal hand injury, but when you meet her, you soon forget her injuries. She is a resolute woman and quite perceptive. I can see why Fox is so taken with her. Soon, I will return to Jurbarkas to develop my last roll of film with Dr. Laukaitis and then go to Tauragė to deliver Filip's greeting to his brother. I am eager to see the happiness on Emil's face when he learns his brother is indeed alive.

February 15

I grieve as I write this last entry for my dear friend Lukas. He was such a talented and intelligent young man, far older than his young years, and brimming with passion for justice and mercy. He came to us as an injured traveler, and he found a place in our hearts.

Last night, a young woman knocked at our door and handed me a knapsack that I recognized as Lukas's traveling case. Inside we found these journals, his camera, and rolls of undeveloped film. The young woman left as quickly as she had arrived, with no explanation. We learned later that Lukas had been arrested by the Cheka for suspicion of terrorist activities

with the band of partisans we know as the Forest Brothers. I am wracked with guilt, for if I had not taken him with me that day, he might never have developed such close ties to the men and women who are fighting for our independence. But I did take him, and he dedicated his work to recording their bravery and seeking recognition for their dignity.

I am told that Lukas was named by an informant and will be taken to Kaunas and interrogated there. It is a gruesome business, and everyone talks sooner or later. The partisans are close to total defeat, and the cause appears lost.

My wife and I were inconsolable, unable to sleep or take nourishment until we could do something, anything, for Lukas. We gathered his supplies and worked throughout the night to develop the film and bring Lukas's work into the world. My beautiful bride Daina, who has never traveled beyond this village, insists on taking these journals and photographs to Lukas's mother in Kaunas. She must meet her and tell her the news, and she is hopeful that they can insist on a visit with him. I must let her go. She is so frail, the authorities will surely let her pass, but I know that hidden beneath her grief, she possesses an iron will and strength beyond her imagination.

There is one photograph that I will keep—that of a beautiful young woman. It was one of the last taken, and I wonder if she may be someone special to him. I will endeavor to find her and deliver the picture myself.

We will forever remember our Lukas, who became our son. His crooked glasses, his intelligent eyes, and his mop of red hair all made him memorable, but it was his kindness, his dedication to justice, and his skill as an artist that made him loveable. Goodbye, my friend. I am bundling this all up for Daina and sending her and your work on to your parents. I enclose this portrait that you so kindly allowed me to take of you. I hope it gives your family peace.

Respectfully,

Dr. Yorus Laukaitis.

CHAPTER THIRTY

BRIGIT AND OTTO, 2010

Brigit arrived at the airport just as runways were cleared and flights were queuing up for takeoff. She ran to the ticket counter, where the line was deep with travelers who had missed their connections during the snowstorm. Inez was texting her updates from Margie's phone, and the news was concerning. Otto had a high fever during the night. His pain was crippling, and none of the medications were having much effect. Inez assured Brigit that they were doing everything they could and that Otto was alert enough to know that she was on her way.

Brigit tapped into her phone:

> Tell him I am at the airport and will be there soon.

> We have already told him. He's cheering up knowing you are on the way. He promises to wait for you. You need to know he is calling you Giti.

Brigit brushed away a tear and took in the airport lounge full of people, none who knew or cared about her. She was going through one of life's most heart-wrenching moments, and she was totally alone in a swelling crowd.

The ticket clerk greeted her with the forced smile of someone who was laboring to remain patient. "Going on holiday?"

Brigit put her hand up to her messy bun and tried to tuck in random strands of flyaway hair. "No, no holiday. I have to get home. I was here, but my dad is dying and I have to get home to the US... to Charleston, South Carolina." It all came rushing out in a jumble, and the ticket clerk lowered the volume on her smile and reached out her hand.

"I'm really sorry. Let's see what we can do." She took Brigit's passport and began tapping loudly on her keyboard, staring into a screen that was positioned so that Brigit couldn't see it. The woman tapped some more, and then rubbed her chin.

"Please," said Brigit. "I need to get on a plane as soon as possible."

The woman kept tapping away, eventually calling over a colleague who also stared wordlessly at the hidden screen. They conferred briefly in Lithuanian.

Brigit was just about to jump on the luggage scale to see the screen for herself when the woman glanced up and said, "You have options. We have a flight leaving in an hour that has two stops—first Reykjavik, then Miami. You can connect from there to Charleston. You would arrive in oh..." she began tapping again. "You would arrive very late tonight Charleston time." Again, she tapped. "Or you can wait until this evening, and take a more direct route through New York and then straight from there to Charleston. You would be there by tomorrow morning."

Her colleague piped up. "Ma'am, you need to make a decision. We are five minutes away from closing the flight to Reykjavik."

"I'll take it," Brigit said briskly, and handed over her credit card without asking the price of the trip.

A series of delays in Reykjavik meant that Brigit arrived in the States several hours after the last flight from Miami to Charleston had left, and she was forced to spend the night among the bottled water and granola vendors at the airport. She called Rachel and got her voicemail, leaving a disjointed message with updates about Otto's condition and her trip. She also inquired about Giedre Shimkus. Just before the message reached its limit, Brigit signed off, all but begging Rachel to come to Charleston and be by her side when Otto died. Pitiful, thought Brigit. My closest friends are people that I just met.

By the time Brigit finally arrived in Charleston, the sun was blazing on a spectacularly warm Lowcountry winter day. She darted out of the taxi and into the hospital, sweating profusely, and holding fast to Inez's last text.

> He is stable and waiting to see you. It appears that you are the medicine he needed.

Brigit didn't wait for the elevator, instead taking the utility stairs two and three at a time until she arrived at the seventh floor. She tried to calm her pounding heart as she navigated the maze of hallways until she finally found her father's room. She could hear Margie's brittle voice as she pushed open the door and swept aside the privacy curtain. Otto lay in the bed, tubes snaking from under his hospital gown and around his face. He had IV lines taped to his bruised and mottled arm. His curly gray hair was plastered to his forehead, but the rest of him was cold and white. Brigit choked back a sob that was part alarm, and part relief to see her father open his eyes and wink at her.

"Oh, Papa!" she cried. "You held on."

Otto touched her hair tenderly, his hand hot with fever. He said, "When was I ever able to refuse a request from you, Liebling?"

Otto rolled over and coughed fiercely, setting off the alarms to all the machines attached to his tubes.

Inez arrived to reset the alarms. "Mrs. Binz," she said softly, "his fever is spiking back up, but his medications are at the maximum dose. I can't give him anything more for a while."

Brigit pulled up a chair next to Otto's bed. "Oh, Papa, please don't leave."

Otto closed his eyes until his coughing abated, then he signaled to Margie and Brigit. "I need to tell you something; it's important and you must listen."

Otto was still for so long that Margie and Brigit stared at the machines to watch for evidence that his heart was still beating. His breathing was ragged, and he was shivering despite the pile of blankets tucked around him. Eventually, he opened his eyes and began to weep.

"Shhhh, Papa, it's okay," Brigit whispered, wiping his brow with her cool fingers.

"No, Brigit," he whispered, "I must tell you what I did. I am so sorry. All for nothing. I never found her."

And then he began. For the first time in his life, Otto told his whole story. He began as a child in the cellar of the farmhouse in Königsberg, playing with his toys and smelling the delightful scents of Mutti and Oma's cooking. He described the soldiers, the screaming, the sensation of reaching out and grasping Giti's hand. He talked about the flames and the shooting. He took them to the train station and described the car, his mother's death, the boy with the mangled ear, and Giti's leap from the train. He described the train door slamming shut, her fingers and the blood. Then how she'd slipped away as the train rounded a corner and crossed the river.

He took them along with him to the Soviet Union, to the gulag, then his release into Lithuania. He spared no details. "Life for me then was made up of bargains—I do this for you, and you do this for me. It wasn't until I was reunited with Stefan that I learned to love and trust again." Otto began to cry. Brigit reached down to hug him, but he waved her off.

"I must do this, Liebling. I must make my peace." He swallowed with difficulty and resumed. "I made a deal with Anton, that he would find my family in exchange for information about the Forest Brothers. I found out really quickly who was stealing supplies, but they were people I knew. Deep down, I cared about them and couldn't turn them in. So, I needed to find someone I could use to gain me that envelope that Anton carried around. I felt sure he had found Giti, and I would have done anything to see her again."

Otto told them about following Joachim and Arne into the clearing, witnessing the trial and the carnage. He paused, his coughing coming in waves. When he finally stopped, he was wheezing and struggling to breathe. Inez stuck her head in the door, but Otto waved her away. Brigit turned around and nodded at her as if to say, *He has stayed alive for this. He needs to keep going.* Inez stepped back out into the hall.

Otto resumed. "I saw a young photographer there. He was easy to spot—a tall, skinny kid with wire-rimmed glasses and a head of red hair. He was taking pictures of the accused, and afterwards, he took pictures of the Captain and the Fox. In my mind, he was just as guilty as the others."

"And then one day, I looked down the road, and there he was. The photographer from the clearing. He was unmistakable. That hair and those glasses. He had a pack slung low on his back, and he came right up to us, asking about our friend Filip.

He introduced himself to us and took our pictures. We took him back to camp to meet Filip."

Otto spoke clearly, his gaze clear but troubled. "All I saw was that envelope in Anton's pocket. All I saw was Giti's face and the chance to see her again. I am so sorry, but I knew his name, and all I wanted to do was give the name Lukas Galinis to Anton."

Margie sat in her chair, her back straight, and her face impassive. She doesn't know what to do with this, thought Brigit, and she felt pity for her mother's limited emotional range.

For Brigit, it was both a shock and confirmation of what she was beginning to suspect, that this search for her aunt was going to yield pain, guilt, and anger. My God, she thought, what a world for a child to have to navigate.

"Did you give his name to the authorities?"

Otto kept his eyes closed, but shook his head. "No, I didn't. I couldn't..." Otto's voice broke, and he began weeping anew. Now Brigit was crying along with him.

"Papa, what happened? Do you know what happened to Lukas?" Brigit asked softly.

Otto didn't respond right away. He struggled to breathe, and he clenched his hands. The only sounds in the room were the whirring of the machines. Brigit gently rubbed the papery skin on Otto's hands. Margie sat unmoving, her eyes in her lap, and her lips pursed with tension.

Otto took a deep breath and opened his eyes, focusing on Bridget. "As we walked back to the *kolkhoz,* he and I talked. He told me about the people he had met on his journeys and how he was trying to help people who had been hurt and separated in the war. He asked me about my story, and I told him. I told him about my search for Giti, about Anton, about following Joachim and Arni to the trial. He had a way about him. He made you trust him, and you knew that he cared. That trial, the horrible events in the woods, had affected him too, and he was wrestling with his part in it. But he had also seen the other side. People killed and tortured for their work with the partisans. He was young and naive yet also very wise. I decided then and there that I would not find Giti if it meant harming another person. I thought that if I took part in his capture, then I wouldn't deserve to see Giti again, so I gave up. I am so sorry, but I just gave up."

Otto pressed on, his voice plaintive, "Even though I didn't turn Lukas in, I later found out who did, and I didn't do anything about it. That's my shame. I allowed him and the Fox to be arrested because I had lost all hope. I just wanted to die, and I gave up. It was Arni who turned him in. He had been working for Anton to infiltrate the Forest Brothers too. I should have known that Anton would not depend on just one person. Arni gave up Lukas's name and then followed him for a few days to try to rope in other partisans. Anton particularly wanted the Fox, and he hoped that Lukas would lead him to more senior partisan officers. Arni followed Lukas to Stubriai and watched from the shadows while Lukas delivered a letter to a woman there. From what I heard, she spied Arni and alerted Lukas. Arni feared exposure and urged Anton to arrest him sooner. Lukas traveled to Jurbarkas, and that's where he was captured."

Brigit asked, "Papa, if you didn't give Anton Lukas's name, how did you get to East Germany?"

"I think Anton was eager to get rid of me. I was a troublemaker between him and Karin. But the envelope didn't have Giti's name. As you know, it contained the name and address of my brother Stefan. It was wonderful to be reunited with him, but it haunted me to have benefited from Lukas's arrest. I hardly remembered Stefan. He left Königsberg when I was so young. I didn't really know him, but he was kind to me, and I lived with him for many years. I tried to be a good person, to atone for my mistakes. We learned to love again, Stefan and I, and I was inconsolable when he drowned."

His confession complete, Otto seemed to retreat into himself. Margie patted his hand absent-mindedly, and Brigit gently rubbed his arm. There was too much weight in the room, too many ghosts, and too many years of things unsaid and unresolved. Together, they remained like that, frozen and depleted, for some time. Once again, only the whooshes and dings of the machines broke the silence.

A soft knock at the door broke the tension in the room. Brigit lifted her head off the bed and responded. "Come on in, Inez, we're all okay right now."

The door opened, but it wasn't Inez. Rachel eased into the room, and Brigit jumped up to embrace her. "I am so glad to see you. You came!" Brigit introduced her to Margie while Otto slipped into a fitful sleep.

Brigit stood up and offered to step out of the room with Rachel, but Rachel hesitated. She said, "Mrs. Penworthy called. Is your father able to talk?"

Brigit rubbed his arm vigorously, and he seemed to stir. "Papa?"

"Giti?' he said. "Is it you?"

Rachel smiled. "Almost, Mr. Binz. Almost. We found her. Brigit found Giti. Her name is Giedre Shimkus Derus, and she lives with her son Jonas Otto in Klaipėda. She is alive and well in Lithuania."

CHAPTER THIRTY-ONE

GITI, 2010

She sat in the overstuffed chair in the music room wearing the lovely pale pink sweater that her daughter-in-law Alice had picked out for her, especially for this day. Giti had protested of course; all of her sweaters would seem new to her niece, but Alice wouldn't hear of it. She insisted, and Giti had to admit that she felt special in the downy cashmere cardigan. The locket that she had carried for so many years hung around her neck and rested on the mother of pearl buttons. Her thick white hair was carefully brushed and, as with most every other day of her life, bound into a tight braid that fell to the middle of her back. She had her right hand, the fingers twisted and gnarled, wrapped in a colorful scarf and lying gently in her lap. Her left hand with the ring fashioned out of brass nails rested serenely on top. Giti wistfully caressed the metal band, its rough edges smoothed over the years. Matis wanted to replace it, but she wouldn't agree to anything other than the loopy version that he had fashioned himself when he was released from prison.

The doorbell rang, and Jonas Otto was there to answer it. In truth, he had been waiting by the front window for an hour eagerly watching out for his cousin. Giti heard pleasantries exchanged and then she looked up to see a beautiful young woman with a bright smile and thick chestnut hair walking across the room. Behind her was a tall, handsome man whose face, framed by copper-colored hair, looked eerily familiar.

Brigit leaned down and kissed Giti gently on the cheek. "That is from my papa," she said in German, and she kissed Giti a second time. "That is from me. I'm Brigit, your niece."

"Dein Vater?" Giti inquired in halting German. It had been a long time since she had spoken her native language.

"He's alive, but fading," Brigit answered. "We almost lost him before, but when he found out you were alive, it gave him a new will to live. He's heavily medicated for the pain, but today, they have eased off the medicines so that he can talk to you clearly. Are you ready?"

Giti nodded, and Jonas Otto handed Brigit the laptop. He had shopped for the fanciest computer with the biggest screen available and had taken great care to set it up and test it so they would be ready for this day. While he logged on, the room filled with people. Alice, Jonas Otto's wife, Matis and Rasa, their grown children. Peter and Agne joined from the back, and Peter asked Jonas Otto again if Giti minded him recording the moment and taking pictures.

Jonas Otto was a jolly man with a quick smile. "Of course not. My mother understands that many people are interested in this." He leaned close to Peter and chuckled. "She is a big reality TV fan!"

Brigit entered the link and watched as the camera and audio lights came on. The connection started slowly, with the audio coming up first. Everyone heard Margie fussing at Inez. "But Brigit promised all you have to do is click! It should have worked!

"Mrs. Binz, let me have the mouse, I can get you connected."

Brigit laughed. "Mama, let Inez have the mouse. We have everyone here waiting." The screen flickered on to show a large picture of Margie peering intently into the camera. "Mama, we see you. Please give Papa the computer."

Back in Klaipėda, Jonas Otto moved a small table in front of Giti and set down the computer. She leaned forward and glared at the screen. "Otto! Otto! Bist du da? *Are you there?*"

In Charleston, Inez set the computer on the table in front of Otto, and with difficulty, she stuffed several pillows behind him so he could lean up to see his sister's face for the first time in sixty-five years. "Hallo, Giti!" he wheezed in German. "How is your hand? Are you all right?"

She held up her hand for Otto to see. She struggled to find the perfect German words that seemed to be on the tip of her tongue. She wiped away a tear and put her left fingers on the screen to try to touch Otto's face. "I hurt my hand, Otto, but all is well now. I have been so worried about you. Your daughter is beautiful, and I am so glad to meet her."

Introductions were made, and there was not a dry eye on either side of the call. Then Brigit and Jonas Otto motioned for everyone to back away. They faded into the background so it was just Giti and Otto, as alone as they could be for the first time since they had huddled in the cellar, terrified. Everyone lurked in the shadows, out of view, afraid to breathe for fear of breaking the spell of the moment.

Giti asked Otto about his symptoms and offered to have Jonas Otto consult with his doctors. Otto touched the computer screen and smiled. "After all these years, Giti, a lifetime ago, you're still my big sister, trying to protect me."

Giti started to share more advice and then she sat back and

smiled, taking in the sight of Otto, still the impish little brother despite his gray hair and wrinkles. Ever the charmer. She asked about Stefan and his injuries, and Otto wanted to know about Giti's children, and her life in Lithuania. That they had lived so close to each other and knew some of the same people amazed them, and they shared regrets. Both went silent and just watched each other, reaching out to touch fingers against the screen, to try to feel each other's warmth and revel in the chance to share the same moment.

Otto was the first to break the silence. He started low and slow, and as his memories came rushing back, he closed his eyes and his voice emerged true and strong as he sang their favorite nursery rhyme in German.

Giti chuckled and joined in.

Soon, Otto started to cough, and Margie reached into the camera view to try to rub his back. Giti held tight to the screen as she tamped down her anxiety. "Margie dear, please take care of my brother," Giti called out in halting German.

Margie peered into the camera, confused, and Brigit leaned over Giti's shoulder. "Mama, Aunt Giti said to please take care of Papa." Margie waved and blew Giti a kiss.

Otto was wracked by spasms of coughing, and Giti continued to stare helplessly at the screen. "Otto, listen to me. You do as those nurses say. You are too young to die, and I want to see you soon. Otto! Otto!" Giti tried to get his attention as he grimaced and shook.

Inez put a syringe in his IV, and he began to quieten down.

"Otto, my son has told me your story. I know it all, and I want you to know that you did the best you could do. It was a terrible time, and you didn't have a family to love you. Mutti and Pappi would be proud of you. Oma and Opa would be proud. Stefan was proud of you, and Otto?"

His eyes tried to focus on the screen, but the medicine was taking effect.

"Otto, I am proud of you. I love you."

Otto looked back at the camera and smiled. "I am proud of you, Giti, and I love you." And then the medicine transported him into a pain-free slumber.

EPILOGUE
THE ZALIUKAS PROJECT

The paint was barely dry, but Brigit and Milo were eager to hang the photographs in the renovated gallery. Milo had designed an arrangement to showcase them along with a massive map commissioned to illustrate Lukas's three journeys. Brigit stood by with a tape measure, spirit level, hammer, and nails. Milo pointed to the first spot, and Brigit readied the hammer to drive the first nail when Milo leaned down and stole a long, slow kiss.

"Hey! Get a room!" Peter teased as he and Agne carried in the desk and set it up in the reception area under Rachel's direction.

They had two days before the grand opening of The Zaliukas Project. Located in an old area of Kaunas, the renovated warehouse had room for four offices, a library, a gallery, and a recording studio. Milo, Brigit, Peter, and Agne had joined forces, with the shared mission of finding Wolfskinder and Forest Brothers and recording their stories. Many had spent a lifetime in hiding, or at least hiding their pasts. They were so much older now, and it was important to preserve their memories and connect family members who had become separated in the years following the war. Rachel made it all possible with her contacts and big donors who were eager to fund the research.

Peter, Rachel, and Agne directed the furniture deliveries while Eljia babbled happily in her playpen. Mrs. Penworthy arranged the chairs and unwrapped new pens for the reception desk. Rachel had flown her over in first class to preside over the office for the grand opening. Giti, Jonas Otto, and his family would be the guests of honor along with Milo's parents, and the media would be there to record the festivities. Thanks to Rachel's cunning marketing, they had already attracted the attention of major news organizations in North America and Europe. There was even a television crew arriving from Japan. All the details needed to be right.

Milo and Brigit reverently hung Lukas's photographs, including a massive enlargement of the image that Dr. Laukaitis had taken of Lukas himself, standing in front of the doctor's horse and buggy with his trademark glasses skewed slightly to the side and his copper-colored hair rumpled and disheveled under a cap. The picture of Fritz and Otto was also hung with bracketed dates under Otto's image, 1933 - 2010. Brigit and Agne had an appointment to visit Fritz the following week, and his and Karin's son was planning to attend the opening.

Late in the afternoon, as Eljia snoozed peacefully amid all the activity, only one last photograph remained. It was the centerpiece of the exhibit, Stubriai photograph #73, the original, on loan from the German Red Cross. Brigit and Milo called the others in, and they opened a bottle of champagne and passed around glasses.

Milo held up his glass. "A toast to Lukas, Giti, and Otto, and to all those who have worked to bring their stories together!" A round of applause erupted, and Milo held up his hand. "But there is one final surprise. Brigit?"

Brigit stepped forward clutching a sheet of paper. "Two days ago, I received an email from our wonderful contacts at the German Red Cross who have confirmed the provenance of our beautiful photograph." A collective gasp rippled through the gathering. Brigit continued, "The original was sent to them in 1995 from a woman named Anna Mickas, and this is the letter that accompanied the photograph." She smiled at Milo and began to read.

"My name is Anna Mickas. I am a wife and a mother who has lived in Lithuania for almost my whole life. Before I was Anna Mickas, I was Anneke Schmidt, and I was born to a German family in what was once East Prussia. After the war, my father was arrested, and our home was taken away from us. My mother, sisters, and I lived in an abandoned barn for some time, and as my mother was ill, my sisters and I foraged for food as best we could. One day, I returned to find them all gone. The ashes from the fire were cold, and there was no sign of them. I never found them, and I think about them every day. I stole away on a train to Lithuania and after much heartache, I found work as a laborer, moving from farm to farm. I learned to speak the language and to hide my identity because Vokietukai, 'Little Germans,' were usually sent away. That is how I became Anna, and at one of the kolkhoz where I worked, I met my husband, Arni.

We married and, as one of the few who did not suffer deportation, we managed to start a family of our own. I never told Arni about my past, and he told me very little about his. We had learned to look ahead and live each day at a time. After we had been married for many years, I found this photograph of a woman buried in a box in the barn along with a pistol and some money. I assumed that Arni kept the picture because he was in love with the woman. As you can see, she is quite beautiful.

I confronted him, and for the first time, I saw him cry like a small child. He finally told me his story. He was ashamed, not because he was unfaithful to me, but because for several years after the war, he served as a spy for the NKVD, the Cheka. The authorities had promised him that in exchange for information, his family would be brought back from Siberia. Yet, he never saw them again, and he was haunted by the fates of his friends and coworkers who were arrested based on the intelligence that he gathered.

In 1952, Arni received this picture from the NKVD. They had captured a brigade of partisans, and a photographer and a physician from Jurbarkas were among those who were arrested for their connections to the freedom fighters. The doctor's house was searched, but nothing was found except for this photograph. It was sent to Arni, and he was ordered to find the woman and watch to see if she would lead them to the partisan commanders. Arni was the one who had followed the photographer and led the authorities to him. The experience broke him, and he vowed never to assist the NKVD again. He confessed to me that he recognized the woman, so he hid the picture and watched her, but not to incriminate her. He wanted to protect her. He begged me for forgiveness and made me promise not to reveal his secret. We reburied the box and never spoke of it again.

Arni died last winter, and the box has begun to call to me. Arni told me one thing about the woman before we sealed those memories away. He had seen the photographer take the picture, and although Arni was a distance away, he thought that the woman had a slight trace of a German accent. What if she is like me? A child lost in the ravages of war, without a family or a proper home? She doesn't deserve to be hidden in a box, buried under soil that may be as foreign to her as it is to me. I share it with you in the hopes that if she is German, you can honor her.

My Arni lived in fear of judgment for his actions. He tried to make amends, but I do not believe he ever truly forgave himself. Do not think ill of him. He was a loving husband and father."

The gathering fell silent.

Rachel slipped her arm around Brigit's waist.

"This is how healing begins. You know that this is all your doing, don't you?" Rachel said.

"Oh, no!" Brigit protested. "It was all of us."

"Yes, in parts, but it was you that brought your story to all of us. In your pain and in your love, you reached out across the decades and collected us together." Rachel lifted her cup and tipped it toward Brigit. "This is for you."

Milo gingerly unwrapped the plain brown paper, and Giti's image peeked out, her hand up to her forehead and her eyes focused just slightly off to the side. He handed the frame to Brigit, and the room burst into cheers as she secured it in place. Brigit stepped back to stand with Milo as they all applauded the significance of the photograph. Underneath was a framed transcript of Giti's interview, the first that Brigit and Agne conducted for the project. It was a complete record of Giti's story, with the final page highlighted.

In the winter of 1952, I was helping out on the farm when I saw a young man approaching on the road. I had never seen him before, but he had an open and honest air and a kind demeanor. He carried a pack on his back and had a camera hanging around his neck, something I had never really seen up close. He asked for Giedre Shimkus, and I said, 'Well that's me!' That was probably foolish on my part because he could have been there to arrest me, but as I said, he seemed very friendly, and I am a pretty good judge of character. He introduced himself as Lukas Galinis, a photographer, and said that he knew my fiancé, Matis Derus. I blushed at this statement because I thought only Matis and I knew that we planned to marry, but Matis had used Lukas to bring me a letter, and so had trusted him with our news. Lukas asked if he could take my picture for Matis, and I immediately agreed even though I had been working on laundry in the barn all day. It was right when Lukas took my picture that I noticed another man farther back on the road. He was attempting to cross into the safety of the underbrush growing in the ditches, but wintertime is a hard time of year to find places to hide in the natural world. I didn't like the look of the second man, and I pointed him out to Lukas. He promised to be careful.

I heard later that Lukas had been arrested near Jurbarkas. It was an awful business to be taken to the Chekas's basement, and we worried for him. We later learned that he was taken in order to force him to divulge the identities of the partisan leaders, the Captain and the Fox. The Fox, of course, was my fiancé, Matis Derus. Once they gained this information, the Cheka executed Lukas and displayed his body to frighten others. That was a common tactic. It was quite horrifying.

Matis managed to evade the Cheka for many months, and during that time, I do not believe I slept a wink. I knew I was under surveillance and had to take precautions not to lead the authorities to him. Thus, Matis and I continued our long separation, and I am glad I did not know at the time how many years we would be apart. Eventually, he was caught near Klaipėda, turned in by a local informant whom he had trusted. Matis was tortured and sentenced to twenty-five years of hard labor. He was put on a train to Vorkuta in Siberia, where he endured horrible conditions in the mines. We were only allowed to exchange one letter a year.

Thankfully, he was released in 1958, but he was forced to remain in exile. He settled in the Omsk region, where I joined him, and we were finally married. He bore scars from his imprisonment, but he was my same Matis, strong, honorable, and kind. We finally returned home in 1965 and lived in Stubriai until Matis's death. Then I moved to Klaipėda to live with my son, the doctor Jonas Otto, and his lovely family. We had four other children: Ruth, Loreta, Titas, and Mikas. Our sweet twins Mikas and Titus died as infants, but our girls are well and living honest lives.

We suffered, those of us who were separated from our families, and we had to learn to survive well before we were old enough to do so. We lost our families, our homes, our language, and our identities. Many of us lost the ability to trust and to love, and survival at that time meant making cold-hearted choices in a cruel world. I pray for peace, love, and tenderness for all of the Wolfskinder. We did the best we could.

THE END

AUTHOR NOTES

In Mikytai, Lithuania, near the Russian town of Sovetsk, formerly known as the German city Tilsit, there is a memorial, *Wolfskinder-Denkmal*, dedicated to the tens of thousands of German children left to wander the countryside at the end of the Second World War. It is a silent witness to the grim conditions for children caught in the crosshairs of hatred and violence for which they bore no responsibility, but for which they endured the unimaginable weight of tragic consequences.

East Prussia, a fabled land of Teutonic Knights, holds a storied place in Germany's history. Though far removed from the halls of power in Berlin, the region was populated by ethnic Germans and thrived on the shores of the Baltic Sea. It held strategic importance in its proximity to Poland, the Baltic regions, and the Soviet Union, and was the only part of Germany to be invaded during the First World War. It was here that Hitler designed and built his *Wolfsschanze,* 'Wolf's Lair,' to safeguard the vital German frontier.

When the Soviet Union invaded in early 1945, East Prussia was a prized conquest strategically and symbolically. Stalin's troops descended on East Prussia with a vengeance, seeking revenge for the war's toll on their own people and carving a swath of destruction in their wake. Men disappeared, never to be heard from again. Women and children were ruthlessly assaulted and killed. Families were turned out of their homes and transported east to labor camps. Others were forced to scavenge for survival. Yet escape from exile was a perverse form of freedom, for without food or shelter, many succumbed to the harsh elements.

In the mayhem that followed the Soviet invasion, thousands of children who were orphaned or separated from their families had to fend for themselves. Called *Wolfskinder* in German or *Vokietukai* in Lithuanian, they endured a feral existence, often fleeing into the Baltic Forest to hide. About one-fifth of the children made it to Lithuania, either traveling back and forth to beg or steal food, or finding refuge with Lithuanian farmers, themselves struggling to survive under a harsh Soviet regime. It was illegal to adopt or foster Germans so the children who settled with families had to melt into a foreign society and hide their heritage. They abandoned their names, their language, and their education to avoid arrest and deportation to gulags or grim orphanages.

The *Wolfskinder* lived in obscurity until the fall of the Soviet Union in 1990, when some of the survivors, by then adults, shared their stories. It is hard to know the exact numbers, and with the passage of time, few are alive to bear witness. Many of those who lived to tell their tales have struggled to locate lost family members, reclaim their heritage, and restore their German citizenship. The society *Edelweiss*, or *Wolfskinder* in Lithuania, is one of the organizations working to preserve and share the survivors' stories. Ursula Dorn, Evelyne Tannehill, and Liesabeth Otto are among the many *Wolfskinder* who committed their stories to print. German historian Ruth Lieserowitz has focused her work on the lives of the

Wolfskinder, yet there are few translations to share their truths with a broader international audience.

German writer and director Rick Ostermann released the harrowing story on film in 2014, with a dramatized account titled *Wolfskinder*. Photographer Claudia Heinermann interviewed and photographed survivors in Lithuania for her book, *Wolfskinder*, which was nominated for the Prix du Livre in Arles in 2016. In 2019, photographer Lukas Kreibig published his record of the *Wolfskinder* in the *National Geographic*. That same year, Lithuanian poet Alvydas Slepikas wrote an unflinching fictionalized account based on the experiences of one *Wolfskind* whom he knew. His novel, *In the Shadow of Wolves*, was named a *Times* Book of the Year. This is not an exhaustive list, but a sampling of the many opportunities to explore the stories.

The few remaining *Wolfskinder* are elderly. They carry with them the ancient traumas and cling tenuously to a harrowing history, an experience that deserves to be remembered.

Readers and book clubs wishing to learn more will find additional resources and discussion questions at carolynnewtonauthor.com.

ACKNOWLEDGMENTS

Writing a story is a rather solitary journey accompanied only by the characters who whisper in your ear and worm their way into your heart. Launching a book, on the other hand, is very much a team sport requiring the support, encouragement, and honesty of a crew of generous and talented souls. I am deeply grateful to my treasured bibliophiles who love to contemplate plot, characters, words and grammar, and who graciously shared their time and expertise poring over drafts and rewrites to help transform this story from rambling scribbles into a novel.

My sincere thanks to: my wonderful editor Rachel Tyrer, for her enthusiasm, kindness, and attention to detail. She brought a keen eye, sharp pen, and full heart to the crafting of this book.

The entire team at Bloodhound books for their imagination, creativity, and tireless efforts.

Gaia Banks for her expertise and insights. Claudia Heinermann for her exquisite book that opened my eyes and heart to the *Wolfskinder*. Her photographs, and documentation of the histories of the very real children who suffered and survived, are a remarkable work of emotional journalism that inspired me to delve deeper into their stories. Benjamin Vengroff for his timely words of encouragement. My dear friends for wading through the first early drafts in acts of abundant generosity. My beloved family who read manuscripts, offered support, and spurred me on. You have touched the heart of the little girl who used to sit on Magpie Lane and invent fantastical tales about the people who strolled by, dreaming that one day, she would write a book.

A NOTE FROM THE PUBLISHER

Thank you for reading this book. If you enjoyed it please do consider leaving a review on Amazon to help others find it too.

We hate typos. All of our books have been rigorously edited and proofread, but sometimes mistakes do slip through. If you have spotted a typo, please do let us know and we can get it amended within hours.

info@bloodhoundbooks.com

Printed in Great Britain
by Amazon

52448457R00178